MY DESPERATE

Highlander

MICHEIL & DIANA

KEIRA MONTCLAIR

Cover Design and Interior format by The Killion Group
http://thekilliongroupinc.com

ALSO AVAILABLE FROM KEIRA MONTCLAIR

CHAPTER ONE

Late summer, 1264, Highlands of Scotland

Never, never, never would she consent to marry that man with a paunch as big as a hog's underbelly.

He was breaking his promise. After all these years, her dear father was breaking his promise, and would, in turn, break her heart. He had pledged her to Baron Ewen Gow of Falkirk.

Diana of Drummond stood in the great hall in front of her sire, the chieftain of the Drummond clan, with her hands on her hips, so exasperated that she didn't know what to say next. A small whisper finally escaped her lips. "How could you?"

Dead silence dominated the hall, nary a servant daring to speak, awaiting their leader's response to his beloved daughter.

"I do what I must, gel. 'Tis my responsibility to all the Drummonds before me. I must see you wed so the Drummond lands will remain with our people. I must." David of Drummond coughed into his linen square.

"But Papa, you said I could marry for love, that I could choose the man I would wed. Why are you being so cruel?"

"Because you have ignored my plea, and the time is nigh upon us. I will not be able to stand on Drummond soil much longer, and 'tis my responsibility to see that it remains within the clan.

I will see you wed before I die. I must know this land will go to a Drummond grandson some day. I have tried to be patient with you, lass, but you have failed to find a suitable husband. You have forced me to choose for you."

"But I will. I promise, I will." Oh, she would have to now, wouldn't she? She could not accept this horrible fate. "His reputation is in tatters. I cannot marry the man."

"'Tis no one to blame but myself. I spoiled you ever since your mama died. I allowed you to hunt, to become an expert horsewoman. Why, I even taught you to read. What lass knows how to read? 'Tis not for the female mind. Now you have the reputation of being a spoiled lass and...forgive me, but you are too old. Most lads do not want a wife past twenty summers. I should have married you off at ten and five, but I could not bear the thought of living without you." He cradled his forehead in his hand for a moment before continuing. "You are all I have left of your sweet mother. I cannot believe it has been ten years since I lost her, bless her soul."

"I am not spoiled. There is naught wrong with having a good mind, even you agreed." Diana crossed her arms in front of her. There had to be a way out of this, there just had to be. She had always been able to convince her father to go along with her, so why was he being this obstinate now?

"Och, but the men of the world say otherwise. 'Struth is they're all afraid of your mind and your talents. But they do not know you as I do. You will be an asset, and you will run this estate better than I ever could."

"Then allow me to choose my own husband." Diana was frantic to convince him.

The wizened old man coughed, hacking up red spittle into his linen square. "Nay, lass. 'Tis too late. I will not be here much longer, and I will see you wed."

"Mayhap you will get better, Papa."

"Sweet Diana, even your cousin, Brenna, renowned as one of the greatest healers in all of the Highlands, has told me there is naught I can do. 'Tis my time. I am happy to see your sweet mama again, but not before I see you settled with a husband who will care for you." He snuggled into the Drummond plaids, one across his shoulders and another across his lap.

Diana banked the fire before turning to him again. "But Papa, they say he is even cruel to his animals. Can I not choose a lad of my own? Please? You must rethink this. What if he is cruel to me, your verra daughter?"

"I spread the word out that I was looking for someone to marry you, but 'tis about the fifth time I have done so, and you have rejected every suitor in the Highlands and the Lowlands. You have even had suitors from almost as far as Edinburgh. He was the only one to offer for you this time, so I accepted. Your cousins will be along to escort you to his castle. They will act in my stead and make sure 'tis a good match. Then you will marry him and return here."

Diana fell to her knees in front of her father and buried her head in his lap. "Please, Papa. Allow me a choice. I beg of you. He is the same age as you."

"Och, he is a few summers younger, and he will bring enough riches to take good care of you. I trust your cousins to judge him well."

"Why not me? Why can you not trust your own daughter?" She swiped at the tears on her cheeks. She chastised herself for being so choosy in the past, for insisting on no less than what her own mother had wanted for her. She would never forget the stories her sweet mama had told her as she plaited her hair. Mama had promised her a braw, handsome knight would come for her one day, a man who would love her and protect her, one who would always support her and understand that she was different and special. Diana's future husband would cherish her for the woman she was and not wish to change her. But she had been waiting for years, with nary a sign of him.

Mama, where is he?

The old man rested his hand on his daughter's head. "I have tried and tried again, Daughter. No one has been good enough for you." He brushed back the hair that had fallen in her face and wiped her tears. "I'm sorry. I only do what I must."

"Papa, promise me you will be here when I return."

"Diana, you must marry him."

"But if the cousins don't agree, I will return to you. Please promise me you will still be here. Please?"

"Daughter, you will marry him. I will stay around long enough to see you wed."

Hellfire, what was she to do now? She may as well accept her fate. Her father would not budge. She would have to work on her cousins. Under no circumstances would she wed that hairy old pot-bellied pig.

~

Micheil Ramsay yelled across the road. "Grant, hold!" He couldn't believe that he had managed to find them this quickly. Micheil's brother, Quade, was married to Brenna Grant, the laird's sister. The Ramsays and the Grants had spent much time together fighting off the Norse a year ago. In fact, Robbie Grant had been in charge of the Grant warriors, a force that had been paramount in sending the enemy forces home.

Laird Alexander Grant and his brother, Robbie, dismounted from their horses in front of the largest inn in all of Perthshire. There was a hooded figure still mounted on another horse, he noticed. Several of the Grant guards were with them, implying their business was important.

"Ramsay," Robbie shouted. "What business have you here?"

Micheil jumped off his horse and clasped Robbie's shoulder. "Looking for you. I was a bit bored at home, what with Logan and Quade both in residence with their wives. Logan wanted a missive brought to Glasgow, so I volunteered to travel. There I heard the Grants were headed to Falkirk. I had to come. Though I know not why you are here, I thought I would investigate and visit my distant kin."

"Are you taking over Logan's wandering tendencies?" Robbie asked.

"Seems I have." He grinned.

Alex reached up for the figure on the horse—a woman, Micheil realized—helping her to dismount and moving her away from the mud. "Family business. Micheil Ramsay, meet Diana Drummond."

Once her feet touched dry ground, her hood fell back and Micheil's senses flared in response to the beauty before him. He took her gloved hand in his and stared into her gorgeous green eyes. She shook her head as soon as her hood fell back, revealing a mass of red curls that tumbled halfway down her back.

Her beauty simply took his breath away. Dark red hair, green eyes that matched the forest in the summer time, and full pink lips reached out to him, commanding his attention in a way he could not refuse. His eyes were drawn to her and a lump lodged in his throat, making him swallow unnecessarily. What the hell was it about this girl? Micheil had always prided himself on having a way with the lassies, but none of his conquests had made him feel like *this*.

"My lady, 'tis a pleasure to make your acquaintance. Why have we never met? You are of the Drummond clan?"

"Aye, I am heir to the Drummond land." Her chin never wavered as she stared into his eyes.

Slud, she was a confident lass on top of it all. Women with backbone drove him to distraction— always had. Judging from the scowl etched into her features, Diana did not seem at all pleased with her circumstances. Micheil shook his head. Something did not ring true about her being heir to the much coveted Drummond keep. "I find that impossible," he said. "'Tis well known the only heir is a spoiled, overage..."

His voice trailed off as he assessed the situation correctly. That spoiled, overage, miserable woman stood directly in front of him. Of course, rumors were not always true, and here was the proof. This woman was absolutely gorgeous. Her sire had kept her well hidden.

She quirked her brow at him. "I'm a what? Overage, spoiled, and what else?" Her hands settled on her hips.

Micheil glanced at Robbie, who presently wore a wicked grin. Clearly his friend was not about to help him out of this situation he had brought upon himself. He must learn to control his tongue some day.

Alex was quick to speak up. "Come. We are going inside for something to eat. Care to join us, Micheil?"

Micheil accepted. He made sure to walk behind the Drummond heir so he could watch the sweet sway of her hips. Where had she been all his life? He prided himself on having personal knowledge of all the beautiful lasses in the Lowlands and the lower end of the Highlands. Surely, he would have remembered if he had met her before. As soon as they were inside, Alex disappeared, searching for the innkeeper.

Robbie said, "Diana's mother, Robina, was our mother's sister. Chief Drummond allowed our cousin to choose her own husband, but since she has been unable to make a choice, he has made it for her."

"Unable to make a choice?" she barked at Robbie, spinning in place to glare at them. "I'm certainly capable, I just have not found the right man yet."

Micheil could not wipe the smile from his face. "How far have you looked, lass?"

"I have not tried verra hard, but now that my sire is ill, I must marry."

"And who is the lucky lad?"Micheil asked.

Robbie coughed and turned his head away, hiding the expression on his face. "Baron Ewen Gow of Falkirk."

Micheil shouted, "Nay!"

CHAPTER TWO

Micheil's eyes widened, and Diana's reaction was swift. "Do you not see, Robbie? I cannot marry the man."

"Alex will be the judge, lass, not me."

Micheil thought carefully about commenting about what he knew of Gow, but decided to wait to hear more about their plan before he shared his thoughts. Thankfully, Alex returned.

Alex grasped his shoulder. "Come, we have a nice dining area to ourselves where we can feast and relax for a few hours before we continue on with our journey. 'Twill be good to catch up."

Once they settled inside, Alex ordered meat pies, cheese, bread, fruit pies, and ale.

As soon as everyone found a place, Diana said, "Tell me, my lord, what hear you of Baron Gow?"

Micheil froze. She stared at him with the deepest green eyes ever, eyes that seemed to dig into his chest and touch his very soul. Lying, he said, "I know little of the gentleman." Gentleman is hardly the word he would use to describe the man. The baron's cruelty was well known throughout the area, primarily because three wives had predeceased him. Many in his employ believe the baron had played a part in each of the timid ladies' death. And his treatment of horseflesh was known to be horrendous. Micheil would have to find an excuse to speak with Grant privately about the matter. It was hardly appropriate dinner conversation.

"Surely, you must have heard something." Her eyes bored into his, searching for the truth.

"I do not know him. I have never met him." At least this was not a lie.

"'Tis bad, is it not?" She glanced at both Alex and Robbie. "Do you see? I cannot marry the man. You cannot make me follow through with this."

Alex leaned back in his chair. "Cousin, we are charged with ensuring your prospective husband is suitable before the marriage takes place. Do not pester us all the way there. Do you not trust Robbie and me to have your best interests in mind?"

She leaned forward over the table. "Aye, perhaps you do and you are well-meaning. I am trying to show you there is no need for us to visit the baron at all. Take me to Edinburgh and I'll find my own husband." Micheil was so shocked he felt his mouth fall open.

Robbie said, "You want us to allow you to walk the streets in Edinburgh until you find a man you deem suitable?"

"Father is too ill to see reason, but I would prefer anyone to that cruel, smelly old goat. Do you truly intend to sentence me to such a life? Besides, I am quite sure my knight is there."

Micheil hid his smile. So Diana Drummond was a wee bit dramatic, or perhaps she had a secret lover in Edinburgh she planned to meet.

She switched her attention from her cousin to Micheil in a second. "And you. Stop looking at me like I am daft. I am not spoiled just because my father wished to allow me to choose my own husband."

Robbie said, "Now, Diana. Your father did permit you to do many things most women are denied."

"Irrelevant." She glared at Robbie. "Now will you take me to Edinburgh, or must I find someone else to help me?"

Alex said, "Diana, we will carry out the plan we agreed upon with your sire. We promised him to take you to Falkirk to your betrothed, see if the two of you are suited, and see you married if you are. We will not bend from that, so cease begging. Your constant demands may have worked on your father until now, but they won't sway me. I will do what I pledged."

A range of emotions flashed through Diana's glorious eyes as she stared at Alex. First Micheil saw anger, then self-righteousness, fear, and finally a spark of determination. Her voice trembled when she spoke. "As you wish." She turned to Micheil. "Just to inform you, I may have been spoiled by a man's definition, but naught was done for me that wasn't done for you, being a male. Were you taught to ride a horse?"

Micheil nodded. "Of course."

"And to hunt?"

"Aye."

"And to read?"

"Aye." He knew he could not pull his gaze from hers if he tried. Something about her was absolutely mesmerizing.

"And I am the only Drummond heir. As such, I am no different than you or either of my cousins. Just because I have a woman's shape does not mean there is aught wrong with my mind."

Micheil nodded in agreement. Yet there was naught wrong with her body either. Her delicious curves were just the type he favored in a woman.

"And I am verra good with numbers, so I will be able to run a keep with no problem. Just because I am as capable as a man does not indicate I am spoiled. I am well-trained. Now, since my cousins refuse," she stared directly at Micheil. "Will you take me to Edinburgh? I am in need of an escort." Then she raked her glance over the three of them, making it clear that her next words were intended for all. "And if he denies me, I'll go on my own. I will not allow my betrothed to touch me."

Diana's confidence waned. Her cousins did not seem as if they were listening, and she was far from sure she would have more luck with this new lad. No one answered her plea, as if they thought she'd made it in jest. They seemed hesitant to believe she had very strong reasons to be concerned. But under no circumstance would she ever end up in Baron Ewen Gow's bed. She would die trying to escape him.

She didn't say that lightly either. There were numerous ways to accomplish her task, beginning with finding her own way to Edinburgh and seeking out her handsome knight. What the gentlemen around her didn't understand, no matter how she laid it out for them, was that she was no weak-kneed little ninny. They thought she was bluffing. Diana Drummond didn't bluff; she acted.

They ate the meal, Diana not speaking, too absorbed in planning her escape. Micheil laughed frequently with Robbie, his white smile lighting up the room. He was a handsome man, and her eyes kept returning to his dark, unkempt hair and that wicked grin. No doubt, he was very experienced with the ladies. Her sire had kept her well protected from lads while she grew up, so she lacked experience with men. Few had possessed the courage to attempt anything with her, even a kiss, but looking at him...well it made her feel *something*. She even found herself considering whether seducing him might have any benefit for her particular situation.

Hell, but how had she ended up in this predicament? It was her own fault. She should have chosen someone long ago, but none of her suitors had inspired her. She had always dreamed of the perfect English knight coming to take her away...and that dream had brought her here. Besides, her father expected her husband to come to her and take over their land upon his death.

Unfortunately, he didn't have much longer. Whatever she did, she needed to do it quickly so she could get home to her papa. The thought of him dying alone, of her never seeing him again, was more than she could bear.

"Well?" she finally asked as the dishes were cleared away from in front of them.

"Well what?" Micheil grinned.

"Will you take me to Edinburgh?" He gave her that winning smile of his, but he did not answer. Those tricks would not work on her. "Why will you not answer my question?"

"Because you have not given me a sound reason to take you there."

His dancing green eyes challenged her. It did not matter; she would not back down. "Because I want to go to Edinburgh. If the reason I already gave you is not enough, I have no other except that it is my desire." She didn't let on that her mother had always told her that she was to meet and marry in Edinburgh. Her mother had seen her destiny in a dream. Diana had to aim for it even if her father had not believed her mother.

"And do you always get what you desire, my lady?" The twinkle in his eye taunted her.

Her eyes narrowed into a gaze intended to intimidate him, though she knew it wouldn't work. "Usually, aye."

His gaze never wavered; he just grinned. Her cousin, Alex, broke the spell. "No one is going to Edinburgh. We're going to Falkirk to meet your betrothed, and I have fifty guards that say you will get there at my side, my lady."

Diana huffed her indignation and flounced in her chair. Micheil just laughed.

Hellfire, her usually tricks weren't going to work on these men. But they were about to see just how stubborn she could be.

CHAPTER THREE

Late in the afternoon, their destination appeared on the horizon. Diana's stomach did somersaults, almost bringing her to the point of gagging.

Diana rode between Alex and Micheil. Robbie brought up the rear, along with three other guards, and her cart was being drawn behind him by one of his men. Alex had directed the other forty some guards to stay back until he beckoned them, though Diana did not comprehend this tactic. As they approached, she noticed a small party leaving the castle gates, headed in their direction. The closer they came, the more her stomach churned. The party was comprised of six horses, and as they came near, she realized she had no idea which of these men she was intended to marry.

The two parties halted, a small distance separating them. The man in the lead of the Baron's party was tall, gray-haired, and thin, though not unattractive. She had been told by a stable boy that Gow had a paunch, but this man did not. He held himself with an air of superiority that Diana did not like. Could he be her betrothed?

The gray-haired man spoke first. "Alexander Grant, I presume. You escort my betrothed, Diana of Drummond?"

Diana glanced at the Grant, who was Laird and Chieftain of his own very large clan in the upper

Highlands. Alex's demeanor changed as the man spoke, his shoulders drawing back, his hand drawing toward the hilt of his sword. It was a subtle move, but she was close enough to detect it. Perhaps she could trust her cousin after all.

"I am Laird Alexander Grant, and aye, I am escorting and protecting Diana of Drummond." His chin lifted at the end of his sentence. "I must see Baron Gow."

The gray-haired man's gaze narrowed, never meeting her gaze or acknowledging her presence. "I am Baron Gow. And if you are in charge of my betrothed, why is she riding a horse? A woman's place is in the cart." He pointed to the cart as if to emphasize his argument.

"Diana prefers to ride," Alex answered, his face void of expression. Alexander Grant was a huge man, much larger than Baron Gow. The fool had to see that, did he not?

Several seconds passed as the two leaders stared at each other, the others waiting with bated breath. Baron Gow moved his horse toward Diana, but Micheil inched his mount closer to her right side and Alex stayed firmly seated to her left. The Baron reached out for her and snarled, "You will get off that horse, woman, and take your proper place. You do not belong alongside men."

Diana gasped and backed away from him, clenching her reins in both hands as two swords swooped down in front of her, one from the Grant, and one from Micheil Ramsay. She had never seen anything happen so quickly.

Alex spoke. "The lady is under my charge. You will not touch her until she is transferred to your charge." His voice radiated with authority.

"Release her to me and be on your way. I did not promise accommodations for all your men. I will see to the lady." The baron stared at her cousin, waiting for a challenge, his men behind him poised to attack.

Alex smiled without budging from his position. "I am sure you would love to have her released to you, but as I just said, she is in my charge, and I will not leave her in your care until I deem that care to be appropriate for a lady of her station."

Gow's mouth twisted in a sneer that made Diana want to vomit. She prayed frantically that her cousins would not desert her with this man.

The baron turned to glare at her. "And who is going to prevent me from taking her now? You and your friends? I think not. She is mine, so she will do as I say. Her land belongs to me. It should have been mine years ago, but my ancestors were fools. You will not stop this from taking place. I have waited too long for this."

Alex whistled and his forty guards galloped full force behind them. Diana released her breath, not realizing until that very moment that she had been holding it. "In the Highlands, honor requires a man to offer a night's stay to parties on the road that are traveling a distance. No honor at your castle, Gow?"

The baron backed off and gave a grim smile. "This move to you, Grant. I will accommodate you and four others. The rest shall remain in the bailey." He nodded to Alex. "I can wait to get my hands on my betrothed. When the time comes, she will learn a wife's proper place." He turned his horse around and headed toward the castle, his five men trailing behind him.

Diana glanced at Alex and whispered, "My thanks, cousin." He nodded in response, his brow furrowed. Emotion welled up inside her, threatening to unseat her.

Robbie spoke up from behind her, though whether he addressed Alex, Micheil, or both was unclear. "This is not going to go at all as I expected. Things will get interesting, will they not?"

The Grant smirked and quirked an eyebrow. "Och, so they will." He then glanced at Diana, who was losing her fight to hold in her tears. "Do not fret, cousin. You remind me of my mother. Protecting you will honor her memory, so 'tis not a duty I will shirk. If you have need of anything, you will come for me. Understood?"

Diana nodded, unable to speak for fear of bursting into wrenching sobs. She would maintain her composure in honor of her mother and his. The look of concern on Micheil Ramsay's face did not go unnoticed. Perhaps she did indeed have an ally in him.

As they entered the gates of the castle, Diana could not help but notice all the threatening glances sent her way by her betrothed. She decided the only way to she could handle her situation was to refrain from looking at him at all. As they walked up the steps to the great hall, she felt an arm brush across her back. She whirled her head around to see her betrothed was touching her, the taunting grin on his face an implied threat. Micheil stood back and gathered her in front of him, for which she was eternally grateful.

Once inside, the baron summoned his servants to feed their guests. Not wanting any more to do with him, Diana said, "My lord, if I may, it has been an exhausting trip. I would like to rest." She wished for anything to get away from his presence.

He smiled at her, "Of course, my dear. Allow me to show you to your chamber." He held his arm out to her so he could escort her.

Diana panicked at the thought of being alone with him and glanced wildly at her cousins. She had hoped there would be a maid to attend to her.

"I would like to see my chamber as well, Baron," Alex said.

"Of course." He led the way up the staircase and down the corridor. He stopped and pointed down the passageway. "Your chamber will be the second on the right, Grant." He stood aside, awaiting the Grant's leave. When the big man did not move, the baron gave him a questioning glance.

Alex stood there for a moment, then headed down the corridor. A moment later, the baron stopped in front of a doorway, motioning for Diana to do the same. "Your chamber, my dear." He opened the door for her and stepped inside. "I'm sure this will please you. It was my former wife's chamber."

As soon as he finished his sentence, Alex, who must not have walked very far down the passageway at all, forced his way into the chamber and searched the room with his gaze. "Where does the door lead, Baron?"

Baron Gow, clearly appalled to be questioned, leveled an intimidating expression at Alex. "As I said, Grant. This was my wife's chamber. The door connects to mine."

Alex grabbed Diana's elbow and ushered her out the door. "Then Diana will not be staying here, and I am offended you would seek to risk her reputation in such a way."

Alex moved down the passageway, but Baron Gow bellowed after him. "Cease your interference. She is to be my wife in less than a sennight. The marriage will happen, whether you approve of it or not."

Alexander Grant turned around slowly, his height and posture even more impressive when he was off his horse. Diana glanced at his face and wanted to take a step back, but she was delighted to see he was in complete control of the situation. The baron could not hope to best such a man. "That is where you are wrong, Baron Gow." He dropped her hand and stalked toward the baron until he was nose to nose with him, although the Grant had to bend over to do so. "She is my charge, and I will do what my kin has requested of me. The future Drummond will *not* marry you without my approval. And if I need to put my sword through your black heart to prevent it, do not doubt that I will." Alex never moved.

The baron spewed hatred. "You are every bit the savage you are reputed to be. Highland savages, all of you. I hated being given land so close to the Highlands. Put her in your chamber if you'd like. She'll be in mine soon enough." He spun on his heel and headed down the passageway, hitting the wall with his fist and growling as he passed.

Alex directed her into his chamber, holding his finger to his lips to encourage her not to speak until they were inside.

"Alex, my thanks, but please remove me from these premises." Diana had progressed to sheer panic after witnessing her betrothed's behavior with a man of Alex's stature. "He frightens me to no end."

"Diana, I cannot just remove you. I must have justification. This union received the king's support, so we cannot break it without a good reason. I will find it, but it will take some time. In the meantime, you will sleep in my chamber, and I will post guards outside your door. Take your rest. He will not bother you today." He kissed her forehead and headed out the door. As soon as it closed behind him, Diana fell onto the bed and cried herself to sleep.

Micheil sat outside Diana's chamber door, leaning against it for support, Alex's two guards standing on either side of him. He had told Alex what he knew of Gow, but now he could see that it was unnecessary. The man had already shown his true colors. Hellfire, but this was not going to be easy. He'd like to shove a fist through the surly bastard's face. It was unbearable to consider the possibility of her marrying that man. He had half a mind to wed her himself just to save her from this sorry situation, but it was not in him to settle down. His own brother, Logan, called him a lover of ladies, and he could not deny it. He loved to play with women. They were all beautiful in their own right—some saucy, some wenchy, and some so innocent. Logan had finally settled down with a powerful woman, Gwyneth, Micheil's new sister-in-law. Micheil wouldn't dare mess with his brother's wife—he knew she'd cut his bollocks off for dinner if provoked—but he had a lot of respect for her.

Diana Drummond reminded him a bit of her. She was strong and confident and not prone to intimidation, except in one area. Something told him Diana was not an experienced lover. How fun it would be to teach her the art of passion.

Which brought him back to the reason he had sworn he would never settle down with one woman—they were each so different in the bed chamber. How could he possibly be expected to stay with just one? One day he loved curvaceous, voluptuous dark-haired women, and the next day he would do most anything to touch a long-limbed, willowy blonde. How did a man ever choose?

No, he could never settle down—it was simply impossible, particularly since he did not take to the notion some men had of it being a man's right to cheat. He knew how sensitive women were, so he could never, ever cheat on his wife. The look on her face would kill him.

Which is precisely why he was destined for the life of a bachelor.

The door flew open and he fell backward into the chamber.

Diana stood with her hand still on the door, staring at him aghast. "Micheil? What are you doing?"

Micheil brushed himself off and jumped up, executing a small bow in her direction. "Why, guarding your honor, my lady. Is that not clear?"

She giggled, a musical sound he vowed to hear again. "Micheil, you cannot help but charm women, can you?"

He wiggled his eyebrows. "I am not in a position to know. Are you charmed?" He flashed a grin her way, hoping it would have its intended effect to take her off her guard. It must have worked because she grabbed him by the tunic and pulled him inside her chamber, closing the door behind them. He stared at her in shock. "You are aware of how this looks, my lady?"

"Do not 'my lady' me, Micheil. It does not suit you. But what am I to do? You can clearly see the man is a beast, a scum, a destroyer of women. I cannot marry him. What would become of me?" She stared at him with her arms crossed in front of her, her green eyes ablaze.

Micheil's grin disappeared. "I must admit he is definitely not an honorable man. My guess is that he has committed dastardly deeds that would astound even me. Nay, I would not like to see you left to his devices. But I trust my cousins to see the same thing." He rubbed his chin in thought.

"Then take me to Edinburgh as I bade you to do."

He could see the lass was completely serious. He had to talk reason into her. Acting without forethought would be unwise around a man like Baron Gow. "Just removing you will not settle this matter. The baron will follow us and demand justice. You are betrothed to him. Alexander Grant is an excellent chieftain and has King Alexander's ear after everything Clan Grant did for the Scots against the Norse. But the Grant understands how to handle situations like this one properly, and always with the end he desires in mind. I trust him to find a way out that will not risk anyone's life. You must be patient."

She paced the room in thought. "He won't take me to Edinburgh. You must."

"And are you really naïve enough to believe you'll find a man who will agree to marry you so quickly? Not to mention he must be acceptable to your father and your cousins."

"Edinburgh is a huge burgh. Why, there must be festivities going on there all the time. All I have to do is flaunt my wares—" her arms swung down her side, "—and I'll find someone who will make a better husband than the baron." She just couldn't admit that her motivation was a dream, her mother's dream from years ago. Her mother had said she would fall in love with her knight in Edinburgh. She must find a way there.

"And just anyone that likes the looks of you will be acceptable? It is a poor plan. You cannot just take anyone who offers himself to you. You could meet a reiver, a murderer. You need to be a wee bit more careful when selecting a mate, don't you agree?"

Her hands flew up to grab her head and she flounced onto the bed. "What else can I do? I have no other alternative. Besides, I am sure I will be able to locate my knight. He is there. I am certain of it." She could not explain how many times her mother's dreams had come true. Perhaps she had possessed the gift of sight. But her mother had warned her against such tales, since they often brought suspicions of witchery.

Micheil gave her a puzzled look. "And who is this knight to whom you keep referring?"

She tossed her curls over her shoulder, pursing her lips. "My knight is the knight my mother told me about many times before she passed. He is the one I want, and I am certain I can find him in Edinburgh." The excitement and possibilities in the city were endless, at least to one kept as sheltered as she had been. Could he not see the potential in such a large place? It must be teeming with handsome knights and young barons, unlike her betrothed.

He strolled over and grabbed her hands, tugging her back onto her feet. "Trust your cousins. Ask Robbie about his wife sometime or about his brother Brodie's wife. She was betrothed to a Norseman and they got her away from him, though it took some time. They are happily married now, and I believe she is carrying their first-born. Come." He held his hand out to her. "I'll escort you below stairs to see about dinner. You must be hungry."

"Nay." She shoved his hands away. "What good will it do me to eat near the disgusting man?"

Micheil reached for her again, but she stepped back, wary. "Can you not see?" he said. "You must inflame the baron with your confidence. The more rudeness your cousins witness from him, the better your chances of being removed from the situation. Incite the baron's temper, raise his ire while you still have protection. Let the man try to touch you again, encourage him to order you about or even grab you. This would only help your case. Your cousins need as much against the man as they can find." He held his hand out to her.

She hesitated but eventually placed her hand in his—her silent agreement to go to dinner. As they moved down the passageway, she took a deep breath. "Mayhap he will be kinder to me when there are more witnesses."

As they descended the staircase, a booming voice caught their ears. "How dare you walk with another man in my own home!"

Diana glanced up to meet Micheil's eyes as she clung to him. "Or mayhap not."

CHAPTER FOUR

Baron Gow reached Diana's side in three long strides and immediately grabbed her arm and yanked her to him. "You will not embarrass me in my own home. Do you hear me?"

She attempted to pull away, momentarily stunned, but he would not release her. "But he was..."

"Silence! How dare you speak without permission. You are a woman, and you must remember it. Women do not speak unless asked."

Diana blushed, glancing around at the room full of guards and servants, embarrassed to be ridiculed in front of the entire great hall. But his servants continued on with their tasks, apparently not surprised at all to see him treat a woman so. No one acted shocked except the Grants. Robbie and Alex were seated at a table, and she could feel Robbie's fury from across the room. Alex showed naught.

Micheil spoke up, each word threaded with a masked threat. "Remove your hand from the lady, Baron."

Baron Gow's eyes narrowed as he turned to look at Micheil. "How dare you attempt to tell me what to do in my own home?"

Although Diana was so overwhelmed she had not even noticed him draw his sword, Alex Grant was suddenly holding the point of his weapon against the baron's side. "I think he told you to remove your hand from the lady."

The baron dropped his hand, swiveling around to glare at Alex. "And what will you do when you are gone, Laird Grant? Who will stop me then? She will be my wife. It was an agreement between her sire and me. Try as you may, you will not stop the marriage. She is mine."

"She is not yours yet, and you would do well to remember that. I am not just here as her protector, Baron. I have been charged by her sire to approve the match," Alex said between clenched teeth. "And I have *not* approved it yet. Leave her be or bear the consequences."

The baron released Diana and stamped his feet all the way over to the dais, acting like a bairn who had been refused a sweet.

Diana and Micheil both glanced at Alex to see his response.

"Alex," Micheil whispered. "Take her home now."

Though she wanted—and even expected—to see Alex nod his head, he did not. Instead he took her arm and led her toward the table. What was he waiting for?

As they passed Micheil, Alex whispered, "Proof. We need proof."

Diana did not know what more evidence of the man's malfeasance he could possibly require, but she could not risk that conversation with him now. Moments later, they sat at the table directly in front of the dais, Diana not wishing to sit next to her intended, and he accepting that a woman's place was not at the dais. Her hands trembled as the servants brought food, but she managed to make eye contact with Micheil and mouth the words, "Help me."

Dinner turned out to be a peaceful affair. A few minstrels arrived to perform, and the baron disappeared, allowing Diana to relax. It had been impossible to feel at ease with that man staring at her, eyeing her as though he were imagining how much he would enjoy beating her into submission. Since he was gone, she made her way to the garderobe alone.

On her way back to the great hall, a hand reached out for her from the shadows of the corridor and someone pulled her into a dark alcove.

Baron Gow smiled at her. "I have been waiting for this moment." His lips descended on hers in a wet kiss. He tasted of mutton and onions, and she pushed at his chest, struggling to get away from him. He grabbed her hands and swung her around until he held her from behind in a vise.

She could feel his hot breath in her ear. "Your cousins may be around to protect you at the moment, but they will not be here for long. I will teach you, my dear, to show me the respect I deserve. You have been spoiled way too much, just as I was warned, but you will kiss my feet before we are done."

Diana struggled to escape, but could not move. He rubbed his hardness against her backside, and she fought to pull away from him. Frantic to escape, she kicked, clawed, and spit—using every maneuver imaginable in an attempt to escape. She brought her foot down hard on his instep and bit his hand.

"You bitch!" he yelled.

Oh, how she hoped he had shouted loud enough for someone to hear.

He let go of her with one arm, but managed to keep hold of her with the other. With his free hand, he swung and slapped her cheek hard enough to leave a mark.

Micheil rounded the corner just in time to see the assault, and he did not pause before slamming his fist into the baron's face and knocking him to the ground.

Gasping for breath, she stared at the lout on the ground and flung herself into Micheil's arms.

***

Diana paced her room, still distraught from the events of the evening. She had to get away, she just had to escape. Where she went did not matter, so long as it was far way from here. She had begged Alex and shared the whole sordid tale with him, but he had flatly refused her and retired to the baron's solar with Robbie at his side. At least Micheil had helped her wash the smell and feel of the man from her by bringing her clean cloths and water. Everything about the baron made her want to retch—his saliva, the feeling of his sex against her, his breath. She had to get out.

But it was the middle of the night, and she did not know what to do. The only way she could get out on her own was if everyone was asleep. But what if the fool caught her unawares again like he had in the passageway? She cringed at the thought of what he would do to her. Pacing again, she reviewed all the alternatives in her mind, coming up empty each time.

A soft knock echoed in her chamber. Her heartbeat sped up, afraid yet hopeful. It could be the baron, but she did not think he would bother to knock. She started to reach for the handle then stopped herself and leaned forward so she could press her ear to the worn wood, hoping for some clue that would tell her the identity of the interloper.

"Aye?" she whispered.

"Open up. It's Micheil."

She sighed in relief and swung the door open, wanting to throw herself into his arms again.

He shut the door behind him and tossed some things at the bed. "Here. Put these on." She reached for them and fingered the worn cloth, a puzzled look on her face.

"Well? You wanted out, did you not? I plan to give you your chance. These clothes are from a young lad, so they should fit you. There is a set of corridors built beneath the keep for the protection of the ruling family. We will use them to sneak out. Hurry."

Diana did not need to be told twice. She grabbed the clothes, but not before tearing off her own and tossing them under the bed. Not even bothering to turn in front of Micheil, whose eyes grew wide at her boldness the instant before he whirled away from her, she pulled on the new clothes. "I don't care, Micheil. Just take me out of here. The man is mad."

Micheil tossed a small saddlebag down. "Here, put whatever else you need in this. It will take us awhile to reach Edinburgh."

Her eyes widened and she threw herself at him, hugging him and kissing his cheek. "Thank you, thank you, Micheil."

He brushed her away. "Hurry, we do not have much time."

She threw a wool gown and a few necessities inside the bag and handed it to Micheil. After looping the bag over his shoulder, he took her hand and paused before opening the door, holding his fingers to his lips. They sneaked down the stairs and into the kitchens without causing a stir. Micheil led her into a dark room at the back of the kitchens, grabbing a torch to light his way.

"Micheil, we must be lost. There is naught here." Her gaze searched the room frantically for a door, but found nothing.

"Patience, my dear." He handed her the torch and pushed at a large chest against one wall. He smiled at her over his shoulder when he pushed the chest, obviously intended to be able to move easily. Once he shoved the cupboard out of the way, they both stared at a rickety old door. Micheil yanked hard on it until it gave way. He stood aside, bowing at the waist to her. "After you, my lovely."

She tiptoed through the door as Micheil took the torch from her, holding it high in the air. As soon as they found the tunnel, he moved back to do his best to hide their escape before he took her hand in his with a grin. And then they ran. Micheil tugged her behind him, and she did her best to keep up. Cobwebs hit her in the face, but she did not care. She had to get away at any cost. The passageway was like a maze, but Micheil never hesitated at any of the corridors. It was as if he knew exactly where they were headed. Didn't matter to her—she would ask him later how he'd come to discover the underground path.

Micheil finally stopped in front of a small staircase and beckoned her to follow him up the steps. He had to heave his shoulder into the door at the top multiple times before it gave way, but it finally opened. They stepped out into a cool evening, and the first thing Diana noticed was the blanket of shining stars in the sky. How had she failed to notice how beautiful they were before now? It was like staring up at a thousand different twinkles of hope. Her eyes misted at what Micheil had risked for her. Just for a moment, she lapsed into a grin at the thought of Baron Gow discovering that she was gone. Alex Grant could handle him, of that she had no doubt.

Diana jumped for joy when she found her beloved horse munching on grass. Micheil helped her mount before climbing into his own horse's saddle, and they galloped off toward the horizon. The direction seemed unimportant compared with the urgency of her need to escape.

She would explain everything to her father later.

Several hours later, they stopped at a clearing near a creek, far off the regular path. Micheil had pushed his horse hard, wanting to ensure they were far away when Gow discovered their absence. He trusted the Grants would be able to delay the chase for a while, but he needed to get Diana to Edinburgh fast so they could disappear into the crowds of the local markets.

He helped her down and said, "See to your needs. I'll keep watch." She disappeared into a nearby group of bushes as he led the two horses over to water. Micheil had to admit he had never done anything this rash or dangerous before. Aye, he had fought during the battle with the Norse, but this was different.

This time, rather than fighting for his clan, he was fighting for the rights of a spoiled young woman. Still, she was beautiful and innocent, and did not deserve the treatment that cruel man had planned for her. Would there be repercussions for Clan Ramsay when his escapade was discovered? It was too late for such a concern, as he was not about to take her back, especially since it could be her death sentence. Sometimes, a man had to stand up for what he believed in, and Micheil believed Baron Gow was beyond reprehensible. Even a spoiled lass did not deserve to call him husband. He also hated to admit it, but the more time he spent with Diana Drummond, the less spoiled she seemed to him. When she returned, her hopeful green eyes pierced his soul. "Do you think we got away? Are we safe?"

"Aye, I think we're fine for now. Sit down. I have oatcakes and ale. We need to let the horses rest for a spell." What he did not tell her was that he had a very good reason for not worrying. Ten guards were in their periphery keeping a watchful eye for Gow and his men. The Grant warriors would follow them all the way to Edinburgh, so they would definitely get away from the boorish man.

He had promised not to tell her that Alex Grant had agreed to this gambit. He had not asked for Alex's reasons for subterfuge; he had been all too eager to get her away from the ugly situation. They sat on a log and ate, the silence deafening between them. While he did not want to speak for fear he would give his secrets away, she was probably in shock.

She played with the pieces of her oatcake. "How did you find out about the hidden passageway?"

He grinned and gave her a sidelong glance. "I have my ways."

She scowled at him. "What does that mean?"

Slud, she really was an innocent. "It means if you sweet talk a saucy kitchen maid, she will tell you anything."

Diana chuckled. "I have an inkling that you are quite experienced at talking sweetly to maids. 'Tis true?"

"Aye." He glanced up at the stars. "I have talked to more than a few maids, lassies, and women—all of the above. I like lasses. Guilty as charged." He turned back to her and could not help but stare at her plump bottom lip. Her teeth chewed that desirable lip in between every bite of oatcake.

Hellfire, he would love to take her into the woods and throw her down on his soft furs and make sweet love to her. Imagining her soft hips, long legs, and how she would look right before he took her over the edge made him hard in an instant. Was not every night meant to be spent in the arms of a saucy wench?

And that thought brought him back to reality. This was no wench seated next to him, but the heir to her clan's lands. An even greater reminder was the memory of her connection to Alexander Grant and the thought of how the Grant would react if he discovered Micheil took his cousin's innocence. *Get control, Ramsay.*

She changed the subject. "What do you think Alex will do when he finds out?"

He sighed, wanting to avoid this entire topic. "Alex was looking for the proof he needed to put an end to the betrothal. He is verra good at getting what he wants and needs. I suspect he will push the baron into betraying his true nature and will then use it against him. That way, he can put an end this whole farce."

Her green eyes crinkled. "Farce? Is that what you call it?"

"One of many things I would call it. Farce, mistake, grave threat to your well-being. Is that enough for a start?" He grinned at her, hoping to see her smile in return.

She did not. "Will you tell my father those things?" she said softly. "He will be furious with me, and he is near death so I do not wish to upset him."

She played with the crumbs of her oatcake before raising her gaze to his.

Micheil frowned. It was not the request of a selfish girl, and the fact that her first concern was for her father made him think more of her. He just hoped the Drummond chieftain was forgiving. "That statement is not something I would expect to hear from a spoiled lass," he murmured.

"It is as I told you," she said, though there was not much fire in her voice at the moment. She sounded lost instead. "Father has allowed me to do things most females do not, but he never had a son. I was his son."

"And you love your sire." He peered at her, staring at her hair, wishing he could run his fingers through the red silky strands of it.

"Aye." She swiped at a tear sliding down her cheek. "Verra much. I love him and I don't want him to leave me."

"Are you sure you want to head to Edinburgh and not home?" He chugged another swish of ale, then handed her the skein.

"Aye, I'm sure. I need to go to Edinburgh first. 'Tis the only way he'll forgive me..." She nodded her head in satisfaction.

"If you bring home a lad?"

Diana stared at Micheil. "I must bring home a husband. I have no choice if I wish to be welcomed back."

CHAPTER FIVE

Several hours later, Diana heaved a sigh of relief as Micheil slowed his horse and cantered off the path in search of a clearing. She had needs, after all. The man had to know that.

Once he helped her to dismount, he said, "We are almost in Edinburgh, so what are your plans?"

"To find my knight, of course." She ran to the stream for some fresh water to wash her face and hands. There had not been much rain lately, so the road was quite dusty. Thankfully, she was still dressed in her lad's clothing and had not ruined the one wool gown she had brought.

"And where are we to find this knight?" He yelled so she could hear him. "You said your mother told you about him, but do you know where he resides? What's his name?"

She turned to stare at him, flummoxed. "How would I know my knight's name?"

"You have not met him yet?" Micheil's eyes widened.

"Of course not. If we had met, we would already be wed." She gave him her back as she leaned over the stream again. Was he daft? That was their entire purpose, to find a knight for her to wed. She had to find the man her mother had seen in her dream. Her mother had been steadfast in predicting she would marry in Edinburgh.

She jumped and turned back in time to see Micheil's hand slap his forehead before he said, "Your mother didn't have someone in mind? So we are here to *find* your husband, and you would like a knight?" His voice echoed in a low timbre that made her almost afraid of him.

"Aye, doesn't every lass?" She was confused by his change in nature. This had been the plan all along, hadn't it? Or had she led him to believe differently?

"I would not know. I am not a lass now, am I?" He took a deep breath before he continued. "And where do you propose we find your knight?" His gaze narrowed, and she turned away, not liking the glare he was sending her way.

She lifted her chin. "I must have an English knight. My beloved mother was English. I have not met any Scots that are knights yet, but I will accept an Englishmen, so long as he has been knighted. I am sure such a man would be acceptable to my father. Perhaps we should go to the royal castle. If the king is in residence at present, I expect there will be parties and minstrels galore. I am sure to find a knight there. As soon as he realizes the land that will come to him as part of my dowry, I am sure he will be agreeable."

She scowled as she thought through her plan. It would be difficult, but now that she had come this far, she was sure to find her knight. Her beloved mama had told her a knight was her destiny as far back as she could remember, and that she would marry in Edinburgh. Why could he not see her reasoning? And now that she had lost her mama, she wanted someone to protect and support her, someone who would always be there for her. Her knight.

Micheil buried his face in his hands. "Why did you not mention this wee fact before? You could at least have mentioned it to Alex, who has actually been to the English Court before. And why must your betrothed be English anyway? Diana, do you truly believe an Englishman will be more willing to leave his country and marry you than a Scottish lad? Does it not make sense to find a husband closer to your home? Just by number alone, I expect we'll meet many more Scotsmen than Englishmen. We are in Edinburgh, for heaven's sake. You're Scottish! Do you not think your clan would be more accepting of a Scot?"

She stared at the clouds above and pondered Micheil's suggestion. Aye, it would be easier if she found a Scottish husband, and her clan would be more accepting. But she knew of no Scottish knights. Had her memory failed her? Had her mother said she would marry a knight or did she just tell her of tales of knights? There had been so many stories of the tourneys. Her beloved mother's bedtime stories suddenly muddled together. Had she said if her husband was Scottish or English? Perhaps Micheil was right and her memories were wrong. Her head rested in her hands, hoping to bring clarity to the issue, especially because it was so important.

She pictured herself sitting in a tented box during a tournament, dressed in her most beautiful blue gown. Her knight would ride over to the tent to accept her scarf as a favor on the end of his lance, and she would lean down to tie it on the tip, blushing as he stared at her. Her handsome knight—blond, he would be blond—would bend over to bestow a kiss upon her cheek, but she would be forced to turn away for propriety's sake. The disappointment in his face would be evident to all who sat with her under the tent, protected from the heat of the sun. Then he would ride off, her scarf fluttering in the wind, but not before swearing his undying love...

"Diana?"

Micheil's voice brought her back to the present. "What?"

"We left quickly. What clothes do you have to attract a knight? Did you manage to squeeze any of your best gowns into the satchel?"

"Err...nay. I have but one wool gown, far from my best." She drummed her fingers on her lips. "Someone in Edinburgh will no doubt be willing to assist us in our plight. There are markets and cloth weavers aplenty in this city. Surely one of them could make me an appropriate gown. Micheil, I am sure I can get the most beautiful gown in all of the land here in Edinburgh. There must be numerous tailors in such a place."

"I suggest we do it quietly. We do not wish to draw attention to our quest. If Baron Gow is as intent on getting his hands on you as I think he is, he will send guards to look for you."

Diana played with her plaited hair. "You are right. We must be careful. Is there not anyone in your family who is nearby?"

"Actually, there is. My father has a sister in Edinburgh. She lost her husband, but she still resides here in a small home. Once I determine exactly where she is, we can at least stay there until we have a better plan." He scowled at her. "Why must you lassies be so besotted with dreams? Sometimes the best lad for you is the closest one to you." He lifted his water skin to his mouth.

Diana gasped and covered her mouth in surprise. He could not be suggesting what she thought he was suggesting, could he? "You do not mean yourself, pray tell, do you?"

Micheil choked on his water. "Nay, I do not mean me. I have no intention of marrying. But there must have been some nice lads near Drummond land. Why have you not chosen one of them? Life would have been much easier for you, and you would be with your dying father now."

Diana blinked back her tears. "Because, I must find my knight. We were meant to be together. 'Tis what my mama told me, that I am destined to marry in Edinburgh. Do you not believe in destiny?"

"Hellfire, nay." He paced in a circle. "But we will try to find my aunt all the same."

Diana ran over and hugged him, planting a kiss on his cheek. "Thank you, Micheil. You will not regret it, I promise."

The next evening, they were seated in the dining hall of the home belonging to Micheil's Aunt Elspeth. She was a lovely lady who had not remarried after losing her husband a few years ago. Elspeth did have two married daughters who had left behind a few gowns that Diana could wear, though they needed to be adjusted a wee bit.

Micheil had sent half of the Grant guards Alex had sent with him to search for any sign of Baron Gow's men. The other half would stay near Elspeth's stables and assist him when necessary. He tried to deal with the men without being conspicuous, and Diana had not suspected their presence yet. Satisfied to have found his beloved aunt so quickly, he began to have a bit of hope that Diana's quest might succeed. Perhaps his aunt could assist them.

Aunt Elspeth's home had three sleeping chambers, a good size hall with a large hearth, plus the kitchens in the back. A large table with benches sat at one end while a circle of chairs sat in front of the hearth. Her cook had come up with a lovely meal for them, and they sat down to enjoy the small feast. He could not hold back a smile as he watched Diana and Aunt Elspeth. His aunt dearly loved to chatter, and he could recall many times when his father would ask her to stop.

She smiled at Diana and clasped her hand before the meal started. "The king is in residence at present, so you have arrived at the perfect time. In fact, I hear they will be opening the portcullis tomorrow and entertaining in the courtyard in the inner bailey. A large wedding is about to take place between an English cousin of the king's with a large dowry and an English knight, a young blond lad who is reputed to be the most handsome in all the land. The wedding is not for a sennight at least, but the king has invited them to wed here with a lavish ceremony. Many English knights will be visiting for the occasion."

"Wonderful, Aunt Elspeth. 'Tis my goal to find a husband, and an English knight is perfect." Diana smiled.

Micheil scowled at the smug look Diana tossed his way when Aunt Elspeth mentioned the knights.

Aunt Elspeth continued, her excitement bubbling over. "If you wish, I will go to the castle with you tomorrow, that is, if we can alter the pale green gown in time, though I don't have many servants to help.

"Aye, my lady, I would be happy to help sew any part that needs adjusting. Micheil and I would love to go with you, wouldn't we, Micheil?" Diana gazed at him from the corner of her eye, clearly hoping he would play along. He grunted. Why the hell not? He might as well attend just to see if he could prevent the lass from making a complete fool of herself. She was overzealous and needed to be brought down a tad.

"Was that an aye or a nay?" Diana tugged on the sleeve of his tunic.

"Aye, I'll go along. I am quite sure you will need someone to protect you from the wolves." His jaw clenched at the thought of some fool grabbing her, using her naivety against her.

"What wolves? There will be no animals present, will there, my lady?"

Micheil stood up and walked away, hiding his reaction to her comment. She was even more naïve than he'd guessed. Intelligent as she was, she was highly ignorant of the ways of men. How could he hope to protect such an innocent?

Elspeth chuckled. "Overzealous lads are often referred to as wolves. My nephew does not want you falling prey to their tricks."

"Tricks?"

"Never mind, Diana. You do not need to know." Micheil's hands covered his face in exasperation.

"I think she does, Micheil," Elspeth said. "I think she needs to be aware of how men can take advantage of an innocent lass."

His hand fell to his sides. "I'll protect her," he barked. Hellfire, he was not about to let her out of his sight. What had caused this miserable feeling in his gut? It was uncharacteristic of him, so he puzzled over the cause of his foulness.

"Micheil, is something bothering you? You don't seem verra agreeable." Aunt Elspeth smiled at him, a sympathetic expression on her face.

Micheil shook his head. What could be bothering him? He was searching for the impossible, Diana of

Drummond's perfect mate—who, based on everything she'd said, had to be a blond-haired English knight. And his blood still boiled at the insult she had thrown his way when she rejected the thought of him pursuing her hand. What was wrong with *him*? Granted he wasn't interested in tying himself down to only one woman, but she hadn't needed to be so crass and candid about her feelings for him. Anyway, a Ramsay was far better than any English knight she could hope to find.

His scowl threatened to become a permanent fixture.

Well, perhaps she would realize the folly of her ways the next day, when her dream knight failed to appear. She would undoubtedly be heartbroken, but Micheil had a gift for taking good care of lasses. He always knew how to make them smile. Somehow, he thought Diana's disappointment would require special skill on his part.

The next day was a flurry of activity as all the women in the house used their needles to alter the gown and matching mantle to fit Diana. When she was finally ready to go, she stared at her reflection in the looking glass, unable to believe it was her.

The over gown was a pale green, with a dark green undergown. The neckline was square and she wore a gold belt around her hips. Her red hair fell in waves down her back that had taken forever to arrange properly since it was often wild and unkempt. Once she was satisfied with what she saw, Micheil settled her mantle over her shoulders and they walked out into the night, not far from the revelry that had already started at the castle.

It was just a short distance, so they had decided to walk. The closer they came to the castle, the louder the music became, and the more butterflies took flight in Diana's stomach. As soon as the festivities came into view, she stopped, drinking in the ambience of the festivities, the flutes and fiddles calling to her like sirens on the high sea.

This would be her night, she was sure of it. The dancing torchlights promised an eve to remember. All of a sudden, Micheil's pace increased.

"Micheil, what is it?"

"Keep going. We are being followed." He glanced over his shoulder as he propelled her toward the castle and throngs of people.

"What are you talking about?" She glanced over her shoulder and noticed two unsavory characters behind them. "Do you think it's his men?" She struggled to keep up with Micheil.

"Aye, could be. We need to get there quickly." Micheil took her elbow and escorted her into the castle bailey, through a crowd of dancers and minstrels, ladies and lassies busy flirting with any lad in sight. They had left Elspeth behind because she had not felt up to traveling with them. Since no one knew them, Diana was not worried about her reputation. This was one of the rare times that she was grateful her sire had kept her hidden. Aye, her name had been out there for suitors, but few had seen her. Micheil would protect her—of that, she had the utmost confidence. She sighed, searching the courtyard for any sign of her knight. He would be here, he had to be.

An hour later, she had been completely unsuccessful at finding anyone suitable to be her betrothed. Discouraged and almost ready to give up for the eve, she turned to Micheil, lifting her skirts to allow for quick movement. Micheil was talking with a curvaceous blonde who reached over to rub his arm on occasion. Diana rolled her eyes and said, "I will return in a moment."

Not ten steps away from Micheil, a hand gripped her elbow and tugged her back until she hit a wall of muscle.

"I thought you would never leave him."

Warm breath scorched her ear as she swung around to see who dared to speak to her in such an intimate manner. The most handsome man she had ever seen gazed into her eyes, and her heart melted. There he was. Unable to speak, she stared into blue eyes that enchanted her with their sparkle. His hair was blonde and straight, falling just over his collar, and an incredible smile stretched across his face.

Her ability to speak finally returned. "I'm sorry, do I know you?"

"Perhaps not, but I *need* to know you. My name is Randall. And what is yours?" His rich English accent threatened to buckle her legs.

"Diana." So entranced was she by Randall, her breath came out with barely a whisper.

"Ah. The goddess, Diana. What an appropriate name for a lady as beautiful as you."

Diana blushed and turned away.

"Do not turn from me, my flower. I thrive when your gaze is upon me and me only." He smiled and reached for her hands, then held them up to his lips. "You are lovely. Please tell me you are not attached to your friend."

Her eyes widened. "Nay, he is...family. He is my cousin."

"Wonderful, because I am in need of a woman in my arms this evening." He headed toward the road outside the bailey, pulling her behind him as he directed her toward a clump of bushes. As soon as they were hidden between the branches, he wrapped his arms around her and pulled her to him. His lips descended on hers and she sighed, so happy to have finally found her knight. His mouth was warm but rough, his teeth knocking against her lips, forcing her to part for him so he could sweep his tongue inside. He pulled back and gazed into her eyes, his desire evident. "I want you, my sweet." He locked his lips on hers again, angling his mouth over hers, his saliva covering half of her face.

This was not quite how she'd envisioned her knight's kiss. He was too bold...too, well, spitty. Granted, he didn't taste awful like the baron, but this was not the kiss of her dreams, nor did he grab her heart as she had expected. Where was the lightning bolt when she met her true love? Naught, there was naught there. She pushed away just so she could wipe his spit from her chin and cheek. Glancing at him, she asked, "Are you an English knight, Randall?"

He grinned as he ran his hands down over her bottom, pulling her in tight. "I can be whatever you want me to be, Goddess Diana."

"But are you? A knight, I mean." She could not help but stare at his plump lips and the golden locks around his face.

"No, but I am English. My father is an earl, so I am nobility. I am looking for a wife while I am here. Are you taken?" He nuzzled her neck as one of his hands reached up to cup her breast.

"Why, nay! That is exactly why I am here." She waited to feel the flutter of her heart as she stared at the man who could possibly solve all her problems, but naught happened. Somehow, she had expected her destiny to feel different than this. Puzzled, she wished to just walk away to clear her mind.

"My pardon!"

Randall jumped back.

Micheil stood there, his hand on the hilt of his sword. "Take your hands from the lady."

"Nay! Micheil, you do not understand." She grabbed his arm, desperate to keep him from pushing Randall away.

"I *do* understand. I see a lad who shoved you back behind some bushes so he could maul you."

"He's not mauling me, he's…"

"His hand was on your breast, Diana. That is my definition of mauling." Micheil's eyes glowed with fury.

CHAPTER SIX

Micheil would kill the man, right then, right there. The bastard had one hand on Diana's breast and the other on her arse. He was a dead man.

"Please, Micheil, listen!" Her hands gripped his arm with enough strength for him to turn and gaze into her eyes.

Hellfire, why did she have to give him that innocent pleading look all the lassies were so talented at giving? He took his hand from the hilt of his sword. "Who is he?"

"This is Randall. He's an Englishmen," Diana whispered, one hand on his arm and the other hand on Randall's arm.

"Randall what? Of where?" He stared at her for a moment before turning his glare on Randall, his hands on his hips now, feet apart in a fighting stance.

She stuttered, unable to respond to his question. He could tell by the confused expression on her face that she had presented him with the entirety of her knowledge about the man. So her only reason for allowing such familiarities was because the man was blond and English. "Diana? Tell me you know something more of him."

Randall held his hands up. "No need to take it out on her. My apologies. Randall Baines, my father is the Earl of Wingate. I'll take my leave now." He nodded to her and ran around Micheil, heading back toward the revelry.

Micheil turned his fury to her. "What in hellfire are you doing? Giving your favors away to anyone who approaches you? Are you that desperate?"

She gave a weak tap to his arms as tears flooded her eyes and slid down her cheeks. "How could you?"

"How could I? He had his hands all over you." He hated it when lassies cried. Why did she have to do that?

"He is my knight! He is my destiny and you just scared him away." She crossed her arms and turned away from him, stomping her foot at the last moment.

"Your destiny? Didn't you just meet him?" he asked.

She whirled around to face him. "Aye, but he is looking for a wife just as I am looking for a husband. I'm not sure of it, but he could be the one. He could assist me out of this wretched situation I am in, could he not?"

"Like hell! A man who wishes to marry a lass doesn't maul her within the first few minutes of meeting her. Men who respect you will not push you behind bushes so they can grab your breasts. He is a wolf, exactly the sort of man Aunt Elspeth and I warned you about."

"Nay, he is not." She whirled around and gave him her back again. "'Struth he did not really seem like my knight. He did appear to be the one, but yet mayhap he is not." She grabbed at her hair in frustration. "How would I know? Where is my mama when I need her? What am I supposed to be looking for in a husband?"

Micheil took a deep breath and stared at the stars, counting to ten until he could speak again without yelling. He reminded himself how innocent she was. Given her circumstances, she was bound to fall for the first handsome man who showed any interest in her. Randall Baines. He growled and crossed his arms. Even the man's name sounded soft and cowardly.

She swung around again and pushed past him. "I want to return to the festivities. Leave me be, Micheil Ramsay."

Micheil followed her, continuing his rampage. "May I remind you that your safety was entrusted to me?"

She stopped and faced him. "By whom? Certainly not by me. Leave me alone, I said."

"You didn't mind having me nearby when you were locked in your chamber by Baron Gow. Or when Baron Gow had his tongue down your throat. And did Randall shove his tongue down your throat, too?"

"Aye, he did, and it was wonderful."

He caught the flash of something different in her expression that told him she was not being exactly truthful. Disgust maybe? He tried to contain his smirk.

She continued on in a huff without looking at him. "You have my thanks for getting me away from the baron, now go. I can take care of myself. I will never find a man with you following me and scaring them all away. Be gone." Her hand waved into the air as she maneuvered amongst the revelers, heading back to the courtyard.

Micheil stopped. Why not just let her go? What did he care? She was one of many lassies in the world. He would just tell Alex Grant how difficult she was, how she wouldn't listen to anything he said.

And Alex Grant would slice his throat for sure or hang him by his bollocks. He growled at the moon in frustration and took off after her. He would just watch her from afar. And if that dirty slime Baines came near her again, he would challenge him to a duel later.

He followed her as she wove through the crowd. He didn't see Baines anywhere nearby, so he relaxed and slowed his steps. He should have forced Aunt Elspeth to come as Diana's escort, though it was a bit late for her and he knew she did not feel well. His hand settled on his sword again, reminding himself he was a Ramsay, and he could handle any fool who dared to mishandle Diana of Drummond.

Unfortunately, he couldn't handle Diana.

Half an hour later, Diana was in deep despair. She sighed as her gaze raked the courtyard once more, searching—but not finding—the man of her dreams. She had to admit it was probably not Randall Baines, though she refused to admit this to Micheil. Randall could, however, be the solution to her dilemma. She tucked her mantle around her against the chill of the night, her pout definitely certain to send anyone else away.

Well, at least Micheil was not openly following her. He was probably not too far, but she did not need him scaring her man away. Drat the brute for his persistence. She moved over to the merchant's table where ribbons were being sold, hoping to find some new ones for her hair, as the green she wore tonight was not quite the shade she preferred.

A hand gripped hers from behind and pulled her away. She whirled around, hoping to see Randall behind her, but instead she found herself gazing into the eyes of a beautiful redheaded woman of about her age. Her hair was a much lighter shade than Diana's.

She smiled and grasped Diana's hand tightly. "You spoke to him. I saw you."

Diana peered at the girl, a wee bit wary since she did not have many female friends her age. "Spoke to whom?"

"The handsome one. Why, he is almost a prince. Have not you heard? All the girls are dying to talk to him, to be the chosen one, and he picked you."

Now she held Diana's attention. "Who is it you speak of? What handsome one?"

"Randall Baines," she whispered. "Do not say his name too loudly or the other lasses will listen."

Diana nodded. "Aye, I did speak with him. What do you know of him?"

Her eyes glittered. "Everyone knows him. He came along with the English crowd for the wedding, and everyone says he searches for his bride. He has not chosen anyone yet. How did you get to be so fortunate? What did he tell you?"

"He told me naught." Diana was secretly pleased that he had chosen to single her out when there were so many lovely women present. "Who are you?"

"I am Clarissa. I saw him drag you away. Tell me, did he kiss you? What was it like? Do you like him? Do you plan to see him again? Will he come back for you?" Her excitement was contagious, her eyes glowing when she spoke of him.

"I don't know anything about him, Clarissa. I just met him. He does look like a prince. I am not certain he is truly looking for a bride. Are you sure?" He had said as much, but Micheil had seemed less than convinced. Besides, she did not want to encourage this other girl to think Randall was seeking a bride. She wanted the man for herself. "Who is the knight getting married? I would like to see him, too. Isn't he handsome as well?" Mayhap she could entice him away. Desperation was a strange motivator.

"Aye, but he is not here. He will be at the tournament tomorrow," Clarissa said.

"The tournament?" Diana's heart fluttered at the thought of such a thing. It was as if all the stories she had loved as a young girl were coming to glorious life. She could feel the flush bloom in her cheeks.

"Aye, there will be a tournament on the fields tomorrow, and jousting is the main event at midday where all the knights showcase their talents with a horse and lance. You can watch from the side. Everyone will be there, hoping to see blood and rooting for the Scots or the English. Surely the knight will ask his betrothed to tie her token on the point of his lance. Even though the lances are dulled, it will be great fun. You should come. Maybe Randall is going to join in as well."

"I would like that. How do I get invited?" Her palms dampened at the thought of attending a tournament and possibly finding her knight in action. Suddenly, Randall did not matter anymore. Her knight would surely be on the field.

"Anyone may attend, but most will be on the fields. The only ones allowed under the tents will be the members of the royal party or the honorees—the groom and his bride. All the others will be on the grounds. But you must come."

"When is it?"

"High noon. Please say you'll be there. I will look for you."

Micheil appeared by her side, a grin on his face. "Good eve to you, my lady." He nodded at Clarissa and kissed the back of her hand. She covered her face quickly with a linen square and ran off, giggling with pleasure.

Micheil was still grinning after Clarissa left, his gaze following the trim hips as they moved through the crowd.

Diana glared at him. He was such a flirt.

"What's wrong, my friend?" Micheil smiled at her, his eyes dancing.

"You chase all the lasses, do you not, Micheil?" She narrowed her gaze, suddenly seeing Micheil a bit differently. He was a handsome and charming man to be sure, but she hadn't realized the depth of his appeal before seeing all the girls swoon over him.

"Well, I would not say all, but I do like to chase a lass or two. Why? Does it bother you? Are you jealous?" He wiggled his eyebrows at her.

She frowned. "Nay! I don't think it's wise to play with Clarissa. I don't trust her for some reason." The girl had been friendly enough to be certain, but Diana did not like her. Something about her seemed strange.

"No matter. She is gone now. Have you met any interesting Scotsmen?"

"Nay, but I did find out some information. There is jousting during a tournament on the morrow and I would like to go. Clarissa said all the knights will be there." She crossed her arms to let Micheil know she would not be dissuaded from her decision.

"Jousting, aye? Och, we should definitely be there." He held his elbow out to her. "Come, enough for this night. We'll need to prepare you another gown for the tourney."

Diana hadn't even thought of that. Of certain, she could not be seen in the same gown. Have mercy, her reputation would be in tatters in an instant. Silently thanking the Lord for Aunt Elspeth, she took his elbow, knowing she would have much work to do that night and on the morrow.

CHAPTER SEVEN

The next morning, Micheil decided to search the town for any news. Edinburgh was large, so it would take him a good while to make the rounds and glean any information he could. In particular, he was determined to discover if any of the visiting Englishmen—or anyone else in the vicinity—were worthy of being her husband.

He had arranged to meet Diana and his aunt at the jousting tourney. He knew he could trust Diana to attend the tournament with Aunt Elspeth, particularly given the fact he'd arranged for a couple of guards to follow them, while he continued his search for information. He was a bit wary about the possibility they had been followed last night, but the guards were on alert. They had reported one unusual group at this point, and they had those men under surveillance and had sent a message to Alex. Aunt Elspeth had raised two daughters, one of whom had been a true hellion, so he felt confident Diana could not convince her to let her run off alone.

He wandered through the streets of Edinburgh in search of the tourney fields. It seemed an appropriate place to start. The market was still full of vendors hawking their pastries and meat pies. He bought a lamb pie and spoke to the vendor as he ate.

"Big tournament with jousting today, aye?"

"Aye, knights always come from England thinking they can embarrass all the Scots, but it never happens. And this particular English knight has declared he will only joust against his fellow Englishmen. Where are ye from?"

"I'm from the western most edge of Lothian, still in the Lowlands, but I have family in the Highlands, so I have trained there often. The Grant lists are brutal."

The vendor's eyes widened. "You've trained with Clan Grant? The ones who chased the Norse away in the West?"

"Aye, my brother married a Grant. We spent time with them, and their training is the most challenging I have ever seen."

The vendor grew hopeful—Micheil could see it in his gaze—but he did not plan to risk injuring himself in the tourney, even if a win would hearten the local Scots in Edinburgh.

The man leaned over the wooden edge of his booth. "Och, we need you in the tourney. Ah, what a shock it would give them. Can you not sneak in as an English challenger?"

"I am here on an assignment, but mayhap I'll find a way to battle for one round. What know you of Randall Baines?"

"The betrothed lad?" The vendor smiled and used a bone to pick his teeth.

"Randall Baines is betrothed?" Micheil tried to hide his surprise, intending to find out all he could about the snake before tearing him apart, limb by limb.

"Aye. He likes the lasses and chases the light skirts, tossing as many as he can every night as if he'll never get another. Ever since he came to

Edinburgh, all we hear is gossip about his escapades."

"Mayhap he prefers Scottish lassies." Though there was one particular lassie who Baines would never touch again—Micheil would see to that.

The vendor shook his head and chuckled. "From what I have heard, anything in a skirt attracts him."

"And his betrothed? Has she not heard about his ways or seen him following other lasses?" Was the woman blind? A man with that kind of reputation clearly did not make much of an effort to try to hide his romantic escapades. The slim efforts he had made to hide his session with Diana last night only provided more evidence of that.

"Strange, but no one has seen the lass yet. It's said she is a passing beauty, good enough, though not as fair as our most notable beauties. She's not like the other lassies, wanting to dance and act frivolous. No' quite sure why because I have never seen her. Her family just came to Edinburgh for the wedding—first time here. She came with a grandmother as her escort. And she appears to prefer going unnoticed."

Micheil thanked the vendor and moved on, asking occasional questions as he toured the center of Edinburgh. The castle was quite a spectacle in the daylight. The battlements spread over half the land, and guards trailed every corner of them. Glorious banners waved everywhere—there more than usual, which he assumed was in honor of the tournament. Many of the visitors had come on strong horses that were being cared for in the daylight, but none that could compete with his horse or any of the Grant destriers.

One thing was certain; this matter needed to be handled very delicately. Though he would love nothing more than to tell Diana the truth about Baines—that he was already betrothed and getting married within a sennight—he knew lassies. She would never believe him. Mayhap she was even naïve enough to believe Randall would marry her instead of his betrothed. After all, she believed everything the lout had told her last night. He would have to somehow force the man to show his true colors in front of her. It was the only way. Hellfire, it made him mad enough to spit when he thought about the situation. The lad would have taken her maidenhead and she would have let him, falling for his promises of marriage.

Aye, Diana needed to know the truth, but she had to learn it the hard way. Otherwise she would hate Micheil for bearing the message, something he didn't want to happen under any circumstances.

He just wasn't quite sure why.

Diana fumbled with the ribbons in her hair in her chamber, unable to steady the trembling that had afflicted her ever since she'd begun the process of readying herself for the tourney. According to one of Elspeth's servants, Randall Baines was indeed jousting this day, and she was sure he would come to her for a favor. She hoped another would, too. She had chosen several wisps of silky material, all of them long enough to tie around the tip of his lance and proudly show the world he had chosen her.

It would show Micheil the truth, she was certain of it. Once he saw Randall on the jousting field, he would know he was the answer to her problem. By the morrow, they could be betrothed, and she would be riding back to her father's home with a man at her side, and it wouldn't be Baron Gow. Somehow, her heart wasn't as certain as her head. How she wished Micheil saw the good side of Randall so he would support her in this quest. She feared she would have to settle instead of finding the man of her dreams. If Gow's men were indeed searching for them, she did not have much time.

She thought about Randall Baines, how his blond hair hung over his collar. He had pretty blue eyes and a soft face, not rough and thick with whiskers like so many lads around Scotland. Perhaps he did lack a certain amount of masculine energy, but no one could deny his appeal. She had known that if she just came to Edinburgh, her knight would find her...and one had. Well, even though he wasn't officially a knight, he could become one. But was he the right one, the one her mother had dreamed of many nights? Mayhap not.

Aunt Elspeth came up behind her, settling her hands on Diana's shoulders. "My dear, you are a true beauty, and you will make all the lads follow you wherever you go. Promise me something."

"Anything, Aunt Elspeth. You have done so much for me and I do appreciate it."

"Promise me you won't fall for the first sweet-talking lad you come upon."

Diana scowled. "Whatever do you mean?"

"I was young once, too, my dear. There were always a few lads who would tell a young lass how beautiful she was just to steal a kiss or mayhap more."

"More?" She glanced at Aunt Elspeth, but then turned away, not wanting Micheil's aunt to see her expression. She had to admit, if only to herself, that Randall sounded quite a bit like those lads.

"Och, lass. A certain type of lad will try to talk a lass into giving her favors away by telling her what she wants to hear."

"What do you mean? What does she want to hear?" Diana had no idea what the older woman meant, but she needed to know so she could avoid attention from ill-meaning lads.

"Why, that she is beautiful, that she is the only one for him. Don't all lassies wish to be promised marriage?"

"So if that is what they want to hear, and the lad promises, why is it wrong? Mayhap 'tis destiny that unites them so quickly."

"Lass, that is exactly of what I speak. A lad will promise anything in order to steal a kiss or an illicit touch, but once he is done, he will change his mind and pursue another. Love does not happen in a few moments, but many young girls think it does. How wrong they are."

"What a terrible thing to happen. I'm so sorry you met a lad who treated you so cruel. Surely there are not many like that." She hated to admit it, but the lad Aunt Elspeth spoke of sounded just like Randall. She regretted not having her mother here to advise her, but would her words be similar to Elspeth's?

Aunt Elspeth gave her a stern look. "There are too many who act that way. And there are plenty of men who would even talk a woman out of her maidenhead."

Diana gasped and her hand flew to her mouth. "How awful! Why, how could anyone be so cruel?"

"Diana." Aunt Elspeth kissed her forehead. "It happens too many times. Just be certain it does not happen to you. No decent lad tries for your innocence or for illicit touches as soon as he meets you. And have no doubt, once a lad like that takes your maidenhead, he will leave you behind. 'Tis something many men boast about to their friends, stealing a woman's virtue. But you must remember 'tis a treasure meant for your husband and no one else."

Aunt Elspeth's words echoed in Diana's mind as they rode their horses to the tournament field, Elspeth's stable lad following behind them along with a couple of other guards she did not know, but Elspeth did. How she wished her mama were here to talk to her about this confusing topic. What did she know about a young lad's desires? Randall would not be like that, would he? Her mind raced with too many thoughts, and though she wanted to sort them all out in her mind before the tournament started, she knew she could not.

As they approached the tournament field, Diana's gaze was drawn to the dazzling display. Spectators and commoners alike wove through brilliantly colored tented pavilions filled with knights and the healers. Banners decorated with lions, hawks, and wolves stood proud, claiming to belong to the victor of the tournament. A light wind rippled the banners for all to see.

To their surprise, someone came along and offered the two of them a seat in one of the smaller grandstands in the shade. Thankful to be out of the sun a bit, Aunt Elspeth accepted readily. "Lass, this is wonderful. I do not know if Micheil will be able to find us when he arrives, but I would never refuse such seating."

Once settled, Diana took in everything about the event. The field was bedecked in color, banners and ribbons waving in the wind as the many knights and horseman practiced to the delight of the audience. The largest grandstand stood proud in gold and red.

"Who sits in the large grandstand, Aunt Elspeth?"

"'Tis for the royals. The king or queen if they are here, along with their court. In this case, I would think the young lass who is engaged to be wed must be inside, along with her family. Any other barons would come next if there was any room left."

The woman who sat in front of them turned around. "This joust is intended to honor the English knight who is betrothed. I heard he has agreed to battle all challengers. 'Tis said that he is a powerful knight on the field. This day is all about showcasing the English knights who are visiting the castle."

Diana sat up in her seat. Mayhap she would get a view of Randall Baines, or even another knight who could be interested in her. With so many here, there were numerous possibilities, and she had no idea what would be best for her. Both excited and confused, her attention flew from one spot to another. She so wanted to see the knight who was brave enough to take on so many challengers. She watched the field, but she could not get a good view of anyone since they were all wearing helms while they practiced. Diana said, "Does anyone ever die from the lance?"

Aunt Elspeth whispered, "Nay, the lances used for the joust have blunt ends."

"Then how do they declare the winner?"

"The winner of each match is whoever remains seated on his horse."

"I'm glad. I do not wish to see bloodshed." Diana tucked her mantle around herself.

"Och, nay, there will be no blood today. There are too many women in the crowd." The woman in front of them snickered. "Though I'd love to see it, I would. The crowd goes wild at the first drawn blood."

The trumpets blared and Diana gasped. The horses were steered to the end of the field as the herald began his announcements. "Any and all challenges from other English are accepted by the English Knight in residence."

At that moment, the knight took to the field and circled the perimeter to the shouts and applause of the spectators. "I wish he would remove his helm. I would like to see how handsome he is," Diana whispered to her companion.

"Don't worry, my dear, he'll remove it at the end of the tourney." Aunt Elspeth held Diana's gloved hand in hers beneath a rabbit pelt she'd brought with her.

"What is he doing now? He seems to just be standing in the middle of the field."

The announcer shouted, "The challengers to the knight."

A train of horses entered the field from the lists and circled the outer edge of the field while the knight stayed in the center.

Diana gasped. "All those men seek to challenge him? But why?"

The woman in front turned around again and said, "A huge purse full of gold will go to the winner of this tourney, not to mention the bragging rights of being the winner and defeating an English knight favored by the King of the Scots. Many hopefuls dream of such gold."

Diana stared at each of the challengers, hoping to catch sight of Randall as well, but she could not identify him among the gathering of helmed men. Her insides turned to jelly at the thought of Randall or another knight coming to her for a token. She squeezed Aunt Elspeth's hand in anticipation and the older woman chuckled.

"Have you never seen a tourney before, lass?"

"Nay, and I am so excited. You do not understand. 'Tis just as my mama told me when I was young.

Every eve before bed, she shared tales of the braw knights and the colorful tourneys, the tokens from the maidens. 'Tis all true, just as mama said."

"Methinks your sire protected you a bit much."

Diana sighed. If she only knew how much her father had protected her from the outside world. Now everything was such a fresh new experience that she couldn't get enough. She had to take advantage of her relative freedom and enjoy herself to the fullest when her kin were not watching.

The challengers exited the field while the English knight stayed in the center.

When he was the lone man on the field, the herald announced, "The knight seeks his tokens for good fortune."

Diana grew wide-eyed. "Is this the part where he gathers scarves and ribbons from the ladies in the crowd?"

Aunt Elspeth nodded. "Since it is his tourney, he will get many, including one from his betrothed. It is tradition. And if the knight sees a lass in the crowd he admires, he may stop in front of her and request a favor. She will either tie one onto his lance or risk insulting him."

The woman in the front chuckled. "Who would dare insult him? You could get speared by the tip of his lance."

Diana squirmed in her seat, so excited by the prospect of seeing such a romantic expression of love between the betrothed couple. He stood in the center and pranced his horse in a circle to the delight of the spectators, feigning an approach in several different directions, much to the excitement of the many lassies in the crowd. Each time he turned toward a group of lassies on the grass, the ladies would jump and scream and wave their scarves in the air, hoping to coax the knight to come to them. He changed directions six times before he finally headed toward the main grandstand.

Diana and Elspeth's grandstand was to the side of the main one, so they could not see inside. How she wished to run out and steal a glimpse at the beautiful bride he had chosen, but to do that, she would have needed to run onto the field.

When he reached the grandstand of his betrothed, he lowered his lance slowly, the blunt end held directly in front of the people who were seated there. His horse bent down onto one knee to the cheers of the audience. Diana could see a lass's delicate hands reach out and tie her scarf on the end of the lance. The crowd applauded and the knight galloped away, circling the field again with his lance held high in the air, showing his token for all to see. The noise from the crowd was deafening, and Diana giggled as she covered her ears for a moment.

He halted in the center again and pranced around in a small circle, playing the same game again.

Diana whispered, "Won't his betrothed be upset?"

"Nay, she was chosen first."

The knight stopped his horse finally, then kneed the beast and headed straight for Diana.

CHAPTER EIGHT

Diana lost the ability to swallow. The world slowed as the knight came in her direction, his lance now pointed at her. Her eyes widened, and she clutched Aunt Elspeth's hand.

The woman in front of her said, "He's coming for you, lass."

Diana shook her head, unable to believe he was singling her out. The faster he came, the louder the roar of the crowd. She fastened her gaze on the knight's and discovered the woman was right. He *was* coming for her.

For her! Just as she had always dreamed! A knight was coming for her. Well, mayhap just for her favor, but still, he had chosen her. The knight stopped in front of her grandstand, and his horse trotted sideways before he calmed him. As soon as his mount was under control, he lowered his lance directly in front of Diana.

Still unable to believe such a thing would happen, she scrambled to pull a scarf out of her sleeve. Leaning toward the knight, she stared directly into his eyes, and she could swear he smiled at her, though it was impossible to know for sure with his helm in place. Her heart melted as the moment she had waited for her entire life finally presented itself. She fumbled with the piece of fine silk, but managed to tie it on the end. The knight bowed his head to her before turning away and holding his lance up for the crowd to celebrate with him again.

He left the field with only two tokens, Diana's and the one from his betrothed. Diana's mind was sheer mush, barely able to concentrate on the tournament in front of her. What did all of this mean? She had asked Aunt Elspeth, but the woman shook her head and shrugged her shoulders. "Mayhap naught, mayhap everything."

She chastised herself for even getting her hopes up. The man was betrothed, and surely not interested in her. However, he must have friends, and his friends would be knights.

The knight defeated challenger after challenger, snapping lances as if they were naught but toy wooden sticks. Each competitor rolled on the ground in pain and agony. She was certain they were making a bigger show of their loss than many Scots would have done, but it didn't matter. It was the best show she had ever seen. The knight did have an occasional break when the field would fill with men on horseback, not in armor but in colorful clothing meant to dazzle the audience with their tricks.

After two hours of jousting and the horse showmanship, the herald came into the center of the field and held his arms up. "The tournament will continue after a one hour break so our competitors can regain their strength. Any new challengers may approach the judge's tent at the end of the field. Please take this time to enjoy our many merchants and their goods in the nearby meadow." He turned toward the end of the field and held up his arm. "Another round of applause for our English knight, the champion at the halfway mark."

The knight came galloping onto the field. Finally, he would remove his helm, and she would get to see him. She stood and leaned toward him, the anticipation almost too keen for her to bear. He pulled off his helm and shook his blond tresses out to the squeal of all his admirers.

Randall Baines grinned and looked directly at her, then nodded briefly before leaving the field.

Diana fell back into her chair in shock. *Randall* was the betrothed knight?

Aunt Elspeth fanned her face. "My dear, you look as if you have seen a ghost. What is it? What happened?"

"I have met him."

"What? What are you talking about? Where did you meet him?"

"Last night. I met him last night." Diana tried to hide the horror growing inside her. She had been kissing a betrothed man. Had she known, it never would have happened.

Aunt Elspeth gave her a suspicious look. "And how did you meet him? He is betrothed."

Diana turned away from Aunt Elspeth, hiding the expression of guilt on her face. How could she have known he was betrothed?

"Just for a moment, Aunt Elspeth. He was at one of the booths I had stopped at, I think the ones with the ribbons. But I had no idea he was the knight who is about to be married."

"Wasn't he with his betrothed?"

"Nay, he was alone."

"Hmm. Not surprising, he was probably out searching for another lass to steal favors from before he marries. Seems to be a tradition within a sennight of the ceremony. Lads run wild right up until the day they are wed." She shook her head.

Aunt Elspeth finally made sense of a few of her comments, apparently, because she looked at her

MY DESPERATE HIGHLANDER   69

with a strange expression on her face. "What exactly happened last eve? The man came for your favor. What prompted him to do that? Did you kiss him or tease him?"

"What?" Diana shook her head and expressed her shock at the crude comment, but then she realized it was exactly what had happened. She blushed and turned away again. Not only had he stolen favors, but he had touched her in inappropriate places. Worst of all, he had lied to her. The niggling doubt she had felt since meeting Randall grew to enormous proportions.

Aye, she had asked him if he was a knight and he'd denied it. Why? Diana could come up with no acceptable reason, but she continued to review everything that had happened between them in her mind. All her hopes were crashing around her, leaving a feeling of utter defeat in their wake.

Aunt Elspeth ushered her out of the grandstand. "Come, I'll buy us some fruit tarts to hold us through to the end of the tourney. There is much more to come. I'm sure the remaining challengers will be much more difficult than the ones he has already met. These rounds were all quite easy for him."

Diana followed Aunt Elspeth through the crowd, her mind still in a daze from all she had discovered. It totally deflated her to realize the man she'd hoped to be honorable was in fact a liar who'd had his hands all over her. Micheil had judged Randall correctly, though she hated to admit it. Here was another example of his good judgment.

Her head was down as she stood in line waiting for a pie. Someone called out her name, and she turned to see Micheil pushing through the crowd toward her. Elspeth bought three strawberry pies and handed them each one.

"Well?" Micheil said, his brow quirked as he stared at her.

She could not answer yet, so the three of them continued on their way with their food until they found a good place to eat—a toppled log among the trees. Now she would have to listen to him gloat. Hellfire, must he always be so wise?

She dropped onto the log in a huff, exasperated by the fast turn of events. This had gone from the best day of her life to one of the worst. A short while ago, there had been a chance for her to find her knight, to become betrothed, to save her father's heritage, but no more. It had all disappeared with the removal of a helm.

The liar.

And now she was just as vulnerable to Baron Gow as ever.

Micheil leaned against a nearby tree, doing his best to stifle his grin. "Well, what did you think of the English knight?" She had to know it was Randall Baines. True, at the beginning he had kept his identity a secret, but he had finally removed his helm for all to see. Having arrived late, Micheil had not managed to find his aunt and Diana during the first half of the tourney. Instead, he'd stood to the side and watched events unfold, checking for the baron's men at the same time. All the women around him had swooned over the knight's good looks, but no matter. Micheil was only interested in the response of one woman—Diana. How had she felt when the knight had removed his helm?

Diana blushed and squirmed on her seat. He gave her a puzzled look. What was she about, and why wasn't she talking to him?

Aunt Elspeth answered, "He was a verra nice looking knight and he fought hard, though I am not sure his competitors fought so hard. Some of them seemed a wee bit louder than necessary for their injuries."

"I agree, Aunt Elspeth." He waited for Diana's assessment of her wonderful knight, but none came. She stared off into space. Then the truth finally dawned on him—she was struggling to hold in tears.

Slud, not tears. That bastard had made Diana cry? But why? She'd known him too short of a time to have genuine feelings for him.

Aunt Elspeth stared at her charge. "Micheil, did you notice who the knight came to for his favors?"

"Nay, I arrived a bit late. I'm sure he went to his betrothed." He shrugged his shoulders.

"Aye, he did. And to one other lass." She tilted her head toward Diana.

Nay, he hadn't... The bastard had actually stood in front of all and asked for her favor? "Aunt, did he remove his helm when he came for his favors?"

"Nay, why does that matter?" She gave him a puzzled look and lifted her chin.

It sure as hell did, but he wasn't going to say anything to his aunt. Now he understood. Baines had come to her with his helm on, and she hadn't realized it was him. Her dreams of a perfect mate had just been squashed by a surly, lying knight.

"Diana." He reached for her, but she dropped her pie and stood. Then, as if she simply could not take it anymore, she ran into the woods away from him and everyone else. "Hellfire." He ran after her. "Diana, he's a bastard, I'm sorry, but he wasn't meant for you."

She ran and ran, and he could hear her sobs. He finally grasped her shoulder from behind. "Diana, please stop."

She spun around and glared at him. "Stop? So what? So you can have your last laugh and tell me about how right you were? Well, I will not give you the satisfaction, Micheil Ramsay."

"He took advantage of you. I'm not here to prove you wrong, just to make sure you don't let him take advantage of you again."

"Well, at least it was someone besides the Baron Gow. I was almost forced to marry that old lout without having been properly kissed. So do not think to tell me what to do. If I wish to kiss someone, I will, and I don't have to check with you!"

"Och, is that so? You think you'll just walk down a path and kiss whomever you wish?" He moved closer to her, making sure no one was about and they were well hidden in the trees. "Do you think your father would like that?" He moved closer until her breasts almost brushed his chest. "And what about your cousin? Would Alex Grant let you kiss just anyone you chose?"

"I do not care. I will kiss whomever I want." Her hands settled on her hips, and she leaned toward him, glaring at him, daring him to do something he knew he shouldn't.

He glowered back at her. How was he to talk sense into her? "Nay, you will not. If you do, I'll return you to Baron Gow." His shout echoed through the trees.

"You would, would you not? You hate me. You don't want me to marry anyone of my choosing or even *talk* to anyone of my choosing." Her finger pointed at his chest. "You wish to choose everything for me, even the men I kiss. Why? Why do you care?"

"Because." Hellfire, but he could breathe in her scent, they stood so close. He glanced at her lips, begging to be kissed. Her breasts touched his chest for a second, and a spark of fire coursed through him. Slud, but she was so beautiful, he could not think straight sometimes.

She still stared at him, but the fury in her gaze had turned to something else. Desire. He saw it and grabbed her, covering her mouth with his. He tugged her close and ran his teeth across her bottom lip until she parted for him so he could sink his tongue into her sweet cavern. Hellfire, he had wanted this for a while. She tasted of strawberries, and when she touched her tongue to his, he groaned and delved deeper. A soft mewling sound erupted from the back of her throat that undid him. He ravished her lips until she rubbed against him, fueling a fire he didn't know if he could put out anytime soon. Finally, his senses returned and he stepped back, placing a good distance between them.

"You wanted a kiss. That's how you kiss, not the insipid way your knight kissed you." With that, he turned on his heel and stalked away. The last thing he noticed was Diana running her fingers across her lips as she stared at him, awestruck.

At least, he hoped she was awestruck. Though he would probably be better off if she were angry, because there was only one way to put out the fire she had just started in him, and he couldn't do that to her. Alex would kill him and so would Aunt Elspeth.

He wanted her more than he had ever wanted anyone, and it scared the hell out of him.

CHAPTER NINE

Diana was spellbound. She rubbed her lips, still able to taste Micheil. That kiss had not been anything like Randall's. Randall had been harsh, rough, and slobbery. Micheil's kiss had been demanding, devouring, but it had set off a spark in her body. It had been the kind of kiss she'd imagined she would get from her knight someday.

Her breathing had increased when she was in Micheil's arms, though she was not sure why. She waited until it slowed before following him out of the woods. To her surprise, Micheil was waiting for her at the edge of the tree line. His harsh breathing made her heart speed back up, and a sense of empowerment came over her because she realized something important. She had caused his harsh breathing—just as he had caused hers—and it had been out of desire, not anger. Desire, which she knew little about, yet suddenly wanted so much more of. But from Micheil Ramsay, not Randall Baines.

She was more confused than ever, and her very heart was now in turmoil. Would it be possible? Could Micheil be the one? Would he consider marrying her to get her out of her dilemma? Nay. She shook her head adamantly at the thought, recalling how he had been appalled when he had misunderstood something she had said earlier. He had declared he would never marry, had he not?

When she reached his side, he said, "I'm sorry. I shouldn't have done that."

She gazed into his green eyes. "*I'm* not sorry you did it." She brushed past him and found her way back to Aunt Elspeth.

Aunt quirked her brow at the two of them, but did not say anything. Diana sat back down on the felled tree and settled her skirts around her. Silence descended on the group, but then Aunt Elspeth said, "Do you think he'll win it all, Micheil? Despite his early efforts, he doesn't seem to be that big of a man or that skilled on the field."

Diana decided to goad the man. Why not? Micheil had enjoyed the fact that Randall had been caught in his lie. Well, how far would he go to make him look bad? After that kiss, she thought she might enjoy watching Micheil on the jousting field.

In fact, after Randall had lied, mayhap he deserved to be beaten by someone.

Micheil sighed. "He's not, Aunt. I'm convinced many of his competitors are not fighting their hardest. It is his wedding tourney, so I am sure he will be the one to win the gold."

"You think he's cheating? Really, Micheil? Your jealousy is showing." Diana rested her elbow on her knee and her chin in her hand. "If you truly believe he was cheating, why do you not challenge him?"

Somehow, he didn't trust the innocent look she gave him. "I would not call it cheating, but I believe it has already been arranged that he will win the tournament. I just hope he remains a gentleman and doesn't truly hurt any of those who have agreed to lose to him. Even though he uses a blunt lance, he can do damage if his opponents do not try to defend themselves at all."

"So challenge him, Micheil." She gave him a sweet smile.

"Since I am not English, 'twould not be allowed, Diana." He paused, catching her gaze with a sparkle he hadn't seen before. "Do you wish to see me trounced? Is that your goal?" What was she about now? The lass changed her mind like the wind. Aunt Elspeth said, "I'm sure he is of sound character and would not intentionally hurt someone. He does have the king and queen as spectators."

"I, for one, would find it more entertaining to watch hand-to-hand combat, but I don't know if he could win any of those matches. And I have to disagree with you, Aunt. I do not think he is of sound character, based on what I have heard of him."

"What have you heard?" Aunt Elspeth asked as her gaze roamed from one to the other. "And I think more goes on than you two are telling. Micheil, what is it? We have a young girl's reputation and feelings at stake here. Please watch your tongue."

He sighed, not wanting to hurt Diana's feelings, but needing to ensure she had no doubts about the fool's lack of character. "I heard that he likes to spend time with different women. Word on the street is that he prefers many women to just one, and he has been sampling all Edinburgh has to offer."

Diana stood up. "You are making that up. Take it back."

He grinned at her. "Now why would I make something such as that up?" Diana sure was a naïve lassie. He chuckled and stared at his feet. "Diana, I am not jealous of him. I am quite proud of my

Scottish heritage, and I am not making anything up. Believe what you wish."

He kissed his aunt's cheek and turned to leave. There was naught more he could do here. "I'm going to find a place to sit for the second half. I'll see you ladies back at home after the tourney ends. If you wish, I'll look for you here so I can escort you back." He gave a slight bow and headed back toward the tournament grounds.

He would have to find another way to show her the scum's true colors if she still didn't fully believe him. Watching Baines in the tourney had been quite sad. Some of the lances had clearly been partially sawed in half so they would snap with the slightest provocation. His competitors appeared to have been carefully chosen in order to make him appear in the best possible light. All this for an Englishmen? A tournament such as this would never be allowed in the Highlands. Tournaments were intended to be a testament to a man's strength, power, and agility. This contest was not demonstrating anything aside from weakness of character.

He found a spot to observe the second half of the afternoon's festivities. Grumbling to himself, he watched that horse's arse parade around the field again to the delight of the crowd. The jousting continued, looking much as it had for the first half of the competition, until a contender appeared that spread a hush over the audience. He did not recognize the man, but he seemed bigger and beefier than the other opponents.

Micheil moved closer, walking up behind a couple of men who were laughing and conversing about the two contestants. These were definitely supporters of Randall's.

"This should be especially fun to watch," the first fool said.

"Why do you say that?" the second fool asked.

"Because this is the first Scotsman he has battled. The rest were all knights from his realm. This is the first true opponent."

"Oh, then he must destroy him." The second fool threw his fist in the air.

"No, he must be careful or he'll rile all the Scots. We are in Edinburgh, after all."

"I thought he was only jousting men he knew."

"Apparently, this one sneaked in past the jousting committee."

Micheil grinned. Finally, a Scotsman. He strolled in the opposite direction, anxious to watch the cowardly knight joust with a horseman who possessed bollocks. The two squared off and took the first run, barely missing each other before resetting at opposite ends of the field.

Both men charged again, and this time, Baines swung at the other man's lance, but he couldn't break it. Many of the others had snapped on contact. Had this lance escaped his tampering? Micheil grinned, hoping the fool would finally get his due.

Baines held his arm to temporarily halt the competition, complaining about his lance. He brought it over to the judges, and he was allowed to switch lances, something that would never have been allowed in the Highlands. He guessed the rules were lax just because of his marriage. Back in the middle of the field, he twirled the lance and spun it again, testing it while his horse trotted around as if spooked by something. Micheil's best guess was that Baines was upset and was passing his anxiety to his horse.

The two braced for another pass. They got into position and spurred their horses on. The Scotsmen was a big, powerful warrior on a destrier. Baines did not stand a chance. As they headed straight at each other with blunted lances at full speed, the crowd roared to life again. When Baines came up in front of his competitor, a sunbeam caught a glint of something. Micheil scowled until he saw the sparkle again—a blade or something similar sticking out of the long stick.

He wasn't sure of it, but Baines must have known it was there, whatever it was. Instead of hitting the Scotsman straight in the chest where his armor was, he struck the side of his chest plate, catching blade to flesh. The Scot fell to the ground, grasping his side, blood escaping through his fingers. The herald declared his victory. The crowd roared to life as soon as the blood seeped out enough to be noticed. They screamed and chanted, seemingly awed by the power of the English knight.

Micheil yelled that the cheat had a blade, but the crowd was too deafening for anyone to hear him. Finally, he made a decision. Unable to watch this farce any longer, he decided to take action. The vendor was not the only Scot he had met that day who'd encouraged him to enter the competition. Others he'd spoken to had promised to provide him with a blunted lance and armor if he decided to enter the competition. After watching this farce Baines called a tourney, he could no longer keep idle. He marched off the field, hopeful he would be able to find what he needed in sufficient time to take part in the jousting. The parade of horses was due up next to give Baines a break. He had time.

After successfully finding his kinsmen and the Grant guards, Micheil returned in armor. His plan was simple: he would take Baines down, but not before he forced him to show his true colors. The fool still circled the perimeter to the cheers of his fans, so there was nothing stopping Micheil from making his way onto the field on his destrier, lance in hand. He'd get on the field before anyone could stop him.

He waited for Baines to acknowledge him. The English knight chose to ignore him and headed toward the opposite end of the field from where Micheil stood. Micheil galloped after him, only stopping when his horse was nudged up against the other man's. The spectators howled in excitement at the new challenge, hoping for anything that might prolong the event or produce more bloodshed. The crowd was covered in waving flags as the spectators did their best to encourage the new challenge.

Baines turned slowly and stared at Micheil. The roar from the audience grew until Baines made his move and put his helm on his head, lowering the face plate. Micheil nodded to him and turned his horse, lowering his face plate and heading toward the other end of the field, as was customary, to set himself up for the first charge.

Micheil knew his competitor was a cheater, so he was ready when the deceitful knight charged him before he had the chance to turn and prepare. Turning, he dodged Baines's first lunge, almost unseating the bastard because he had pushed himself so.

Thundering applause echoed across the field, so Micheil returned to his spot and waited for the cheater to take his. Baines wouldn't dare back out now. The knight held his arm up once again, and the judges halted the tournament so Baines could exchange lances.

Just as Micheil had hoped, he went for the lance that had felled the Scotsman before. If he could get him to graze him with the weapon a few times, someone would surely notice and Baines's cheating would be laid bare for all to see. Diana had to know what kind of man she was falling for before it was too late.

Because Micheil Ramsay wanted Diana of Drummond for himself.

There, he'd admitted it. He wanted her and not just as another plaything. While his instant desire for her had not surprised him, the feeling had only grown and grown, as had the realization that he never wanted to part from her. It was time to end her ridiculous dream of marrying an English knight, and he intended to do so with this joust.

Baines came at him and hit him in the shoulder with his first pass. Micheil had turned at the last minute to prevent the blade from catching him in the face. The rotten bastard could have taken out his eye. Now he would pay for his deception. He hid his lance next to a grandstand and waited for the next pass, the crowd erupting in joy. He was determined to take out the dissembler with his bare hands.

The next pass, the third, Micheil grabbed for his opponent's lance to keep it away from his face, causing the blade to catch the inside of his unprotected arm, leaving a trail of blood. The crowd went wild at the drawn blood, no one apparently noticing the blade yet.

The next pass, Baines went for his face again. Ramsay grabbed the lance and tugged on it, almost unseating his opponent, though the blade caught him in the chest in his armor. The cheating knight was weakening. One more pass and he'd have Baines on the ground.

The next pass, Baines fooled him completely and aimed for his groin, something totally unexpected. Micheil was able to fend him off, but a small sting bit his belly. His armor had protected him, but whatever he had in his lance had pushed the plate inward. However, it served him well because it was enough to piss him off. When he reached the end of the field, he picked up his lance leaning against one of the grandstands and turned his horse, heading straight for Baines, more furious than he had ever been. The piece of shit had no honor, none. He could hear the crowd shouting for him, yelling "Scot, Scot, Scot." He was almost on Baines when someone yelled, "Blade, he's got a blade."

Baines heard it, too, and knew he had been discovered. Panic crossed his face as Micheil swung his lance with all his might and sent him flying off his horse. The crowd roared and Micheil turned back to the center of the field, only to look down and notice something for the first time.

He was covered in blood.

CHAPTER TEN

Diana was shocked when she first saw Micheil at the end of the field challenging Randall Baines. Aunt Elspeth noticed him and grabbed Diana's hand. "Oh, dear Lord, please protect him."

"Why is he doing this, Auntie?" Diana stared at him, dressed in armor and a helm in his hand to protect his face. Her mouth went dry as she realized just how handsome he looked when he entered the field. But he was going up against a liar and a cheat. Her heart hammered inside her chest at the thought of Micheil getting hurt, a telling sign she wanted to ignore. She should never have goaded the man. Diana wanted to stand up and shout to the treetops that she believed him now. Baines would kill him if given the chance. Her stomach twisted in knots as the scene played out in front of her, and she grabbed Elspeth's hand for comfort.

When he rode his horse up behind Randall, Micheil towered over the other man, appearing larger than the English knight. There wasn't anything soft about Micheil Ramsay, particularly not his eyes, which were ablaze with fury and hatred as he beheld Randall Baines.

"I do not know, but I pray this ends well." Aunt Elspeth was watching Micheil, too, her face lined with worry. "I think 'tis more to it than you or I can understand, though you may know a bit more than I do. That's hatred in my nephew's eyes, and I don't know if I have ever seen him look this way."

Diana watched as she gripped her companion's hand. As the two men started to do battle, she was more agitated than ever. When Randall first hurt Micheil, a lump formed in her throat that she was unable to swallow. Her gut clenched each time they passed each other, and she could only hope and pray they would both survive the encounter unscathed.

After he foolishly gave up his lance to take on Baines bare-handed, Micheil's arm was injured by his opponent's lance. As he turned at the end of the field, she noticed the stream of blood running down his limb. Her hand came up to cover her mouth as she gasped in fright.

Aunt Elspeth squeezed her hand. "I know, my dear. I noticed the same thing. Why is he bleeding so from a lance and with armor on? The jousting sticks are blunted, though I know there are open spots in any armor. Only one of the other opponents bled at all and it was a small amount. Micheil is bleeding heavily, though he does not seem to notice or care. It certainly has not slowed him."

Two more passes and Randall headed for his end of the field. He had aimed for Micheil's man parts on his last pass, and the entire crowd had erupted in fury at such a dishonorable attempt. She stared at Randall Baines, wondering what he was about. Micheil had accused him of being exactly the kind of man Aunt Elspeth had warned her about. She knew him to be a liar, but now he was revealing himself to be something so much worse. Randall Baines *was* a wolf.

Randall was heading down the field toward Ramsay when Diana saw it. The reflection of sun off steel caught her eye, and she was dumbfounded.

"Blade! He has a blade. Micheil, watch out!" she screamed.

Baines fell to the ground first, unseated from his horse. Though Micheil made it to the end of the field, he grasped at his horse's mane and toppled off the side of his horse. He was covered in blood.

Diana dashed over to Micheil—a most telling sign, she knew—but she could not stop herself. He was covered in blood. Randall, the swine, had apparently instructed someone to place a blade or a sharp piece of metal off the end of his blunted lance. He was the worst kind of cheat.

She stooped down next to him. "Micheil, Micheil." His eyes were closed, but he groaned and his hand moved, reaching for hers. "Are you all right?"

Micheil rolled onto his side and groaned again.

She shook his shoulder. "He had a blade, 'tis why you are bleeding. I saw it. I saw the blade when he came at you in the last pass."

He opened his eyes and whispered, "I know. I saw it in his other challenge. 'Tis not the first time he has used it. I wanted everyone to see his true nature."

Diana's eyes widened. "You knew? You did this on purpose?" She swung lightly at his leg. "You did, didn't you? This was all meant to show me how poor my taste is. Now I understand, anything to make him look bad in my eyes. Damn you, Micheil Ramsay. You would not see yourself settled with one lady, so you think everyone who seeks a spouse is ridiculous."

She ran down the field to Randall Baines, but then stopped herself. She did not want to see the liar and the cheat either. He had just pulled one of the lowest stunts she had ever seen, and yet she wanted to see him? Nay, she did not. Aye, she was angry with Micheil Ramsay for making her look so foolish, but she wasn't interested in Randall Baines at all. Her only chance was if he could introduce her to one of his friends. Unable to decide what to do next, she stood there while activity pushed her from one spot to another.

Randall passed right in front of her, and he pointed to her and said, "I want you, only you." He continued on his way, smiling at her over his shoulder, surrounded by his many guards.

She stepped back, shocked. What did he mean by that? It didn't matter if he wanted her or not. She no longer had any interest in *him*. She managed to find her way through the crowds back to Aunt Elspeth's side. Just before she caught up with Elspeth, a voice called out to her. She turned to see Clarissa hiding across the road.

"He wants to see you. I heard him when they brought him by. He was delirious and talking about his new love. Surely, you will go see him tonight?" Her eyes were wide with innocence.

Diana scowled at Clarissa, not trusting anything she said. First of all, he hadn't been delirious when she had seen him. Deciding to be blunt with the lass, she put her on the spot. "You were the one who told me Randall Baines was *not* the one getting married."

"I know. My apologies, but I did not know any better than you. I just listened to the gossip. But now I think he wants you instead of his betrothed. My guess is it was you he was calling for." She grinned at Diana. "You're so fortunate. All the girls followed him because he is so handsome, but he wants you."

"Well, he's not going to get me. I watched him at the jousting, and he is not the man for me. So don't bother updating me on his condition, Clarissa. I am not interested." Diana crossed her arms in front of her.

"Too bad," Clarissa smiled. "He has a heavy purse of gold now, and he has many friends, some quite handsome."

Diana turned away from her before Clarissa could see her pursed lips. She had said the one possibility that could change her mind about visiting him one last time. Could he lead her to another knight?

Diana walked over to Aunt Elspeth, unsure of what or who to believe.

Micheil was not seriously hurt. Though there was a lot of blood, most of his injuries were superficial. His pride was more damaged than anything, if Diana were asked her opinion. He could not stop accusing Randall Baines of being a cheat and complaining about all the luck the other man had. Even though Micheil had unseated him, Barnes had still been chosen as the winner of the tourney.

Aunt Elspeth said, "Micheil, I have told you several times by now. The man was chosen because he is set to wed the cousin of the Scots king. The purse was already slated to be his. A lone horseman who came into the competition uninvited was not about to change the entire reason for the tourney."

Thus, Micheil had sulked, furious that it had taken him so long to unseat the fool. "He has no skills. 'Tis why he needed a blade in his lance to make his job easy. Aye, and I am certain he weakened his opponents' lances before the match." Once they got him into bed and took care of his wounds, he spent the better part of the evening muttering in between lapses of snoring, so Diana just sat and stared at him as he slept. She had to admit, she was far more entranced by Micheil

Ramsay than she'd ever been by Randall Baines, or any other man, for that matter. But what was she to do? Micheil had very clearly said he was not interested in marriage.

At first she had been quite angry with Micheil, but now, as she watched him, she realized he had competed in the tourney for her and only her. He had tried to warn her away from Randall with words, but she had not listened. So he had risked his own life to help her, to prove to her that the Englishman was not worthy of her.

Diana sighed, not knowing what to do.

Aunt Elspeth came into the chamber to check on Micheil and brushed his hair back off his face. "My dear, he is a handsome lad. Why have you not considered my nephew? He would make a wonderful husband."

"You are absolutely correct, Aunt." Diana looked into the older woman's hopeful eyes. "But Micheil made it verra clear to me that he does not wish to marry. Ever."

Scowling, Aunt Elspeth covered Micheil with a plaid. "Are you sure he did not say that in passing? He cannot be serious."

Diana took Elspeth's hand. "'Tis what he told me." She dropped her hand and walked into the kitchens, leaving Elspeth to fuss over Micheil.

Sensing her opportunity, Diana slipped out the back door of the cottage. Her mind was made up; she had decided to see Randall one last time. She didn't care about him anymore, but perhaps he would feel guilty enough to lead her to another knight. There was no alternative to Baron Gow at this point. She needed to marry and soon.

Standing opposite the portcullis and the gatehouse, she stared at the imposing castle of

Edinburgh, so regal in the night sky. The towers sat so high that she could not count how many stories they were. The archways and the stonework were absolutely glorious, the carefully carved decorations visible even at night. Guards marched across the battlements, moving between the circular turrets and the proudly waving banners.

A young lad approached her and said, "This way, he is looking for you."

"What?" She stared at the stranger, uncertain whether to follow him or not.

He grabbed her by the hand. "Hush, Randall wishes to see you and only you."

Diana allowed him to pull her down the walkway and through the portcullis, eventually switching to the back side of the keep. He ushered her through a confusing maze of passageways until he knocked on a door and said, "Baines, it's me."

He then pushed her into the chamber and left, shutting the door behind him. She leaned against the heavy wooden door, flustered and confused, as her eyes adjusted to the darkness inside the chamber, which was lit by only two small tallows. Randall Baines leaned against the window casing, a small smile on his face. "Good, you came."

Diana said, "You are hearty? No serious injuries?"

"Of course I am hearty, lass." He stood and sauntered toward her. "I am the champion of Edinburgh, aren't I? I believe I was declared winner of all, and I have the gold coins to show for it." He wrapped his arms around her and pulled her close, dipping his head to kiss her.

She pushed him away, not at all interested in his advances. "Your methods were quite unsavory."

"I know not what you are about, but I won the contest with many witnesses. 'Twas your *friend* who used unsavory methods, not I." An edge that she did not like crept into his voice.

She turned her back to him, fearing he would sense her disgust if she were to look into his eyes. It was time to turn this to a discussion about his friends. "Why did you ask me here?"

"Isn't it obvious? Because I want you. Because we belong together." He came up behind her and nuzzled her neck. "Can we not just enjoy each other?"

"But you are betrothed to another."

He stood back, anger flashing in his gaze. "Oh, is that your problem? Yes, I am engaged to a cow. But I don't want her, I want you." He grasped her hand in his again and kissed each of her fingers.

"I'm sorry, but I cannot do this when you are soon to be wed to another." Diana was losing her self-confidence. She was in a room alone with a man she didn't trust. How had she allowed this to happen? Because she was desperate, and she had little time to lose. *Think, Diana, think!*

Grinning, he moved her over to his bed and tried to draw her down beside him. "Relax, my sweet. Help me forget my ugly betrothed." He kissed her again and ran his hands down to her waist, rubbing her back as he talked.

She turned her neck to avoid his embrace. "What of your friends? Where are they this eve?"

"I do not wish to speak of my friends." Taking her lips with his again, he kissed her while her mind jumped from one thing to another. She wanted more than anything to push him back, but she did not wish to antagonize him. He could be violent, she suddenly realized. Oh, how foolish she had been to come here.

Without speaking, he reached up to her shoulders and shrugged her gown down over her arms, exposing her breasts.

"Oh, my, you have a beautiful set, don't you?" He cupped her breasts in his hands.

Diana gasped. What had just happened? How had he untied her gown in the back? And what was he doing now? She dropped her gaze and saw his hands on her breasts and attempted to cover them and push him away, but her hands were all caught up in her gown.

"Relax, little one. I promise you will enjoy yourself. I pride myself on being an excellent lover."

Diana forced herself to stay focused. "This is not what I want!" she said, her voice quavering with fear. "I came here to find out if you had a friend for me. Another knight? You are betrothed. I must find another."

"I shall consider your request, but I would never recommend you to a friend without testing you for myself." He rucked her skirts up and grazed his hands up her legs. "I must see and feel all of you. You must let me inside you."

Aunt Elspeth popped into her head, her words suddenly taking on a vivid new meaning. The man in front of her was making all kinds of promises to her, but he would only make good on them if he could see her unclothed. And how could he be inside her? His comments baffled her. Everything was happening too fast. "But your friends, surely you must have one seeking a wife."

His hands brushed across her nipples and she jumped. He made the move to unclothe himself from his breeks, and she gasped when she caught sight of his manhood.

He wanted her maidenhead. She shoved against him and cried, "Nay." Standing, she tried to pull her gown up over her shoulders, but he yanked her back to the bed.

"Oh, you think you can tease me like that and then just leave? I do not think so. You will not get away from me so easily."

"Please, nay. I need to think. This is not right. Please let me go, Randall." She was barely able to get her breasts covered before the door flew open and Micheil raged inside. He grabbed Randall by the throat, and the two fell onto the bed.

"I heard the lady say nay, swine." Micheil punched him in the face and blood flew. The two fell off the bed onto the floor, and Micheil continued to pummel the knight.

Diana straightened her clothing and closed her eyes, unable to watch the two men fighting over her. She ran out the door.

She never wanted to see Randall Baines again.

CHAPTER ELEVEN

When she reached the end of the corridor, Micheil came up behind her and shoved her into an alcove. "Shhh." She gasped for air, fighting not to sob. "We have to sneak back out though the kitchens, or the castle guards will be upon us."

She nodded, her breath hitching, doing her best to calm down. Her big doe eyes stared at him with such trust, it wrenched his gut. Lassies usually stared at him with flirting or teasing eyes—her gaze was so much more powerful.

"Ready?" he asked. He grabbed her hand. "I will not let anything happen to you."

She nodded again.

He headed down the passageway, hanging onto her hand, just then realizing how fragile she felt. The rogue would pay even more if he saw him again. Though he doubted the great Randall Baines would look very good for his wedding ceremony in two days. The scum would blame the tourney for his bruises and none would be the wiser.

They made their way through the kitchens and out through a small gate in the back of the huge fortress. As soon as they were far enough away, he stopped and pulled her into his arms. He brushed a tear from her cheek and said, "Are you all right? He did not hurt you, did he?"

She shook her head but avoided his gaze, gripping his arms as if she would never let go.

He did not like that she was not being forthcoming about whatever hideous things the lout had done to her. As upset as she was, let alone the fact Baines had been in almost a complete state of undress, he did not believe she was all right. Had he gotten there in time? "Did he take your maidenhead? Because if he did, I will kill him."

"Nay." She shook her head and the tears spilled over onto her cheeks, followed by wrenching sobs, and she buried her face in his chest, still grasping his arms.

He breathed in her scent, trying to calm his own fury at what he had found when he opened that chamber door. "I'll protect you, Diana, but you have to stop sneaking off. What were you thinking?" He tucked her head under his chin and rubbed her back as he spoke, using a soothing voice in an attempt to calm her trembling body.

After a few minutes, she pulled back and stared at him, her breath hitching again. "I was just trying to find out about his friends. I thought one of his knights could be interested in marrying me. But he wouldn't do it without testing me first." The last sentence came out in a wail, and she leaned against him again, sobbing. Then she jerked back. "I'm sorry, am I hurting...you...where you were cut?" She hiccupped at the end.

"Nay, you can't hurt me, wee one. I'm just proud of you for stopping and pushing him away." He tucked his finger on her chin. "I heard you tell him nay, and he was wrong to ignore you. You must be more careful." He pressed a light kiss on her lips.

She stared at his chest. "Aunt Elspeth was right. He just wanted my favors. He said....he said...he wanted to see all of me first." She wailed again. "How could I have been foolish enough to go in there with him? My papa raised me to be strong, to fight, to believe in myself. I am surely daft."

Micheil tucked her close again, a sly grin on his face. The bastard had finally shown his true colors to her. Thank God he had gotten there in time to protect her from an even worse situation.

"Thank you for following me, Micheil." She mopped her face with a linen square he gave her, finally calming her breathing a bit. "I was worse than foolish."

"How did you end up there? Hellfire, I try to keep an eye on you, but you always seem to get away. Promise to stop doing that?"

She nodded. "Clarissa."

"Who's Clarissa?"

"She's the lass who told me in the courtyard that Randall wanted me. But she didn't even know he was betrothed at the time. She told me she overheard him talking about me when he left his tent at the field, saying something about how he had found a new love. All the lassies followed him to make sure he was all right, I guess. 'Tis when she overheard him. I just thought I could meet one of his friends. I need a knight, Micheil. I need a husband."

"Diana, a lass cannot walk alone in Edinburgh. You have to stop. You're not on your lands where everyone knows you're the chieftain's daughter. Any lad could go after you here. You are too beautiful."

"I am? You think I'm beautiful?" She gazed at him with a pout in her lips.

He lifted her chin with his finger. "Aye, of course you are beautiful. 'Tis why the knight wants you."

"My apologies. I won't ever do it again. He had some lad pull me into the castle and into his chamber. Next thing you know he was kissing me and pulling at my gown, doing things I did not want, making me promises of introducing me to his friends."

"Are you sure he didn't take your maidenhead?"

"I think I would know, Micheil. As soon as he rucked my skirts up, I pushed him away. That's when you came in. If you hadn't come, I do not know if I could have gotten away."

He almost laughed at her haughty look. As beautiful and strong as she was, it was hard to believe she was such an innocent.

"Your father kept you well protected, aye?"

"Aye, 'tis true. And I am just realizing 'twas mayhap not such a good thing. A lass needs to understand certain things. I can do numbers, read, and go hunting, but I know little about the ways of lads and lassies. And how exactly does one go about learning these things without getting into situations that are unsafe?" She gave him a saucy look.

He tucked a loose lock of hair behind her ear. Slud, but she was lovely. He wanted naught more than to kiss her senseless right now, but he knew it would be taking advantage of her when she was most vulnerable. He didn't want to kiss her when Randall Baines was still in her mind. He rubbed his thumb across her bottom lip.

She peeked up at him through her lashes. "I like your kisses better, Micheil. He slobbers like a deerhound."

He barked out a laugh and hugged her. "I guess that's as good a reason as any to stay away from him." When he glanced at her again, he said, "But why the sad face? He won't bother you again. I will not allow it, I promise."

She rested her head on his shoulder. "I know. I will be forever grateful to you, but now what will I do? He was my solution to my problem. Now I do not have a knight to solve my problem."

Micheil sighed. If she was still determined to find herself an English knight, he had no hope of making a relationship work with her. Well, at least he could try and help her find a man who was worthy of her.

"We're going back to Auntie's cottage, and we'll think more on it in the morning."

Once they had Diana calmed down, he and Aunt Elspeth tucked her into bed. They moved into the main chamber. He was about to walk out the door for some fresh air, but Auntie called out to him.

"Micheil, a moment please."

He turned. "Of course, Auntie. What is it?"

Elspeth strode over to her nephew and grasped his hand in hers. "Why do you not do the right thing and marry her yourself? Would that not solve the problem?"

Micheil's insides clenched at the suggestion. He had been thinking of little else these past hours, but there were a couple of serious issues. "Because she wants an English knight."

"But, Micheil, she is young. She doesn't know what she wants. Why not court her a bit and see if you two suit?"

Micheil shook his head. "Aunt Elspeth, I can't court her in earnest because I do not know if that is what I want." Aye, he had just lied to his aunt, but he didn't wish to admit his fear of rejection. Rarely had a lass turned him away. What if Diana did not want him?

"Have you not thought of it? She is a beautiful Scottish lass, and you would have your own land, the two of you."

"I have considered it. I am just not sure if I am ready to settle down with one woman." He stared at the heavens, promising to start being honest soon—with others and with himself. He wanted Diana more than he had ever wanted any woman. Seeing her every day and not acting on his desire for her was sheer torture. He breathed out through pursed lips, hoping to somehow gain the courage to do what he should do, court Diana of Drummond.

"Your father died when you were young, and you and Avelina have verra few memories of him, but your sire would have wanted to see you settled down with a wife."

"You cannot know that." Micheil scowled at her.

"Aye, I can."

"How? My sire has been dead for many years." Micheil was trying to be patient with her, but he always had difficulty talking about his father. It had been a hard loss.

"He was my brother, Micheil, and he told me. He wanted you to be as happy with your future life as he was with Arlene. He adored her and loved all of you. He said if he could wish anything for his bairns, it would be for them to find someone to truly love and settle down, just as he did."

"I just do not know that I am ready. Besides that, her sire wants her to marry nobility, and I am a last son, so I am naught." This truth he could voice to his aunt. Diana was heir to Drummond lands. Would she and her sire think him beneath them?

"Mayhap, but in view of the circumstances, I think he would consider you. He probably wishes to see her happy, and if she is in love with you, which I think she is...or is well on her way to being, then he would approve. He does not need someone with a title, just someone to help his daughter run the clan. Why not give it a try? You never allow any woman close enough, Micheil. Mayhap it is time."

"Neither did Logan."

"Nay, he did not, but look at him now. He is happier than I have ever seen him. Gwyneth completes him. Have you not seen how he is with their wee daughter? Sorcha is delightful. I'm so happy for them, and I want to see the same happiness for you and Avelina. The two of you were without your father for so long. I fear that is why you spend so much time with the lassies. Please try, for me. You cannot deny there is something between you and Diana. I know you feel it as much as I see it."

"I promise to think on all you have said. Do not forget there are two of us in this, and I do not meet all her requirements. I know I am not the sort of man she seeks to marry."

Elspeth moved over to embrace him and kiss his cheek. "I can ask no more than for you to consider it."

Micheil headed out the door and down the road, eager to walk off some of his unease and discontent. His aunt had just given him plenty to think about. Was she right? Did he prefer the company of women because he had spent most of his childhood without a father? He had to admit, many of his younger days had been spent around women. Though he had two brothers, his eldest brother, Quade, had spent the years before his second marriage in a depressed haze. And Logan. Logan he adored, but he had spent much of Micheil's boyhood away from home. He used to disappear, not telling anyone where he was headed or when he would return. Aye, he had spent quite a bit of time around lasses throughout his life.

Micheil found a local inn and entered, seeking an ale to quench his thirst and the time to think seriously about courting Diana. He allowed his eyes to adjust to the dark and found a stool at a table. His eyes wandered the room.

There were several bawdy Scots enjoying their drinks and the lovely lassies waiting on them. One lass came over to offer him a drink, and she gave him a lusty smile. "My, but I have not seen you here before. If you are looking for a warm bed tonight, stranger, I know where you can find one."

Micheil chuckled. "That is the most exciting invitation I have received in a sennight, lass. Do not go too far without me tonight."

Though he enjoyed flirting with her, as he always enjoyed sparring with women, he felt nothing when she brought his ale and brushed against him, giving him a soft sample of her generous curves. He did not stir as he usually did when close to a beautiful woman.

A lad at the nearby table said, "Och, 'tis the Scot who forced that English knight to show his true colors today." He walked over and patted Micheil on the back. "Well done, lad. I offer a thank you for all the Scots today. The knight was a fool to take you on."

Micheil laughed off the comment, not really wanting to rehash the day. The other lass came over, a dark-haired, willowy girl with the kind of legs that could wrap around him completely.

He was still staring at her long limbs when she said, "Och, and I know how to reward him proper, if you understand me, Scot." She smiled and raised her eyebrows at him. "You can give me the come hither anytime. I heard all about you today."

While she wasn't a beauty, she was attractive enough, but she wasn't exciting him either. He winked at her. "I promise I'll remember that someday." She giggled and went to retrieve more drinks for the customers.

What the hell was wrong with him? He scowled, and a red-haired lass popped into his mind, her eyes all teary from being treated poorly. Diana truly had infiltrated his heart and soul, so why was he still hesitant to make his feelings known to her?

There was his fear of rejection, of course. While she had always appreciated his help, she had never come on to him like the other lasses did. Just like tonight, he could walk into any room and some lass would offer herself to him, all it took was a smile and a few kind words. He credited his luck with ladies more to his kind words than to his other attributes. Women were not used to hearing them. Sweet words could indeed get him far, but not far with Diana. She required a larger gesture, but it was no less than she deserved.

Perhaps the bigger issue remained the improbability of getting her father's blessing. A chieftain usually did not want his daughter married to a third son. Her father had wanted her to marry into nobility enough to agree to give his only daughter to an old baron of questionable ethics that the King of the Scots had approved. There was no title attached to Micheil Ramsay and no king nearby telling him to court Diana. He would need the king's approval to continue.

He stared at the table of lads next to him. "Are the knights still around?"

The same man answered. "Aye, they are staying until the big wedding. None of them are as bad as the one you unseated today."

Another said, "And you should have gotten that purse. Not him. What does the English boy need it for? He probably has plenty of money, plus his betrothed is wealthy."

"Is she now?" Micheil asked. "It makes sense that the king gave him that purse. I was not supposed to take part in the tourney." He pondered the lad's words. "So the lass has plenty of coin?" That explained a few things about Baines—why he was marrying a woman who didn't interest him, why he didn't have any respect enough for her to stay away from others. Wealth, simply put—wealth.

"Aye, they say 'tis why he is marrying her. He is too randy to settle."

"Are any of the other knights with him marrying?"

"Nay." One looked at the lad next to him. "From what I've heard, the betrothed is the one searching for the lassies, not the rest of them. Some came with lassies."

Hellfire, that wouldn't help. Since he knew Diana's father would never accept him as a son, he needed to find another knight for her. So why did he not feel like asking any more questions?

Because none of them would be good enough for his Diana.

CHAPTER TWELVE

Diana awakened to a dismal morning. Micheil had disappeared, and she had only one more day to find a husband. Once Baines married on the morrow, the English would be leaving. Since she wasn't invited to the wedding, it was imperative that she find a lad today. She knew she was running out of time. Baron Gow would not be agreeable to releasing his claim on her hand if she did not have a husband's protection, and her cousin, Alex, would only be able to delay them for a while. She would be called to task soon for her actions, she was sure of it. A backup plan was essential, or she would find herself marrying the mean old man.

Once she finished her ablutions and broke her fast with Aunt Elspeth, she decided to go to the market with Elspeth. Within an hour, Clarissa found her and tugged her back behind a tent. She waved to Elspeth, who was busy bargaining for some bread.

"Did you see him last night? I know he wants you." Clarissa's eyes lit with excitement.

"Mayhap so, but I do not want him, Clarissa. I am no longer interested in discussing him, so please stop."

"Why not? Do you not think he is handsome?" Clarissa looked at her as though she were daft.

Diana sighed. "Aye, I do, but he is marrying his betrothed tomorrow. I want naught to do with the lout. I want a knight who is unencumbered."

"I thought you wished to marry?"

"I do, but he is already betrothed."

"Perhaps he could find you another. He has plenty of knights who are his friends. Why don't you ask?" Clarissa gripped her hand.

"Because I do not wish to ever see him again, Clarissa. Please stop bothering me about him." Diana spun on her heel and left, locating Elspeth within seconds.

Diana walked and walked through the crowd. After a time, Aunt Elspeth grabbed her hand and said, "What are you looking for, child? You wander on and on. We must return home soon."

"Nay." She stopped in the middle of a courtyard and searched the crowd around her. "Nay, Auntie. Do you not understand? If I do not find a knight today, 'twill be hopeless. The big wedding is on the morrow. Who will I find after that?"

Elspeth continued to walk with her until it was almost dark. "Come, child. We must go home. 'Tis not safe for two females after dark."

Diana hung her head and trudged behind Elspeth, feeling as if her world was crumbling around her. Where would she go? What would she do?

Micheil flew in from behind them and grabbed her around the waist. "Come, you need to get back to Aunt Elspeth's. Gow's men are in the courtyard today."

Diana's panic was obvious, but Micheil moved her forward at a steady pace, making sure his aunt was able to keep up with them.

"And as soon as we get home, I shall to teach you how to use a dagger. After last night, I would feel better if you had some skills."

"What happened last night, Micheil?" Aunt Elspeth frowned.

Diana's cheeks pinked prettily, but he stepped in to ease her shame. "It does not matter now, Auntie. She must be prepared to defend herself."

As soon as they arrived home, they assisted Aunt Elspeth with her purchases, then Micheil led Diana back through the kitchens and into the small copse of trees behind the house.

"Micheil, I do not know how to use a dagger at all," she said, her voice soft. "I'll surely cut myself. I do not even possess a dagger."

"Which is exactly why I bought one for you at the market. 'Twill fit nicely in the folds of your skirt. You can sew a pocket to hold it." He held it out for her to examine.

He had purchased the nicest one he could find. The handle had a smooth black finish and was encrusted with small gemstones.

She fingered the beautiful stones, then stared into his eyes. "Micheil, 'tis beautiful. My thanks for your gift."

He stood close enough to inhale her scent, but vowed not to let it distract him from his purpose. Gow's men were in the area. She needed to know how to repel them if she were attacked.

She stood up on her tiptoes and placed a chaste kiss on his lips. "I love it."

Micheil couldn't resist. He cupped her face in his hands and kissed her tenderly. Their first kiss had been too rough for her. Her lips were soft and warm, and she tasted as sweet as he remembered. She opened for him, touching her tongue to his with an innocence that threatened to unman him, but he maintained control. Wee steps. If he had to court her slowly to convince her she did not need to wed an Englishman, he would.

He stood back and saw how flustered she was, but kept himself from puffing his chest out like a peacock. She liked his kisses, and if the smoldering heat in her gaze was any indication, this one had been even better for her. He turned her around and tucked her in close to him.

"Now, your right hand is stronger?" he whispered in her ear.

"Aye." Her voice came out in a lusty moan, and he smirked. Mayhap he did stand a chance with her.

"Then the pocket in your skirt must be sewed on the right-hand side so you can reach it quickly. It comes with a cover, if you wish to use it, to keep you from slicing your hand. This is the move I want you to practice." He showed her how to grip the dagger in such a way that she would be able to pull it out and use it fast. "This is a small knife—you won't kill anyone unless you plunge it into their neck just so." He showed her the cut he meant.

"I don't want to kill anyone."

"You will if they're trying to kill you. Even if you cannot get to their neck, embedding a dagger in a man's belly will cause enough pain and bleeding to slow him. To wound your attacker in the chest, you must be lucky enough to miss the rib, and until you are practiced, I wouldn't recommend it. Remember that any strike from a wee lass will take a man off his guard, possibly giving you the time to run away."

"But men are so much bigger than me."

"You fight and kick as hard as you can, just as you did with the baron and with Randall. You don't want to make it easy for them. Even a slice under the arm can catch a major vessel and cause severe bleeding."

Diana leaned back against Micheil, wishing she could just stay in his arms like this forever. Micheil was strong and protective, just as her mother had said her knight would be. He smelled like leather and a scent she had come to recognize as Micheil, one that made her want to rub against him just to absorb more of him.

She wiped the sweat from her brow. "Awfully warm out here, is it not?"

He grinned. "Aye." It was a deep, throaty answer that ran a path down her spine and into her core, making her want to curl into him and never move.

He turned her around to face him, grasping her shoulders. "Diana, I know I am taking a chance here, but would your father ever consider someone who wasn't nobility or a knight? Would he ever allow you to marry a man like me?"

Her eyes widened, shocked but beyond pleased at his backwards proposal. She nodded and smiled. "I think he would consider it. Truly, Micheil? You would want me?"

Hope blossomed in her heart. Micheil was someone she could depend on, someone who made her heart stir. Would he truly consider it? "I thought you never wanted to marry?"

"Well, I never did before. But you are changing my mind. I'm afraid I don't wish to let you go. May I court you to see if we suit?"

She threw her arms around his neck. "Aye, Micheil. Naught would make me happier."

He kissed her soundly, then the door opened and a servant came outside. The kiss ended sooner than Diana would have liked.

It did not matter. Micheil had just made her blissfully happy. Now there was hope for her...and for countless more kisses.

⁓

It was early the next morning and the wedding was not set to take place until noon. Even though he had promised to court Diana, and she had agreed, Micheil decided to head into the market again to see if he could learn anything more about the baron's men. He also sensed something was off about the wedding—both the groom *and* the bride—so he decided to keep an ear open to see what he could discover. But his primary purpose was protection. He had to make sure Gow's men were not on to their location. He left one guard at the house, took a couple with him, and sent a few out to scout the area.

Starting at the market, he found one vendor selling animal furs who was quite eager to chat. "What say you about the lass betrothed to Baines? I never saw her at the tourney. Is she fair?"

"Och, they say she is a beauty. She should be since she is King Alexander's cousin, but no one has seen her. We all thought she was yellow-haired, but the one in the stands yesterday appeared to be flame-haired."

"Was she fair?"

"Who could tell? Her face and hair were almost completely covered and hidden. As you know, the Scottish tradition would be for her to show her face at her betrothed's jousting tournament, especially. But she never allowed anyone the full view of her beauty."

Micheil stroked his chin. "'Tis true, that is unusual. Many have come from far and wide to set their eyes on the married couple. Has she not been out with the king at all? Has she not appeared on the steps of the great hall to greet the Scottish guests?"

"Nay, I have not seen the lass, and I have not come upon anyone who has. Some suggest 'twas planned that way so more will attend the ceremony. Apparently, King Alexander fears the Scots will not attend an English wedding ceremony or greet the newly wedded couple after they take their vows."

A scowl felt permanently engraved on Micheil's face after their conversation. Something was not right, and there were too many uncertainties. Alex would go direct to the king and ask him questions. Unfortunately, he had no idea where Robbie and Alex were, and the king would probably not see him, but he did know the location of someone else who might help.

Logan. It was time to send for his brother, the expert at ferreting out information. Gwyneth had given birth to their wee daughter not long ago. Would he be willing to travel without Gwynie?

He had to try. He sent a messenger after Logan.

<hr>

"Please, Aunt Elspeth, please? There are so many vendors at the market for the wedding."

Elspeth glared at her charge with her hands on her hips. "Micheil said we were to stay in. He's worried about Baron Gow's men."

"Aye, but we can take the guard with us. I just want to go to the cloth vendors. I'll never find such fine cloth in Crieff. If Micheil and I marry, wouldn't you like me to have the best possible gown?"

Elspeth sighed. "Lass, you know how to play at my heartstrings. Agreed. The guard goes with us, one hour, and cloth and ribbons only."

"And slippers?"

"Only if we pass one."

Diana squealed and hugged Aunt Elspeth. Now that the possibility of marrying Micheil was on the horizon, she had to be prepared with a gown. They would have to marry quickly to dissuade Baron Gow's suit, but she still wanted to feel beautiful.

"All right, but this is the last time. I would like to see the wedding procession later. Mayhap we'll run into Micheil, and he can help us carry home our packages, though he promised to shop for food in case Logan arrived."

So they headed off to the market again toward the wares with one guard behind them. An hour later, she had found one bolt of cloth and some ribbons, but no slippers. "Come along, my dear. We are running out of time. We must go. " Diana, happy with the cloth but disappointed that she hadn't found her slippers, trudged along next to Aunt Elspeth, sniffling all the way.

They almost made it back to the cottage when something hard struck Diana in the back of the head, and her entire world went black.

Micheil had almost reached his aunt's home, his arms full of purchases, when he saw something that was like a fist punching him square in the gut. Straight ahead, a woman he thought to be Aunt Elspeth lay prone on the ground in front of him. Diana was nowhere to be seen. He dropped the goods and knelt down next to his aunt and rubbed her shoulder. "Auntie, Auntie, wake up, please."

He was relieved to feel a pounding on the side of her neck, but though her heart still beat, she would not awaken. Searching the area for the guard, he finally noticed another lump not far away. The guard was arousable and able to move, though he admitted he had no idea what had happened. Micheil shook his head and returned to get his aunt. He picked her up in his arms and made his way back to her house, hoping he would find Diana inside. A sinking feeling in his gut told him otherwise. Diana would never leave her like this. Something must have happened. He settled Elspeth onto her bed in her small chamber, while the guard assisted with the packages. He managed to get his aunt to sip on some ale, enough to wake her up sputtering.

"Diana? Where is she? I saw someone hit her in the head, but I do not remember anything afterwards." She grasped Micheil's hand. "I must see her, please, or I will not rest." The words were like a knife stabbed into his heart.

He shook his head. "I was hoping you would tell me she wasn't with you. There was no sign of her either in the street or here in the house. I don't know where she is, Aunt Elspeth. Try to remember as much as you can."

Thank goodness he had sent a message to Logan and Gwyneth earlier. Though he did not fully understand the situation, he did not like what was going on here, and he no longer felt he could handle it on his own.

He tucked Elspeth into bed and she fell fast asleep. He ran outside to search the nearby area for any clues, but found nothing before returning to check on his aunt. Not sure what to do next, he was pacing in her front room when a solid knock interrupted his thoughts. The door flew open and much to his relief, Logan and Gwyneth stood on the other side, both grinning at the wee bairn, their new daughter Sorcha. The babe was attached to the front of Logan, facing out, swinging her arms in delight at the antics of her mother.

"Och, thank God. Come inside, quick. I need your help."

Logan barked, "And a good day to you, too, brother. What has you in knots?"

"Diana of Drummond is missing, and I have no idea where to look for her. I am supposed to be protecting her and helping her find a husband, as Alex Grant bade me to do, but now everything is a mess." His hands waved back and forth as he spoke.

Logan shouted, "Micheil, get hold of yourself. And where is Aunt Elspeth?"

Micheil stared at his brother for a long moment, mouth gaping, before escorting them to a table in the dining area. Elspeth's maid brought ale for the guests. Then he explained everything as succinctly as he could. He began pacing again before stopping in the middle of the small hall to stare at Logan still at the table. "Well?"

"Well what?"

"What do we do next? We have to go after her. Hellfire, we cannot just sit here and hope she returns. She was probably kidnapped. We must do something."

Logan said, "First, you need to give us time to eat something. I cannot work on an empty stomach. From the sounds of things, it's one of two people. If it's Baron Gow, Alex Grant and his guards will be on his trail in no time and they will take care of him."

"Alex has guards here in the city just to watch for the baron. I'll have to find them and see what they know while you are eating. And the other person it could be?"

"Your knight wanted a taste of her before his wedding. Though it's unlikely he's involved since he marries at noon, you cannot dismiss him if the randy lad truly does not desire his intended. Then again, it might very well be someone you do not suspect at all, so we have to go into this with an open mind. But we must make a plan, because I'm not just running across all of Edinburgh without any sort of preparation. Get food for us and we'll think this through. We will also need a map of the castle."

"How did you get here so quickly?" Micheil asked.

"We were already on our way when we caught your messenger," Gwyneth said. "Dougal Hamilton had asked us to check on Edinburgh. He got wind of something strange going on here with this wedding—some form of deceit." She undid the plaid securing her daughter to Logan's chest and turned to Micheil. "Here, would you mind holding your niece for a moment?" She held wee Sorcha up for her uncle.

Micheil stared at the bairn and finally took her, wondering what he was supposed to do next. She gave him a small smile in between sucking on her fingers. "You brought your wean with you when the Crown asked you to do covert work for them?" His brother and sister-in-law were both spies for the Scottish Crown and had met while on assignment, marrying shortly thereafter. Dougal Hamilton was their contact.

Gwyneth laughed. "Of course, 'tis the only way Logan and I work. And since I was housebound for a couple of months, we were anxious to leave. Sorcha goes everywhere with us. Sorcha, do you remember Uncle Micheil?"

Sorcha gave him another grin before shoving her fist in her mouth and waving her other arm. "Here, I'll feed her while you and Logan plan. I can sit over here and listen to everything. Tell us all you can about Diana's character as well. We have to know whether she is a fighter, how bold she can be."

Gwyneth sat down near the hearth to nurse wee Sorcha. Logan grabbed Gwyneth a goblet of cider along with an apple and a chunk of cheese to munch on while she fed the bairn. He kissed Gwyneth's cheek. "Stay strong for me, love. I think I'll need you." He leaned down to kiss Sorcha's cheek, and she popped off her mother's breast for long enough to give her sire a big grin. "Aye, papa loves you, too, sweet Sorcha." She went back to eating, but her gaze followed her father as she gripped her mama's finger.

Micheil and Logan discussed everything and made their plan. Part way through, Elspeth found her way to the door of her chamber and said, "Thank goodness you're here, Logan. We need you."

Lunging out of his chair, Micheil helped her out into the room. "Aunt Elspeth, please use due care. You took a terrible fall. Come sit by Gwyneth while we talk."

Elspeth sat down with tears in her eyes. "Gwyneth, you look wonderful, and the bairn is so beautiful. I cannot wait to hold her."

"Auntie, are you well? That is a terrible bump on your head." Gwyneth leaned toward her.

"Aye, I am fine, but please do all you can to find Diana. She is a lovely lass, and I think someone is taking advantage of her." Then she put her hand to the side of her mouth and whispered. "And I think she truly loves Micheil. They belong together in my opinion."

Micheil could only scowl.

CHAPTER THIRTEEN

Diana awakened to a huge headache. She moved her hand up to check her bump gingerly, only to wince in immediate pain. She was atop a bed in a large circular chamber, possibly a tower room. One window cast morning light across the chamber, enough for her to notice she was not alone. An old woman sat in a chair next to the bed, and there were two guards in the room, one on either side of the door.

When the old woman noticed she was awake, she said, "If you give me your word not to scream, I will send the guards away and explain your purpose. But if you scream or fight, I'll have them tie you to the bed and gag you. The choice is entirely yours."

The woman's beady eyes bored into Diana's as she awaited her response.

Diana thought for a moment, but then decided she had to find out why she was here. She could fight and scream later.

"I'll stay quiet. Who are you?"

"You'll find that out when you need to know." She tipped her head to the two guards, "Leave us, but keep an ear out in case I need you back to tie her up. And if she makes any sounds, you'll return to gag her."

The two men left, and the old woman walked to the bed. "I'm sure you are wondering why you are

here. First and foremost, I need to tell you that you
are the chosen one, that many young girls would
love to be in your place, so you need to be thankful
and appreciate your position."

Diana's gaze searched her chamber, searching for
any clues of her whereabouts. Her fingers managed
to locate the knife in her pocket, so she breathed a
sigh of relief that she wasn't without any hope, but
decided to leave it there for now. Hellfire, she had
enough of being a victim. She had to get herself out
of this situation. The bedchamber belonged to
someone of wealth, someone who could afford the
very best furnishings, tapestries, and wall coverings.
"But I cannot leave?" she finally asked the old
woman.

"Nay, you may not. Eventually, once you have
acquiesced to your position and accepted it, you will
be allowed to go out on your own. But you need not
worry, you will be given everything you ever want or
need. You are fortunate because you are the choice
of two people."

"I don't understand. Who has chosen me?" She
gripped the coverlet in her hands as the woman
continued to talk, and her eyes roamed the bed
chamber for anything she could use as a weapon.
"Whose chamber is this?"

"This will be your home for the next few nights.
When we return to England, you will have a
chamber similar to this, but much more luxurious."

"England? I am not going to England. *Who has
chosen me?*"

"Why, my grandson-to-be, of course. His wife, my
granddaughter, is allowing him one mistress and
you are the one he selected. Remember, there are
many who would love to take your place. We will
take very good care of you."

Diana could not believe her ears. "And the name of the gentleman?"

"Randall Baines, of course. You know him very well, I am told. In fact, if you would like, you can watch the wedding processional from the window. But again, only if you agree not to scream."

The old woman raised a bony finger to point at the window. "See for yourself how handsome Randall looks."

Diana put her feet to the floor and stood, a wave of dizziness assaulting her. She sat back down and waited for it to clear.

"Be careful, my dear, you took a nasty blow to the head."

Once her head cleared, she returned to the window and moved the furs back, clutching the shutters as she searched the area for the marrying couple. Finally she saw them, riding matching white horses. There Randall sat, his shoulders back and his head held high, looking most regal. His bride—the secretive lass no one had seen—was by his side.

She gasped as soon as she recognized the woman.

"What's wrong? Why are you so surprised?"

Diana spun around to the old woman, then grabbed the post of the bed to hold herself upright. "His wife...I know her."

"Yes, you do. She said she tried to convince you to go along with their plan so you wouldn't have to be hit on the head."

"Clarissa told me he wanted to marry me, but Clarissa was his betrothed all along, wasn't she?"

"Yes, that's true, but her true name is Clarice, not Clarissa. She told you a lie, did she? Well, she is a spoiled little girl." The old crone chuckled as she settled back into her seat.

Diana moved back to the window and stared at the beautiful pair, prancing in the courtyard to the delight of the crowd. "I don't understand. Why would she want her husband to have a mistress? Does she not want him for herself and no one else? 'Tis what I would want."

"She has her reasons, and they agreed."

Diana turned back from the window, glancing over her shoulder at the woman. "They agreed? He insisted on having me as his mistress, and she said it was all right?"

"More than all right. She wants you as his mistress, as well." A smug look crossed her face as she waited for Diana's response.

Diana scowled. "I still do not understand. She has a knight who wants her."

"Aye, but she does not wish to carry any children, so you are selected to do this for her."

"Nay...then why would she marry at all?"

"She must because the King of England has decreed it, and the coin must pass hands. The betrothal agreement was made long ago. An agreement is an agreement."

Diana covered her mouth as the reality of her situation finally sunk in. "But why me? There are many more beautiful."

"Because your hair is almost the same color as hers and you have green eyes. You must bear Randall's children. If they are your children, they will resemble Clarice enough to pass as hers. As soon as you are carrying his heir, you will both go in hiding, you as her maid, and you will not come out until the child is born. Then you will give up the babe to be raised as nobility. What more could you ask for?"

Diana stumbled back to the bed, holding her head as the ache increased. Nay, she could not do this. No way would she give up her bairn. She had to escape. *Micheil, please help me.*

✧

"Aunt Elspeth, are you sure you are comfortable with watching Sorcha for a spell?" Logan asked. "Micheil and I are going to gather information about town before returning here for Gwyneth. She will return as soon as she can, but we will need her to get into the castle later. Guards do not question women with big bellies or weans at their sides."

"What wean?"

"There must be street urchins in Edinburgh. Gwyneth has gone in search of a young lass to help us in exchange for some coin. After we meet back here, we will be off. I do not know how long it will take."

Elspeth nodded. "No worries. I'm quite happy with the bairn on my lap." As if she understood her compliment, Sorcha gazed up at her with a smile.

Micheil paced the floor as his brother spoke. They had to find Diana, they just had to. Everything was finally starting to fall in place. His life was about to take a huge turn, and he had been interrupted too soon. He wanted time to spend with Diana, to learn more about her. Would they ever have the opportunity to just laugh and enjoy each other?

"Micheil and I will return shortly." Logan placed a huge kiss on Sorcha's cheek, which was all it took to get her smiling and kicking, and ushered Micheil out the door.

Once they made it down the road, Micheil sighed, unsure of which direction to take.

Logan placed his hands on his hips. "Do you want to tell me exactly what this lass means to you? Does Auntie have the truth of it?"

"Naught," he answered too quickly. *Too much* is what he should have answered. "Alexander Grant asked me to keep watch over her and bring her home safe to her sire. I do not care to be speared at the end of his sword if anything happens to her. Presently, the situation does not speak well of me, does it? She disappeared out from under my nose."

They headed toward the center of town. "You're lying. You're in love with her."

"What?" Micheil yelped. "Nay." He hesitated. This was his brother. "Och, 'struth is I am unsure, but I would like to court her. Unfortunately, there are too many obstacles."

"That was not convincing enough, so that tells me that while you love her, you are not yet ready to admit it to anyone else. Are you as pig-headed as I was over Gwyneth?"

"What are you talking about? You and Gwyneth were meant for each other. I'm sure you knew it from the start."

Logan grinned. "In a sense, aye, she set a fire in me, but I didn't have any feelings for her right away. These things take time, brother."

"And was she receptive to your attentions?"

Logan coughed. "Receptive? Hellfire, she threatened to rip my bollocks in two, and I didn't doubt her at her word."

Micheil laughed. "Och, I would have loved to see that."

"Ask Robbie Grant the next time you see him. He's my witness." Logan grinned at the memory of meeting his wife for the first time. "Aye, there was a spark there from the beginning, but I chose to ignore it at first. Had I continued to do so, I would have missed out on the greatest pleasure in my life."

Micheil glanced at his brother. "Which is?"

"Watching my wife and daughter together. Now I understand Quade better than I ever did before."

"You always had a soft spot for bairns, especially our niece and nephew."

"'Tis true, but my feelings go beyond that. I cannot explain it. Now tell me why you left Falkirk for Edinburgh. How did you convince Alex Grant to let you leave with just his niece, a male and a female alone?"

"Because there are rumors Baron Gow killed his first three wives, and his behavior suggests they are true. The man is every bit as cruel as he is reputed to be. Alex did not want Diana to know we had staged her escape together. She and I left alone, but Alex sent ten guards to follow us. Once I got to Aunt Elspeth's, I sent most of them out to watch for Baron Gow's men. I realize now I shouldn't have done that."

"Why Edinburgh and not back to her father?"

"Because Diana was convinced she could find a better husband here. Saints above, the certainty with which she spoke of it made us all thing she already had someone in mind. I think we were all in such a rush to get her away from Baron Gow, we did not think this through. That man is a cruel beast. I would never have given my daughter to him."

"Rushing anything doesn't sound like Alex Grant to me."

They reached the center of town, so the two split—Micheil heading toward the castle, Logan heading toward the Cathedral where the wedding was to take place, searching out the Grant guards.

Micheil had to admit he was shocked at Logan's confession. Gwyneth was such a perfect match for his brother that he would have guessed they had sensed their rightness for each other immediately.

Could he and Diana really be as perfectly suited as his brother and sister-in-law were? The kiss they had shared in the woods near the tournament had taken him completely by surprise. Though it had been intended to frighten her off Randall, he'd frightened himself instead. It had infuriated him to listen to her talking about kissing the other man, so he'd wanted to prove to her that the Englishman couldn't possibly be the best kisser. The electricity between him and Diana had surprised both of them, he knew. She had melted in his arms and shown a passion that had made him want to throw her down on the ground and take her right there. Had they not been so close to the tournament, he might not have stopped.

It was totally out of character for him. He had always been under control, regardless of which lass kept him company. His experience had shown him that no one could unman him.

Until Diana. No matter how he assessed the situation, he came up with the same conclusion. He was in love with her, he just wasn't ready to admit it to his brother or anyone else.

Outside the kitchens, he sauntered over to a couple of urchins searching for food. Micheil leaned against the fence and pulled a couple of gold coins out of his pocket. As soon as the gold flashed in the sun, two lads charged over to him.

"Anyone notice anything unusual about a fire-haired girl?" Micheil asked as he flipped the coins in the air.

"Aye, I did, my lord."

"Do tell, and I'll see if you're deserving of the coin."

"Someone struck two people on the head on the other side of town. I saw him do it. Then he threw the flame-haired lass in a cart and covered her with a plaid."

"Continue. Who did it and where did they take her?"

The one lad glanced at his friend. "We dinnae ken who did it, but they brought her to the back of the castle."

The other said, "Aye, around to the kitchens. And they left the old woman on the ground. Two castle guards, they were. English. They came with the Englishman."

Micheil smiled as he flipped one coin to each lad.

They'd have to take care of Randall Baines, the bastard.

CHAPTER FOURTEEN

When Micheil arrived back at the home, Logan and Gwyneth were already there with a young dark-haired lass around ten or eleven summers. He stopped as soon as he stepped inside the door, frozen in place by the sight of the bruises on the young girl's face.

Micheil stared at Logan with his eyebrows raised in question. Gwyneth sat in the corner feeding Sorcha.

Logan placed his hands on the lassie's shoulders. "This is Molly. Molly worked for the English family that brought Randall Baines and his betrothed here to town."

"But no longer?" Micheil asked.

"Nay. Molly dropped a trencher on the floor, and the grandmother of Clarice, the girl to be married, slapped her and ordered for her to be beaten with a switch. Gwynie found her outside sobbing after her beating. Ena, the grandmother, thought if they sent her out into the cold without any protection, she would learn her lesson better. She was tethered to a tree."

Molly hung her head, tears rolling down her cheeks in humiliation.

Aunt Elspeth said, "Molly, please do not cry," she said softly. "I promise we will never beat you."

Micheil said, "Nay, we will not beat you. Where are your parents?"

"In England," Logan answered. "Tell Micheil why they sent you away," he added, his voice gentle.

Her gaze remained staring at the floor. "My sire said there were too many mouths to feed, so my younger sister and I were sent out. He wouldn't part with his sons."

"Where is your sister?" Micheil was almost afraid to ask.

"Maggie is still inside." Her eyes turned hopeful eyes at the mention of her sister.

"Do you have information about Diana, a lady with red hair?"

Logan smiled. "Why, aye, she does. Molly can lead us to Diana. She knows exactly where she is being kept. Diana was kidnapped to be taken back to England as Randall Baines's mistress." He tipped his head at his brother.

Micheil's eyes widened. Lord, he could hardly believe it, but judging from the expression on Logan's face, it was true. "His mistress?"

Molly nodded, her eyes still cast down. "His new wife agreed."

Micheil knelt in front of the lass and placed his finger under her chin, forcing her to look into his eyes. "My thanks, Molly, for helping us. Is Lady Diana alive and well?"

"Aye, they have her guarded until Randall returns from the wedding ceremony."

Gwyneth announced, "We also have another job to do."

"And that is?" Micheil asked.

"We're going to find Maggie and bring her with us. I have need of a couple of helpers with my bairn, especially since my husband has made me with child again." She glared at Logan. "Molly said she would prefer to go with us instead of back to England with that family. Logan and I thought it was a wonderful idea."

Molly spoke up. "I can clean clothes, too, my lord." She stood stiff as a board, not moving a muscle, probably sore from her beating.

Micheil stared into space, envisioning wrapping his hands around Baines's neck so he could choke him slowly. "That sounds wonderful, Gwyneth. I think Molly and Maggie will like the Ramsay keep, and I'm sure mama would love to have them."

"Come eat more, lassie," Aunt Elspeth said, grabbing Molly by the hand. "You are too thin." She sat her down at the table, but Molly jumped back out of the chair.

"Must I sit, my lady?" Her hands protected her backside.

Elspeth found a soft plaid and set it atop the chair. "Try this, lass."

Micheil spun around to Gwyneth. "Are you two ready? 'Tis time to prepare ourselves and do this." He wrung his hands as he stood in the middle of the small hall.

He just couldn't wait any longer. How the hell could someone take a switch to such a wee lass? "And Molly? Do not forget to show us which one is the grandmother who ordered your punishment."

❧

Diana was in a panic, but there was still a most crushing ache in her head. The old biddy sat down in her chair again—she clearly had no intention of leaving—so Diana turned to the other side and closed her eyes, feigning sleep. She needed time to think. Micheil would come for her, wouldn't he? And she desperately hoped Aunt Elspeth was all right.

A short time later, the door opened and quietly closed. "Is she behaving, Grandmama?"

Diana turned toward the door. Clarice moved over to her side of the bed and sat on the edge.

"I'm sorry we had to hurt you, my dear. If you had only given in to Randall, we wouldn't have needed to kidnap you." Clarice ran her finger down the side of Diana's cheek. "I tried to get you to be agreeable."

Diana pulled away from her, cringing from her touch, but Clarice grabbed her hair. Pain shot through Diana's head since it was so close to her lump. "You will learn not to look down your nose at me, but for now I will forgive you since you are probably a bit...bewildered...by the changes in your circumstances. Just remember there are many who would be grateful to take your place."

"Then please pick one of them. I want naught to do with you or Randall. You lied to me and now you are holding me against my will. I will never give in to you."

Clarice smiled and released her hair, then rubbed her cheek with the back of her hand, following the caress with a brisk slap. "We'll see. Randall will have his way with you, don't you doubt it."

She stood and walked over to her grandmother. "Keep her quiet for another hour or two. We must participate in the feast. If you need the guards to tie her up, do it. There must be no chance of her breaking free while the castle is still full of Scots."

As soon as she left, Diana took stock of her surroundings. It would not be difficult to overpower the old biddy, and she did have her dagger. She needed to distract the woman.

"Would it be possible to have something to eat, my lady?"

"Here's some cheese. That's all I have. Foolish serving girl spilled the porridge."

"But my head hurts so much and it will be painful to chew. Porridge would be better." She had to get out of here. The crony groaned, but she got up to speak to the guards and sent one to the great hall for food.

Diana needed a distraction. She needed to get out of this nightmare and back to Micheil. Why had she not appreciated Micheil for all he had done for her? She'd been blinded by stories and her own imagination. Now she realized *he* was the true knight, always protecting and taking care of her. To hell with foolish English knights. She wanted a Scot, and Micheil Ramsay was the man for her. Bringing her to Edinburgh, saving her from the lout Randall, holding her while she cried, standing up against the cheat at the jousting tournament, he had helped her so much. Why hadn't she seen him for what he was?

She finally realized Micheil Ramsay was her knight, and that she fell in love with him in Edinburgh, just as her dear mother had predicted. If only she had a way to tell him.

Gwyneth helped Molly get dressed in a bed chamber in Aunt Elspeth's house. The men were still in the dining hall, planning a strategy based on the detailed description Molly had given them of the layout of the castle.

Gwyneth sat on her heels in front of the lass, fitting her hair into a lad's cap. They had decided the only way to get in was disguised as kitchen lads. A huge feast, to which King Alexander had invited most of the town, offered the perfect cover for them. There would be many in and out of the bailey, so no one would suspect them. Their only problem was ensuring that Molly was not recognized by any of the inside helpers.

"My lady?" Molly whispered.

"What, sweeting?" Gwyneth asked her, smiling in the hopes of soothing some of the girl's fear.

"Promise not to leave us behind, my sister and me?" Her voice trembled as she stared at her feet. "We'll go anywhere with you if you won't beat us. Or I can take Maggie's beatings. As long as you do not beat my sister, I'll do whatever you ask. She's too young."

Gwyneth set her finger under Molly's chin and lifted the girl's gaze to hers. "I promise not to leave you two behind, and I promise not to beat either of you. If we are separated, I will come back for you. Do you believe me?"

"I'll try my best," she whispered, her voice breaking.

"Tell me, who are you most afraid of—Randall, Clarice, or her grandmother?"

Molly averted her gaze. "Lord Baines. I did not know the other two before coming to Edinburgh."

"But was it not the grandmother who had you beaten?" Gwyneth had a bad feeling in her gut all of a sudden.

"Aye, but I understand that kind of beating. I had them back in England, too." She stared at the ceiling as her toe began tapping on the floor.

Gwyneth stopped fussing with the lass's disguise and brought Molly's gaze back to hers. "And what kind of beating do you not understand?"

Molly did not answer, but tears slid down her cheek as her lower lip trembled.

"Molly, I was once forced aboard a ship where a man tried to touch me in a place that is my private area alone. He made me feel verra uncomfortable and dirty. Was that what happened?"

The lass nodded, her hands wringing behind her slim body. "Lord Baines made me undress, and he felt my chest. He said I was not quite ready yet, but soon. I did not like it. I fear for Maggie."

Gwyneth's belly was suddenly squeezed in a familiar grip—one she hadn't felt in a long time. It would serve her well for the task that lay ahead of her. She hugged Molly tight even though she stood as stiff as a board. "Don't you worry, lassie. Randall Baines will never touch you again, I'll see to it. And neither will the old woman."

Molly relaxed and laid her head on Gwyneth's shoulders, her soft cries echoing in Gwyneth's ear. "I'm sorry we must take you when you are so sore," she said, "but we need your guidance. Come, lass, we've work to do. Let's go get your sis, aye?"

Molly nodded and stood erect so Gwyneth could finish perfecting her disguise. "I don't mind hurting as long as we find Maggie." Once they were ready, Gwyneth strode out into the dining hall, Molly's hand in hers. They stopped in front of the others, and Gwyneth stared at her husband and tugged Molly in close so she could wrap an arm around her shoulders.

Everyone quieted and waited for her to speak.

Her gaze never leaving Logan's, she said, "Husband, we have work to do."

Logan froze. "Och, I've seen that look before." He glanced at Molly and gave his wife a pointed look.

Gwyneth nodded.

"Bastard will pay." Logan turned to his brother. "This will be sheer pleasure, I promise you."

Micheil stared at Gwyneth and Molly, hoping he had misinterpreted the silent conversation between husband and wife, but something told him he hadn't. "Baines is a liar and a cheat. He proved that in front of a crowd of English and Scots on the jousting field."

Gwyneth closed her eyes. "Och, but the man is so, so much more than that."

Her eyes flew open again, a fury in them Micheil had only seen there once before, the night many moons ago when Gwyneth had hunted down the man who had murdered her father and brother. His brother's wife was a master archer, and she always carried her bow and arrows. He had seen the proof of her ability that night.

Before they stepped out, Gwyneth turned to her husband. "Logan, place this mantle so it appears I have a hunched back. I need to hide my quiver."

Molly watched her carefully as Logan assisted her. "You use a bow and arrow, my lady?"

Gwyneth nodded as she ran her hand down her back. "Aye. I promised to get your sister back, and I will." Once she was suitably arranged, Gwyneth moved over to Aunt Elspeth, who held Sorcha in her arms, and kissed her sleeping daughter on the cheek, then strode to the door. "Come, we must rescue the two lassies."

Aunt Elspeth smiled, nodding in satisfaction. "Bless you, my dear."

CHAPTER FIFTEEN

The old lady had another serving girl bring in the porridge. As the woman walked over to the window, Diana made her move, managing to reach into her pocket and remove the cover from her dagger. She hoped not to cut her leg, but she needed it ready.

"Well, the nobility are moving into the great hall. Wonderful. Randall and Clarice should be able to find their way here soon. I would like to go down to the festivities for a while." She turned from the window to stare at Diana. "And I do not care to be here whence your lessons begin. They'll have a time with you." She shook her bent finger at her. "They should have heeded my words and chosen someone willing in exchange for the coin. But that Randall has some unique views. Perhaps it is best you are here so he can use you instead of my beautiful granddaughter."

The door to the chamber swung open and Randall marched in. "Well, Ena, I see you have my pretty one." He stood in front of her with his arms crossed over his chest. "My, my, I believe I am grateful I decided to wait until my wedding night to take you. It will make me feel like I have a true bride instead of the cold one I wed."

Diana glared at him and he chuckled. "We will definitely have fun tonight. You will not be the only one screaming, so no one will heed your cries." He spun on his heel and called in the guards. "Bring the woman to the room off my chamber within the next few moments. Be discreet and gag her if you must. Though with all the revelry in the hall and the courtyard, no one will pay her any mind."

He walked over and tipped her head back to kiss her. Diana sealed her lips together, refusing to return the kiss until he bit her and she yelped. He chucked her under the chin and said, "If I need to have someone tie you to the bed, I will, you can count on that." He grinned and sauntered out the door.

Diana spit on the floor after he left, glaring at the old crone who laughed in the corner, wondering how she could ever have been attracted to the vile lout. She had considered stabbing the man with her dagger, but she would have to use it on two people since the old bitch was still present. She would only have one chance, and she was not ready to gamble it yet. The guards were still outside the room. She thought her best opportunity would arise while she was being moved or when she was in the other chamber.

Where was Micheil?

❧

Gwyneth gave Logan a fast kiss behind the castle.

Micheil said, "Plan in place. Are you solid with it, Gwyneth?"

"Aye, Molly and I will do our part, don't you worry. We'll be looking for you, either outside or inside." Gwyneth, dressed in her favored tunic and leggings, had her bow across her back and her quiver within easy reach, hidden by her mantle. Since it was a cool night, she hoped it would escape notice by the cook.

Logan said, "Micheil, you wait out here for Gwyneth's call."

The group split and Gwyneth trudged around to the back of the kitchens with Molly. She found two platters and they wove their way out to the roasted pig outside and stood in line. As soon as the cook loaded their platters, they moved into the kitchens.

"Hurry with the pork, lads. They are eating everything inside the hall. There is not enough to hold them," one cook shouted. "Remove your mantle, lad."

"Aye, Cook." She mumbled over her shoulder but hurried along, counting on the chaos to cover her.

Gwyneth moved out of the kitchens and into the corridor leading to the great hall. Molly stayed right beside her. Just before they entered the great hall, Molly stopped and pointed. "There, that way."

They made their way through a large maze of passageways littered with scraps of food, lovers kissing, and an occasional drunken soul passed out on the floor. The torches were scattered so their faces stayed quite hidden. Molly pointed to a doorway, and Gwyneth stole inside. It was a small deserted chamber that would serve their purposes perfectly. Molly was definitely an asset.

"Here, lass," she said, pulling a small bottle out of her satchel. "Put some of this powder over the meat you have there. Be careful not to get any on your skin or we must wash it off." Finished with their task, they sneaked back out of the door and down the dark passageway, then up the stairs at the end of the corridor.

They stole up two flights without encountering anyone. Once they reached the door at the top of the steps, Gwyneth glanced back down the damp staircase. Seeing no one, she stuck her head out of the doorway and noticed the two guards outside a chamber, just as Molly had said they would be.

Molly whispered, "Are they close or way down the passageway?"

Gwyneth answered, "They are not close."

"Then they must have her in the wedding chamber. That is the largest one at the end of the passageway. There are two connected rooms inside, and a small one with a large tub for bathing and dressing."

"Then off we go. Are you ready?"

Molly nodded, a serious expression on her face, and began carrying her platter toward the guards. Satisfied, Gwyneth walked beside her.

The guard on the left stopped them. "Lord Baines is in his room, and he has decreed no one is allowed inside either chamber."

Gwyneth glared at him. "Lord Baines himself caught us on his way up and told us to bring meat platters with us. We brought two, one for you and one for him."

One guard stared at the food, his mouth drooling. "Glen, I have not eaten in a while. Let them in so we can eat. What harm could two such slight lads be?"

The other guard nodded, his eyes on the huge chunks of steaming meat in front of him.

"Aye. Let them in. Here, give us ours first."

Gwyneth handed over the platter and reached for the door. As soon as they stepped inside, she closed the door behind them. A woman who met the description of Diana was on a bed on the far wall set between two windows. Both windows had fur coverings, and the farther one had a heavy chest under it. An old woman sat on a chair near the bed, a chest of drawers not far from her. She held her fingers to her lips as the old woman had not noticed them yet. To the far side of the room sat another door. She smiled as she gripped Molly's hand. This would be easy.

∞

Diana stared at the two lads who had just entered. Randall had gone into his chamber, promising to change, but presently singing in a deep voice and creating all kinds of noise inside his chamber. Then who were these two?

One of the lads, who appeared to be built like a lass, set down a platter of meat and stepped over to the old woman. Then he yanked her up and held a dagger to her throat.

"Do not say a word or you're a dead woman."

Ena started to yell, but the lad squeezed her throat with his hand until she wheezed, finally falling silent.

The lad whispered over his shoulder to her. "I'm married to Micheil's brother, and my name is Gwyneth. Diana, can you handle tying this bitch up?"

Diana wanted to shout for joy, but instead she chose to hop off the bed, nodding her head. "Aye, with pleasure." She smiled at Ena.

"Good, here's rope. Tie her up and I'll take care of Baines."

Diana's eyes misted but she did as Gwyneth bade her to do. Micheil had come through for her. Hellfire, she loved the man! They dropped Ena onto the bed, and the smaller lad helped by holding the crone's legs. While Diana was busy tying the old woman's hands, Gwyneth went to the window at the far end of the chamber, tied a rope to a hunk of metal on the chest, then pulled the furs back and dropped the rope outside.

Ena stared at the smaller lad and said, "You're no lad. You're the daft servant I had whipped for being lazy and dropping the trencher. I'll have you...."

The speed with which Gwyneth moved from the window made Diana jump. Grasping Ena by the hair, the fierce woman pulled out her dagger and held it at Ena's throat. "Say another word to that lass and I'll cut your tongue out. I'm going to let her whip you in return for what you did to her."

The old woman's eyes bugged out, and her mouth snapped shut.

"Better. If I see or hear that tongue again, it'll be gone. Don't doubt it. Naught would give me more pleasure after what you did to this defenseless lassie." She jerked her head toward the lass, who was staring at the floor now. "Take a good look at her, because now your life is in her hands." Gwyneth glared at the woman before she finally dropped her head back on the mattress and stepped away.

Diana peered from Gwyneth to the lad, only then realizing she was indeed a young lass close to tears. Retrieving her own dagger from where she'd hidden it, Diana said, "I'll take care of this. Do what you need to do to get us out of here. Randall is in the next chamber and may emerge at any moment."

Gwyneth nodded and rushed over to peek through the corridor door just as Micheil dropped over the sash at the window. Diana wished to shout to the heavens when his gaze caught hers. He grinned and her heart fluttered, but she forced herself to complete her task. She blinked several times to eliminate the misting in her eyes.

"I will take care of the guards, Gwyneth. Don't you touch them in your condition. Logan would have my arse." He no doubt tried his best to whisper, but fortunately, Baines continued to sing and was oblivious to them.

Micheil leaned over to kiss Diana's cheek as he passed her on his way to the door, and she wanted to swoon. She had never expected to have such strong feelings for a man, and to have it happen so fast, boggled her mind. How she wished she could tell her papa.

She had finished gagging the old woman when Micheil said to the lass. "Molly, hold open the door." The lass ran over and did as she was told. Micheil dragged the two motionless guards into the room and tied one up.

"Are they dead?" the lass whispered as he continued working.

Gwyneth shook her head. "Nay, just asleep. Diana, are you all right with her?"

Diana nodded. "Aye, she's not going anywhere."

As Gwyneth moved toward the door to the next chamber, Micheil said, "Let me. These fools are not going anywhere." He gestured to the guards, who were already trussed up.

Gwyneth shook her head slowly and deliberately. "Not a chance. This bastard is all mine." She strode back and kissed Molly's cheek, then pivoted back toward the door, a large grin on her face.

CHAPTER SIXTEEN

As soon as Gwyneth stepped inside the chamber, Diana launched herself at Micheil, throwing herself into his arms. She wrapped her arms around his neck and planted a kiss on his lips.

"My knight, finally my knight is here."

Micheil could hardly believe his ears. Had she just said what he thought she had? If he was her knight, did that mean she wanted him? "Truly? You want me?"

"Aye. Micheil, do you not see? You are the one my mama told me about."

He shook his head. "I'm not a knight, Diana. I cannot be all you had hoped for."

"I've had much time to think on it, and I was confused. My mother told me I would fall in love in Edinburgh. Aye, she told tales of braw knights and jousts, but she never said my husband was a knight. She said she had a dream where I met a man and fell in love in Edinburgh. 'Tis you. I have fallen in love with you here in Edinburgh, just as my mama said." Micheil kissed her, a long deep kiss that made him daft, a kiss that made him want so much more. She tasted so sweet, yet she lit a fire in him like no one else ever could. He had to admit, his daft brother was right about one thing. He was in love with Diana.

He pulled back and stared at her, happy to finally have her in his arms again. "You frightened the hell out of me, Diana. I had no idea where you were."

"I have been such a fool. Thank you for coming for me. You wouldn't believe what they wanted me to do."

"Molly here—" he nodded his head in her direction, "—gave us a wee idea of their plans. There was no way we would ever have let them steal you away to England."

"Thank you, Molly." Diana smiled at the shy girl.

Molly smiled and stared at her feet, her hands clasped in front of her.

The door flew open, revealing Logan in the doorway. As soon as he took in the situation in the room, he nodded to a person outside the door. The next moment, King Alexander strode in, followed by two guards. His eyes grew wide at the sight of the guards on the floor before finally settling on the old woman on the bed. "Ena, what have you gotten yourself into this time?"

His gaze fell on Diana, who had stepped away from Micheil, but still hung onto his hand.

"Untie the foolish woman, Ramsay. She has some explaining to do. I warned her she could not have everything her way, but she never listens."

The king looked at Ena again, a furrow in his brow. A loud crash sounded from inside the adjoining chamber.

Logan yelled, "Gwynie? You need help?"

"Nay, we'll be out in a second," she shouted back.

Logan smiled, but then his eyes landed on King Alexander, who was scratching his jaw, seemingly puzzled by the woman on the bed. "Isn't she your relation?" he asked the king. "I thought Clarice was your cousin?"

King Alexander sighed. "Aye she is. But Ena is not a blood relative, and she has always had unusual ideas. Apparently Clarice is much like her. I'll see them both in my solar for a full explanation. The guards will escort her." He nodded to one guard, and he helped Ena up and guided her out into the corridor.

Gwyneth opened the door to the chamber and said, "You're welcome to enter if you would like. Please bring Molly with you."

Placing an arm around Diana, Micheil took Molly's hand into his free one and ushered her inside the other room. She clung to him, refusing to move away, which broke his heart. Gwyneth stood next to the bed, a bit in front of Randall, who was crouched over in what appeared to be exquisite pain. She had a plaid over her arm that extended toward Randall's midsection.

"Apologize, Randall." Gwyneth didn't look at the man, but she moved her arm a touch, making Randall squirm.

Micheil thought Baines looked a wee bit green, but he was quite enjoying the sight. Rather than interfere, King Alexander watched the scene from the back of the room, his arms folded as he took in the tableau before him.

"Sorry," Baines whispered.

"That's not good enough. Molly, come up here close to me, please."

Molly kept her head down, but she moved toward Gwyneth.

"Again, Randall. And you need to address her."

"I'm sorry, Molly." He stared at the top of Molly's head.

Gwyneth gripped tighter.

"For?"

"For touching you inappropriately. I'll never do it again."

"That's better. Molly, you may step out of the room if you wish, sweet."

Molly whirled around, clearly anxious to get away from the man. Clearly sensing her anxiety, Diana followed her out, her hands on Molly's shoulders and closed the door behind them. Micheil stared at Baines, still puzzled by what exactly Gwyneth was doing to him. Dagger in his belly?

Logan sighed. "Gwyneth. Did you truss him like a turkey?"

Gwyneth smiled at her husband. "He deserved it, Logan."

"Mayhap, he did." He stood next to his wife and kissed her forehead. "Let go of the man's bollocks, would you please?"

Micheil's eyes widened. That would explain why Baines looked as if he were on the verge of fainting.

Logan laughed. "Besides, he is no Scot. I think you could have bested him without any need for that."

Gwyneth scowled and stared at Baines, fear and pain still oozing from his pores. "Fine, you're probably right." She let go of whatever she held and dropped the plaid, releasing a cloth with ties on it and allowing it to fall to the floor.

Baines let out a deep sigh and held his middle.

Gwyneth's elbow snapped him in the face, breaking his nose with a loud crack. He fell back onto the bed, his eyes rolling back into his sockets. She wrapped her arms around her husband's neck. "I guess you were right, Logan."

Logan glanced over her shoulder at Randall on the bed. "He won't be quite so pretty anymore, will he?"

The king whispered, "I understand why Hamilton employs the two of you. Ruthless, my dear, but deserved. You may guard me anytime."

A wee voice interrupted them from the other chamber. "No, no, please, someone help her! Clarice has my sister, and she is taking her away." They opened the door between the rooms and Micheil rushed over to join Molly at the window, arriving just in time to see Clarice running through the courtyard dragging a wee lass behind her.

Gwyneth tore into the chamber after him, heading straight toward Molly. Logan and the king were fast behind her.

"Diana, stay with Molly," Micheil yelled. "We'll be back." He assumed he and Logan would head down the stairs, but Gwyneth went straight for the window, dropping her mantle on the way.

"Husband, hold the rope for me." As she climbed out, Logan grabbed the rope to steady it and make sure it held.

"Hellfire, you are letting her go first, Logan?"

"I accept her strengths, she accepts mine," he said over his shoulder.

Gwyneth couldn't help but smirk in response to Logan's comment. She shimmied down the rope, thanking God for her wonderful husband. She would get Maggie back. He knew it, and so did she. Fortunately, she didn't have much of a belly with this bairn yet.

She landed and took off after Clarice, still able to hear her husband's conversation with his brother.

"Hell, Micheil, can you not see she is faster than I am? She's lithe and quick."

She had to block him out and focus on her goal, focusing all her energy onto her target. Her fingers caressed the end of her bow, making sure it was where she expected it to be. When she needed, it would be in her hands in seconds.

The wind had come up and was whipping all around her, which better helped her follow Clarice with her voluminous skirts billowing around her. Wee Maggie kept up with the daft woman as best she could.

"Hang on, Maggie," she cried out. "I'll get you back with Molly."

The lassie's head turned back to see who was following them, and Gwyneth hoped she had the courage to stay strong. Clarice headed straight for the stables, causing a painful memory to creep back into her mind—the day she had failed to kill the man who murdered her brother and father. Eventually she had succeeded, but the memory of that day still smarted.

Well, she would not fail today, she assured herself. She would be strong for two wee lassies who deserved a better life. The bitch dragging Maggie would be stopped, no doubt. The opening to the stables was on the far side of the building. Clarice would have to run half the length of the building to get to the end, which gave Gwyneth the most perfect target she had ever seen.

She smiled and reached for an arrow in her quiver.

CHAPTER SEVENTEEN

Gwyneth nocked her arrow and released it just before Clarice reached the corner. She made a direct hit, right into the dress billowing behind the woman. The material pinned her to the wooden wall. She jerked backwards as Gwyneth sent two more arrows flying, one hitting Clarice's hand, forcing her to release Maggie, and the other securing her bell sleeve to the wall above the skirt of her gown.

Logan and Micheil, who must have been running fast behind her, passed her as she made her way to her quarry. The wee girl who had been Clarice's captive headed straight for Gwyneth and threw her arms around her waist, burying her face into her tunic.

"Where's my sister? I want Molly," she cried out as Micheil and Logan grabbed Clarice and tied her hands so they could lead her back into the castle.

"Do not worry, lass," Gwyneth said. "We'll get you together." Maggie had beautiful chestnut hair and the bluest eyes Gwynie had ever seen. She knelt in front of the wee lass and said, "I promise. I will not allow anyone to separate you two again."

As the rest of the group moved on toward the king's solar, Micheil tugged Diana into an alcove.

She gazed up at him with an expression that humbled him. He took his hands in hers and rubbed his thumbs across her soft skin.

"Micheil, what is it?"

He cleared his throat, trying to come up with the right words. Everything had happened so fast, but that did not matter. He knew in his bones this was right. "I..." He glanced up at the ceiling, and started again. "I knew I was developing strong feelings for you, but I had no idea how strong. 'Twas my brother who recognized my love for you, even before I did. For so long, I had no interest in settling down in marriage."

Diana stared at him, her eyes misting at his words. The beautiful smile on her face told him they were happy tears, which gave him the strength to continue.

"You came into my life and turned everything upside down. I love you, and I want to spend a lifetime showing you how much I care. I want to run from here, show you the moon and the stars and have you at my side always. Diana of Drummond, will you marry me?"

Diana squealed and threw her arms around his shoulders, jumping into his embrace. "Aye, Micheil. Naught would make me happier." She settled back onto her tiptoes and cupped his face in her hands. "I love you, too. Aye, aye, aye."

He kissed her tenderly, so ecstatic that she had accepted. He ended the kiss and leaned his forehead against hers. "Will you marry me here in Edinburgh or would you prefer to talk to your sire first?"

Tears slid down her cheeks. "Here, Micheil. 'Tis the last part of my mama's dream to come true. She said I would fall in love and marry in Edinburgh."

He smiled and brushed the wetness from her face. "Then as soon as we finish in the king's solar, I'll search out a priest if the king agrees."

Diana's gaze searched the chamber as she tried to process everything that had transpired in such a short time. With the exception of the young girls, the entire group was squeezed together in the king's solar as King Alexander paced behind his desk and his guards at the periphery and the door. "All right. Who wishes to start explaining this disaster to me?"

No one spoke. While Logan held Baines in front of him, Micheil stood near Clarice. Ena sat in a chair, refusing to look at anyone.

Randall finally spoke. "I have no idea what has happened. I married my betrothed Clarice today, but I have no idea who these people are." He jerked his head toward Logan and Micheil. "I would prefer to be allowed to spend my evening with my bride. I am totally innocent."

"Innocent?" Diana huffed out. "If you are innocent, then why was I kidnapped and held captive in the chamber next to yours?"

"All right. So I made one mistake. There is no reason you should not release me. I have not taken her innocence."

Gwyneth snarled and took three steps toward him. "Give him to me again, husband."

His eyes frantic, Baines held his hands out in front of him. "All right. Two mistakes." He pointed at Gwyneth. "Just keep her away from me." He took a moment to regain his composure, then continued. "I apologized to the lassie, but this one," he pointed to Diana. "She has been chasing me for two days. I was just giving her what she wanted."

Diana's reaction was swift. "Aye, you fooled me once, but not again, especially after your shenanigans on the jousting field showed your true colors."

Micheil let go of Clarice and strode over, his fist connecting with the English knight's face. Baines was quick to cover his broken nose, so Micheil's fist slid off his cheek and knocked him backwards.

"Enough!" King Alexander bellowed. "I care nothing for this English fool. Take him out of the room for now, guards. I want to talk to the other two." He motioned to Clarice and Ena. "Now what foolish plan did you instigate, Ena?"

Ena gave the king a haughty stare. "Clarice is in love with another, and she did not wish to marry this fool. We checked into his background. He would never stay true to her. I didn't blame her. I knew you insisted they wed, Alexander..."

"Ena?" The king gave her a piercing look.

"As you wish, though I knew you when you were in swaddling cloth. Your Grace. Clarice is my only granddaughter, and I seek her happiness. She did not care to have relations with Baines or carry his child, so we kidnapped a redhead to stand in her place. What harm could it be? 'Tis done all the time in England."

"The harm is you kidnapped the daughter of a Scottish chieftain."

Clarice's eyes widened. "What?"

King Alexander bellowed. "She'll be chieftain of the Drummond clan. And why did you take the poor wee lass and run with her?"

"I do not wish to be married to Baines. I do not like him, and I decided to run to my beloved," Clarice answered, her arms crossed in front of her.

The king waited, glowering at her.

In a small voice, she added, "I wanted a maid. My beloved doesn't have one for me. She's just a wee lass, and she does not belong to anyone. I checked. Can't I have her?"

"Nay!" the king shouted. "If I dissolve the marriage, will the two of you behave?"

Diana saw Ena lean forward from her chair, staring at her granddaughter. The old woman fussed with her skirts for a moment before she finally spoke "We'll go home. If you could share the gold purse with us, Alexander…"

"Ena. I will throttle you yet." He leaned toward her, clearly exasperated with the old woman.

"*King* Alexander. My pardon. We could use the coin."

"Nay, no coin. You will get enough to get you home with my guards as escort." He turned to stare at Clarice. "And no servants. Arrange your own back in England. Wait until I see your mother again."

Shaking his head, King Alexander turned to his guards. "Take them away and put them in a chamber somewhere. Do not let them leave until I say so. Logan, you will locate the priest so I can have this marriage annulled. What a disaster.

Micheil and Gwyneth, go get your aunt and your daughter and bring them here. God only knows what other blackguards may be out there tonight." He stepped out into the corridor and called more guards. "Clear the courtyard and the great hall. The festivities are over." The men disappeared to carry out their instructions.

Logan left with the guards to do as he'd been ordered. The king shook his head and turned his attention to Gwyneth. "I commend you for your service to the Crown, my dear. I am proud to say I have seen you in action with my own eyes. When your family arrives, you will have your own hall for the night. There is plenty of food."

"My king, I would like to petition the Crown for a boon, if I may," Gwyneth whispered.

The king nodded. "Name it and it is yours."

"I would like to request to have Molly and Maggie added to our family. According to Molly, they were sent away by their own father out of need, and they were treated abominably by Randall's family."

The king considered her request, rubbing his chin. "The two lassies are with my housekeeper. When I have the opportunity, I will speak to the two girls and the Baines family to verify your statement and consider your petition. Tonight they will remain under the protection of my staff and the ministrations of my personal healer. You will have your answer on the morrow. Is this acceptable to you, Lady Ramsay?"

"Aye, and many thanks."

Micheil had made his way over to Diana and now held her hand. "My king, if I may have a word?"

The king's eyes narrowed as he turned to Micheil. "Aye, Ramsay?"

"I would like to request the honor of taking Diana of Drummond as my wife. If possible, I would like to do this here, with your priest, with you as a witness."

Diana held her breath, hoping the king would agree.

King Alexander turned to Diana. "Stay a moment in my solar. Gwyneth, if you'd prefer, you may take a couple of guards back and retrieve your family."

Gwyneth gave Micheil a kiss and a squeeze on his shoulder before she left. "'Tis the right thing." She disappeared with a few guards.

Now that the others had left, the king ushered them both into chairs. Silence settled over the group for the moment. She stole a glance at Micheil and he caught her staring, sending her a look that melted her heart. Could they marry and put an end to all her troubles? She could hardly have imagined a better conclusion to the past several days.

She blushed and stared at her king, awaiting his command.

"Diana of Drummond, the last I heard from your father was that he had betrothed you to Baron Gow. I also received a missive stating that the baron was happy with the arrangement. I thought you to be wed by now, but I have not had the opportunity to speak with you on the matter with all this madness. What say you?"

Micheil said, "If I may, your..."

Alexander held his hand up to silence Micheil. "From Diana, please."

Diana cleared her throat. "You are correct. My sire has not been well, and he wished for me to marry so our lands would stay within our bloodline, since I am heir to them. When I did not find a suitable partner, he settled on the arrangement with the baron."

"And you did not agree to this? Is your sire not gravely ill?"

Tears misted in her eyes. "Aye, I did agree before I met the baron. But..."

He stopped her. "There is nae but. You agreed to this marriage."

Diana burst into tears and Micheil reached for her hand, rubbing his thumb across the back of her palm.

"Go ahead, speak what you will." The king waved his hand.

"I did agree, Your Grace, but when I finally met the baron, he frightened me. He was cruel and made some verra crude suggestions to me. I am certain we would not suit. I ran away." She stared at the ground, embarrassed by her actions.

"And how did you get to the baron's lands if your sire was so ill?"

"I was escorted by my cousins, Alexander and Robbie Grant."

"Hmmm." The king scratched his cheek, his lips pursed. "And how did the Grant feel about the baron?"

"I'm not sure. You see, Micheil and I left..."

"If I may interrupt, Your Grace." Micheil cleared his throat.

The king stared at him for a moment before finally motioning for him to speak.

"Alex Grant asked me to escort her to Edinburgh in search of an English knight to take to husband. We thought she knew one, but when we arrived..."

Diana's head jerked to stare at Micheil. Had she heard him correctly? Alex had supported her journey to Edinburgh?

The king held up his hand. "Never mind." He was silent a moment before returning his gaze to Micheil. "Would the Grant support your request for her hand?"

Micheil nodded. "I believe he would. He did not support the marriage to Baron Gow."

Diana moved to the edge of her seat. "Aye, Your Grace. He would, I am sure of it. And my sire would as well. He wants me to be happy. The only reason he forced my hand was because I had not yet found anyone who fit my idea of an ideal husband."

He glanced at her with one eyebrow raised. "And does Micheil Ramsay suit you?"

Diana blushed, realizing how spoiled she sounded. "Aye. Your Grace, I was young, and did not understand much of the world. My sire was almost too vigilant in protecting me from lads and anything outside of our lands and our clan."

He smiled. "And now?"

She knew she sounded daft. "After my time in Falkirk and Edinburgh, I understand what qualities I seek in a husband."

"Do tell."

She glanced at Micheil. "I want someone who will protect me, who will listen to me and support me. The Drummond clan is mine and the land is where I was raised. I wish to have a say in how our clan is run, not to be wed to someone like the baron who would come in and order my people around. He would never have asked my input. I am proud of my clan, and Micheil would help me to do what is best for them. He is kind and wise and patient." Tears clogged her throat as she spoke.

"And this is what you want?"

"Aye." She stared at her lap before looking up at Micheil. "I wish to marry someone who would manage our clan like my sire, and I think that man is Micheil. My people would be happy to accept him and so would my father."

King Alexander smiled. "It appears to me that your jaunt in Edinburgh has taught you quite a bit, young lady."

"Aye, it has. I am embarrassed by some of my actions, but I am wiser because of them."

The king thought for a moment. "Why do you wish to marry here instead of your home?"

"Because I fear Baron Gow will be searching for me, and if Micheil and I are already wed when he finds us, he cannot hope to tear us apart."

After several minutes, King Alexander stood. He held his arms wide and said, "I support this marriage. It would please me to have one good marriage come of all this preparation. It will please me even more for the Drummond land to remain under the control of two loyal Scots. Will you consider marrying within a few hours while the priest is still here?"

Micheil gazed at Diana with a smile and she nodded. "Aye, Sire."

"Then let's prepare for a wedding. We'll use the small hall, and I will find an appropriate chamber for you this night if you are agreeable."

She nodded. "Thank you, Your Grace." Tears of joy slid down her face, realizing her dreams were all about to come true. Her marriage to Micheil was what she wanted, what her father would want, and what her mother would want if she were here. This was the best decision for her clan.

The king held out his arm. "Come, Diana of Drummond. We will find my dressmaker. Micheil, I am sure your family will arrive soon, if they have not already. They should be in the east hall."

CHAPTER EIGHTEEN

A few hours later, Micheil stood at the end of one of the king's halls, pacing in front of his brother. "I cannot believe this is happening. Where is she? Mayhap she has changed her mind?"

Logan chuckled. "I doubt that. You make a good match, in my opinion."

"Do you think so? I have chosen well?"

Logan leaned closer to his brother, making sure they would not be overheard. "Micheil, I know you love the lassies, but how much longer could you have continued to go on like that? You sampled everyone near the Ramsay keep, then moved on to Glasgow, Ayr, and now Edinburgh. Did you plan on moving to England soon?"

Micheil laughed. "Nay, I like women. I cannot help it. But now that I've met Diana, I have no desire for another. I look at other women, but I do not see them in the same way I once did. Sometimes it frightens me, the hold she has on me. Am I daft? Do you have any regrets? You never used to stay in one place for long." Micheil searched his brother's gaze, hoping for an honest answer. Did he regret marrying Gwyneth and settling down?

"Nay, Micheil. Not for one moment of any day have I felt regret. My wife makes me a better person. And Sorcha? I never thought I could feel so much love. Nay, you have found the right lass for you and will feel no regret. Besides, her lands are not far from the Ramsay lands, so Gwynie and I can go back and forth. Neither of us likes to stay in one place for long. She is definitely the other half to my soul."

"This has all happened so fast. Mayhap we are rushing things, but we both fear the baron could push for his rights. If you were to meet the bastard, you would understand why I cannot allow him to come near Diana... Quade and mother will be furious when they find out I married without them. "

Logan shook his head. "Nay. They will be happy for you. It will make for more merriment at holiday festivities. 'Tis time." He clasped his younger brother on the shoulder and tilted his head toward the doorway.

Micheil swallowed the thickening lump in his throat. Diana had arrived. Beaming with happiness, she strode across the hall on the arm of King Alexander, dressed in a deep blue dress that perfectly set off her red tresses. When she finally reached his side, he held his arm out for her and she grasped it. His heart flooded with happiness, but he noticed her eyes were misting.

"Something wrong? Do you wish to talk in private?" he whispered in her ear.

"Nay. I just wish my papa was here. But I know he is not strong enough to make it. My mama is here with me in spirit, I can feel her here with us."

Moments later, they stood in front of the priest, Gwyneth and Aunt Elspeth at Diana's side and Logan at Micheil's. When the priest wrapped their hands in the blue Ramsay plaid, Micheil could feel Diana's hand trembling, so he squeezed it a wee bit. She gazed up at him and mouthed, "I love you."

Before he knew it, the ceremony was finished and he kissed Diana, shocked by the sense of serenity and fulfillment he felt. He cupped her face and kissed her again to the cheers of his family. He whispered in her ear, "I love you, too. I do not know when it happened, but I do, truly."

The king raised his arms to speak. Turning to the bride and groom, he congratulated them first. "My best wishes for a wonderful future for your marriage. It has come to my attention that parts of the jousting tourney were conducted in less than a fair manner. I am shocked that it happened here in the land of Scots, but there is one man who acted and fought with the most admirable qualities."

He stopped to move to the side of the chamber and pulled out a heavy bag from a wooden chest.

"Micheil Ramsay, I thank you for conducting yourself most honorably on Scottish soil. It is my belief that this coin was previously given in error, and it pleases me to bestow such coin as your wedding gift from the Crown." King Alexander handed Micheil and Diana a bag of gold coins, and when Micheil tried to object, he said, "They go to the winner of the jousting tournament, and I no longer feel Baines deserves. Won fairly and respectably."

Micheil accepted with a smile, bowing to his king.

Once the festivities began, Logan whispered in Micheil's ear, "Found the dastardly saw he used for the lances."

Micheil stared his brother in shock. "I'm satisfied his dishonesty was caught, but somehow, this does not seem right."

Logan clasped his brother's shoulder. "It is. Accept it with pride. I heard about your accomplishments on the field. All the Scots are boasting their countryman. You deserve it."

Micheil wrapped his arms around his wife and kissed her. "Are you happy, love?"

She rested her head on his shoulder. "Micheil, this day that started so horribly has turned wondrous. I could not be happier."

They ate a marvelous meal. Platters of venison, pork, and turkey were served on beautiful silver serving dishes. Crusty brown breads and bowls of minted peas sat on each table, along with a wide variety of cheeses. At one point, Diana leaned over and said. "Micheil, I am happy this is our wedding day. I like this small cozy atmosphere, and we are in a beautiful castle. We can celebrate with the clan and my sire later. This moment is for us."

Aunt Elspeth cried many tears. "I knew it all along. Why did it take you two so much longer to finally realize you were meant to be together?"

Diana gave Aunt Elspeth a sheepish look. "Someday you'll come to realize how stubborn I can be, Auntie."

Micheil quirked his brow at her. "You agree you are a wee bit stubborn? I tried many, many times to dissuade you from the English knights."

"Aye, but you did not offer yourself as a candidate."

"Nay, but I am not stubborn, just foolish."

Aunt Elspeth said, "Micheil, do not try to deny a lass her dreams. She just needed some guidance." She kissed each of them on the cheek. "You are perfect for each other. You are together now, and that is what's important."

Smiling at Auntie, Diana picked Sorcha up from Logan's lap and said, "By the way, does this bairn ever cry? I have not heard a peep from her yet."

Logan scowled. "Nay, she's my daughter. She's perfect. And mayhap I'll have a son the next time you see us, Aunt Elspeth."

Gwyneth whispered, "Um, and two more daughters, husband?"

"Hellfire, lass, you want to do things that quick?"

"Och, there's something I forgot to tell you," Gwyneth said with a smile.

"What?"

All the talk at the table stopped.

"I asked the king for Molly and Maggie. I could not bear the possibility of them being returned to Randall Baines family. They may be returning to Lothian with us." She stared up at Logan, awaiting his reaction.

Micheil smiled, knowing Logan would gladly give Gwyneth anything she wanted.

Logan tipped his head and chewed on his lip for a moment. Then his eyes brightened. "Do you think they will be agreeable? They *are* English."

Leaning over, Gwyneth wrapped her arms around him and said, "Thank you. You know they need to have a home. I think they'll be agreeable."

Logan whispered, "Mayhap they can help you with the cooking and the sewing."

Gwyneth scowled, but then her face lit up. "Aye, you're correct. Mayhap they can teach me something. My womanly skills are quite poor."

"But you have so many skills that I love," Logan said with a wide smile, then raised his goblet. "To Micheil and Diana, my new sister, and to two new daughters."

∞

The king escorted the new couple to their chamber. He kissed Diana on the cheek and held the door open for her. "If you have need of anything, please let me know." With another smile, he left them.

Diana gasped as she and Micheil stepped into the room, closing the door behind them. "This is so beautiful."

A large canopied bed sat in between two fur covered windows. A fire burned in the hearth, and two cushioned chairs sat in front with a small chest between them. A bowl of apples and a bottle of wine sat atop the chest, next to two gold studded goblets.

The bed was covered with more pillows and furs than Diana had ever seen. If she fell asleep there, she feared she would never want to leave it.

Micheil took her hand and led her over to the table and chairs, then poured them each a goblet of wine. "Diana, 'tis a beautiful dress, but may I help you remove it?"

Her reaction must have shown on her face, for he quickly added, "Nay, just to make you more comfortable. There's a white night rail across the bed I can help you into if you would like. We have had little opportunity to talk, and I would like to."

The words filled her heart with warmth. She gave him her back and swept her long tendrils up and out of the way. "Aye, I am ready to get out of these bindings." She glanced over her shoulder at him as he untied her ribbons, hoping she would please him.

Once the dress fell to her feet and she stepped out of it, Micheil's gaze roamed over her whole body. Her flimsy shift did little to conceal her figure. "Lass, you are beautiful." He gathered her in his arms and kissed her.

When he ended the kiss, Diana chuckled. "Do you know how much better you are at this than Randall or Baron Gow? They were terrible. Your kisses are wonderful, Micheil."

He touched his fingers to her lips and said, "Shush. Thank you for the compliment, but I would prefer not to hear those two names again tonight.

"Agreed, or forever if it pleases you."

Micheil sat in the chair and tugged her into the chair next to his. "Tell me your thoughts. Are you truly happy, Diana?" he asked, giving her one of the goblets of wine. "I asked you before in front of others. Now I ask you privately."

Diana sipped her wine. Was she happy? Aye, more than she had ever thought possible, though she was a trifle nervous at the moment. She stared at Micheil's long dark hair, at the sparkle in his eye, at his wonderful smile. What more could she ask for than to see his handsome face first thing in the morning every day for the rest of her life?

Licking her lips, she had to admit curiosity was getting the best of her. What she most wanted at this very moment was to see him without his clothes. Her gaze ran down his chest and his muscular arms to his flat belly and below. Chugging her wine, she set her goblet down.

"Lass, if you continue to look at me like that, I make no promises as to the consequences of your actions."

Heat spread through her body and settled between her thighs. Her mind could not release one thought. She wanted her husband to make love to her; she had been patient long enough. Diana stood directly in front of Micheil and hooked her thumb under the edge of her chemise, dropping it down over her shoulder to free one breast from its confinement.

She paused, unsure of what to do next, but Micheil's heavy lidded gaze gave her the confidence to continue.

His gaze followed her bare skin. "Do not stop there, lass. I wish to see more of you."

Diana tossed her shoulders back and released her other breast, shimmying her shift down to her waist where she held it. "Your turn. I wish to see your skin, Micheil." She peeked at him through her lashes, shocked at her boldness, but laughed as he first removed his boots and stockings, then his leine before he jumped out of the chair. He was about to remove his plaid, but she stopped him with her hand. Fueled with a newfound power, she shook her finger at him. "Not yet."

Micheil's eyes widened. "Och, you will kill me if you make me wait much longer."

She grinned at him and held her arms in the air as she wiggled her hips enough to cause the shift to slowly drop lower, stopping it every few inches or so to tease him a bit more. Cupping her breasts from underneath, she held them out, rubbing her thumbs over her sensitive nipples, making them erect. She could not help but notice his plaid stood out a bit more than it had a few moments ago. Even though she was inexperienced, she had wondered about the act of loving a man for a long time, asking her maids many questions. She oft had overheard them whisper about how to tease a man. It seems they had given her sound advice.

"Wife, do you know how long I have waited for this?" he growled, still holding back.

"Nay, I do not. Tell me please, husband." Her wiggling dropped the shift to her hips, so she reached down and moved it until it stopped just over her thatch of curls, wanting to tease him a bit more before she let it tumble to the ground. She could tell by the look in her husband's gaze that her plan was successful.

His voice, deep and husky, sent a shiver down her spine. "Forever. I have wanted you since I first met you. Please allow me to touch you." His gaze raked over her belly and down to her thighs as he waited for that last bit of clothing to disappear. "Hellfire, you are so beautiful, Diana. Those curves, your breasts, I want those lovely nipples in my mouth. Let me cherish you as you should be cherished."

She chuckled and stood back. "Wait." Still holding the fine cloth in her hands, she turned around slowly until her backside faced Micheil. She glanced over her shoulder and couldn't stop from giggling. Why, the man was almost drooling.

His eyes followed the curve of her hip to the very top of her bum, the bottom still covered. "Diana, please stop. I must touch you."

She wiggled her bottom and said, "You may touch me lightly, but only if you drop your plaid first."

His plaid fell away in a second, and Micheil stood facing her backside with naught on, just as she'd wanted, giving herself the opportunity to turn her gaze away if she was embarrassed. Her eyes widened at the proud way his erection jutted out toward her. Her gaze wished to stay there, but she forced it away, choosing instead to drink in everything else about him, his muscles, his fine abdomen, the spattering of dark chest hairs that led down his belly, before returning to his cock. He looked absolutely magnificent.

He reached over and caressed each cheek of her bottom and she moaned, realizing how wonderful a tender touch could feel. No longer able to think clearly, she let the cloth slip to the floor and fell back against him in sheer wantonness, unable to control her desire.

His hand reached around to the front of her curls, and he parted them, groaning. "I knew you would be wet for me." He inserted one finger inside her and her legs nearly buckled with pleasure. Only by clinging to his arms did she manage to stay upright.

"That's it, wife," he whispered in her ear. "Nae more teasing." Micheil scooped her up in his arms and dropped her on the bed. "My turn now, lass."

CHAPTER NINETEEN

Diana fell into the plump cushioning of the bed and reached for her husband, spreading her legs wide in an open invitation.

She reached for his hard sex, but he held her hand back. "Not yet." Before she could argue, he kissed her, ravaging her mouth, tasting every corner with his tongue until she responded in kind. He angled his mouth over hers and slowly caressed her until she moaned in the back of her throat, just as he had wanted.

He ended the kiss and gazed down at her, pleased with the passion he saw in her gaze. Trailing a line down her neck, he kissed her earlobe, traced a path across her fine bone, and finally settled in the valley between her luscious breasts. He licked her nipple until it stood erect, then he took the taut peak into his mouth, suckling her until she cried out. Her fingers dug into his shoulders, and he smiled.

"That's right, now it's my turn to tease you, wee one. How does it feel to be at my mercy?"

"Micheil, please?"

"Please, what, my sweet?"

"Please, just please. Ohhh," she moaned and gripped the sheets at her side as his tongue traveled over to her other breast, repeating everything until she cried out again. "Please, I need you."

"Where do you need me, love?" His gaze caught hers, and he could not help but tease her some more, her excitement so delighting him. Hellfire, she was a passionate one. His hand grazed down her belly until he found her core. Teasing her clit, he entered her with one finger, then two, until she moved her hips on his fingers, trying to reach her peak.

"Slow down, Diana. We have all night."

"Nay, I cannot take any more of this torture. I want you now. Please, Micheil. Stop playing and do whatever you need to do." She ground her hips against him, then managed to move away enough to reach down and grasp his rod, sliding her hand down the smooth surface.

"Och, not yet. You are not ready. This will hurt, you are aware."

"I am ready. I need something. You know what to do. Can you not finish this, please?" She reached for him, a tentative touch that indicated her uncertainty of what was to come.

Micheil growled. "Enough, lass. I need to worry about your first time." He pulled away from her grasp and moved down the surface of the bed until he found her clit with his tongue. He flicked her pleasure spot until she gasped, then entered her with his finger again.

"Micheil? What are...? Ohhh...."

Her legs spread wide, and he suckled her until she fell over the edge, yelling his name as she pulsed around his finger.

When she finished, he kissed a path back up across her skin until he could gaze into her eyes while he leaned his head on his elbow. Her satisfied expression pleased him. "Better? Did I give you what you begged for?"

She glanced at him and whimpered, then grabbed his bicep. "I want more."

He chuckled and settled himself on top of her, resting his weight on his elbows and entering her just a touch. "This will hurt, love, but I'll be quick."

"Aye."

Micheil plunged ahead, and she gasped at the intrusion as he broke through her barrier. He kissed her forehead and stilled. "Are you all right? I'll wait until you are ready." He ran his fingers through her hair and gritted his teeth, forcing himself to wait until she could handle him. He swore he would not move a muscle until she told him she was ready.

A moment later, she tipped her hips to take him in further, then pulled away from him again. "Aye, again, Micheil."

Micheil grasped her hips and drove into her, letting her set the pace until he could sense her desire return. She arched her back and spread wider, allowing him better access. He called her name out, thrusting into her until they moved perfectly together, panting and grasping for the same pleasure. He rode her until he could tell she was close, then reached down and caressed her nub until she convulsed again, this time squeezing his dick until he followed her. A deep growl let loose as he erupted inside of her, intense waves of pleasure shooting through him until he collapsed on top of her.

When he was able to think again, he pushed himself up on his elbows and rolled over, taking her with him and kissing her cheek. He held her close, not wanting the moment to end.

"Did I please you, Diana? Did I give you what you were searching for?"

She leaned up on her elbow and cupped his face to kiss him. "Aye, and much more." She dropped her head on his chest and fell fast asleep.

The next morning, they were all seated for breakfast when the king strode in followed by his guards. He made his way first to Micheil and Diana. "Did the accommodations please you, Diana and Micheil of Drummond?"

"Aye." Diana nodded and blushed, thinking how pleased she was indeed with her newfound love. She leaned in to Micheil and he kissed her cheek.

"Wonderful, thank you, Your Grace." Micheil smiled.

The king nodded in acknowledgement and turned to Gwyneth and Logan. "As you requested, I have given a great deal of thought to your proposal."

Diana could not help but notice everyone in the hall stopped to listen to the king's decision about the two sisters.

He continued with his hands clasped behind his back. "I have also talked to Randall Baines' mother, who took the girls from their home. While she was sad to relinquish them, I gave her no choice in the matter. She did inform me that the lassies' family did not wish to have them returned. The couple believed they had too many bairns, and their father apparently did not approve of Molly's looks, saying he would never be able to marry her off. His wife only sent Maggie along so Molly would not be alone."

The king beckoned to the guards at the door, and they opened them, ushering the two girls inside. Molly and Maggie stepped into the chamber clinging to each other, but they only moved forward a couple of steps. There was a package in Molly's arms, and she set it in on the table before returning to her sister's side.

The king continued, "The lassies are quite happy with your proposal, and if you still agree, would like to go along as your maids."

"But that's not what I want," Gwyneth said, standing and moving in front of King Alexander. "Your Grace, I wish to treat them as our daughters, to raise them right and include them as family, to live with us forever or until they marry, not as maids. They will have chores, but they will not be servants."

Diana glanced at the two adorable sisters, unable to believe a parent would turn them out. She thought of the love her mother and father both had for her. How awful it must be to grow up without a parent's love. When Gwyneth explained she wanted them as daughters, both girls' faces beamed as if illuminated by a sudden ray of sunshine.

The king considered Gwyneth's request and finally turned to her husband. "Logan, does this meet with your approval?"

"Aye, I wish to gain two more daughters. We promise not to beat them or treat them poorly, and we will keep them together."

Molly tried to hold back her smile, but could not. Maggie jumped up and down, her straight brown hair bouncing with her as she clung to her sister.

The king turned to the girls. "Then it is done. Molly and Maggie, I will have the priest bless you as Molly and Maggie Ramsay." He turned back to Logan and Micheil. "When do you plan to leave?"

"On the morrow," Logan answered. "We wish to return home, especially now that we have two new daughters to introduce to our clan."

Micheil nodded. "We will travel with them, along with the remaining Grant warriors, and head back to Diana's clan. We're hoping to find her father is still well."

King Alexander strode to the door, then stopped to address the group again. "I will send missives to Baron Gow, Alexander Grant, and to your father, Diana, explaining that I have approved this match. I do not want any further troubles for you."

"May we carry a missive from you on the morrow, Your Grace?" Micheil asked. "In case the other letters do not reach their intended? I do not wish for my wife to have any difficulties should we encounter Baron Gow or his men on the road. They may still be in pursuit of her."

"Aye, I will see to it. The other missives will depart this morn. If you are in need of aught else before you leave, please ask." He bowed and stepped out of the chamber, his guards following.

As soon as he left, Gwyneth turned to the sisters and held out her arms. The two jumped into her embrace, squealing with excitement. They both hugged Logan, too, and everyone else joined in to welcome them to the family.

Molly picked up her package and brought it over to Gwyneth, a shy look on her face. "We made this for you while we waited. Maggie is good with a needle, so she did most of it. I am a better cook so I can help with preparing food." Her hands kneaded in front of her as Gwyneth took the gift. "But I did help to the best of my ability. I wanted to thank you for what you did for me and my sister. I did not want to lose her." Her gaze dropped to the floor.

Diana peered over Molly's mass of dark curls, watching as Gwyneth pulled out a beautiful dark blue tunic with silver threads in it and blue leggings. She gasped when she fingered the careful stitches the girls had placed. What caught everyone's eyes the most was what sat beneath the larger pair of leggings—a matching tunic and leggings in Sorcha's size.

Gwyneth held them up for all to see, then squeezed both girls, kissing the tops of their heads. "Perfect, just as you two lassies are."

The following morning, the group gathered at the stables, ready to move on. The king had given them the requested missive declaring his approval of their marriage. Diana prayed her father would accept it and that he would still be alive to meet Micheil. He had declined quickly before the trip to Falkirk, which gave her concern.

On their return journey to her home south of Crieff, they would need to circumvent Falkirk to stay out of Baron Gow's territory.

Micheil held his arm out to his wife. "Come, ride with me, Diana."

"Micheil, nay. Can I not ride alone? You know how I love riding. I have not been able to do it much lately. Please let me ride alone for a while."

Logan scowled. "Micheil, we have enough guards. She should be fine."

"Aye, but Sorcha and Maggie will both ride with you. Molly will ride with Gwyneth. We have quite a few lassies with us. I worry we will attract the wrong kind of notice."

"Gwyneth can handle her own. We already talked to the lassies about what to do if we are attacked. Is that not correct, Molly?"

Molly nodded. "Aye, Maggie will bring Sorcha to me and we will hide in the bushes until everything is safe again. We promise to take good care of Sorcha."

Micheil stared at Diana. His gaze narrowed, but apparently he could not refuse her. "Fine. We should be far from trouble today. On the morrow, you will ride with me. And no argument in the morning. Agreed?"

Diana smiled and hugged her husband. "Aye, I will ride with you on the morrow, no arguing. I promise."

"You agree to follow the wee lassies if there's trouble?"

She pursed her lips, set to argue. "I can use my arrow."

Micheil's hand shot up to stop her. "Nay, you will be the target. You and the girls will go off into the forest or the bushes."

Diana scowled and stared at Logan. "But Gwyneth won't go with us, will she?"

"Gwyneth is the best archer in the land of the Scots," Logan said. "Nay, she fights at my side. Always." He walked over and kissed his wife, who was settling the bags onto the mounts as Molly held Sorcha.

Sensing her upset, Gwyneth strode over and hugged her. "I know you are offended, Diana, but you *are* a target."

"Then I shouldn't go with the lassies. I'll draw the attackers with me."

"But the goal is for you to get away before they are close enough to grab you. If we are ambushed, you will need to run off before they are close. I'll take care of them if they follow you." Micheil's expression turned dark, as if the mere thought of such an attack made him sick.

Diana stared at the ground. "As you wish. But once we are past Falkirk, you must all stop fussing over me."

They rode through most of the day, stopping once or twice to feed Sorcha and take repast. They had ten guards with them, the Grant guards who had followed them to Edinburgh. Alex had insisted they remain near them.

Sorcha was quite happy riding in her sling in front of her sire. Truly, Diana had never seen a less fussy baby. Maggie rode behind Logan and played peeking games with the bairn whenever she was awake. The sight of the new sisters playing together was enough to swell her heart.

Micheil spent more of his time gazing at his beautiful wife than he did watching in the distance for predators. Diana was a true beauty, and she sat her horse regally, as if she was born there. He had been a bit concerned she would be too sore to ride today, but she was steadfast as ever. Every once in a while, he would pull up close to her and wink at her. It didn't matter how many times he did it, she still blushed a deep shade of pink and tossed her mantle off her shoulder at him.

"Micheil, stop embarrassing me," she finally whispered.

"What am I doing, love?" His grin would only embarrass her more—he knew that.

"You are thinking about our lovemaking," she whispered.

"Aye," he winked again. "I cannot help but recall such wonderful memories. You are so beautiful. Do you wish to know my favorite part of your curves, wife?"

"Och, Micheil! How I wish I had something to throw at you. Stop teasing me."

He chuckled and said, "Only if you promise to tell me later."

"I will. Now cease your incessant blather." She arched her chin into the air and spurred her horse ahead.

And that is when disaster struck. Near dusk, somewhere between fifteen and twenty horses came out of the forest headed straight for them.

CHAPTER TWENTY

Gwyneth almost choked on her own saliva when she first noticed the warriors on horseback headed toward them. Baron Gow's men. They had to be his, since they wore no plaid and seemed to be undisciplined.

Moments before, she had been listening to Micheil and Diana's charming banter, but now that idyllic moment had been shattered.

Everything happened at once. Two horses headed straight for Diana. One rider grabbed for her reins while the other reached for her and threw her over his horse. Four others flanked them to prevent Micheil or Logan from reaching her, forcing them to fight through them first. Though she wanted nothing more than to immediately ride into battle, Gwyneth was worried for her own family's safety. She lowered Molly onto the ground and rode in front of Logan, drawing her sword to protect him and the girls as he lowered Maggie to the ground and placed Sorcha into her arms. The girls ran into the forest, Sorcha yelling a bit, but Gwyneth sighed when they ducked behind a large rock off to the side.

Gwyneth swung her sword at one horseman and caught him in the side, enough to send him sailing off his horse. The rest of the Grant guards riding behind them jumped into the melee, and the clashing of steel on steel rang through the land as the two groups battled. Logan headed into the middle of the fight while Gwyneth hung back, another move they had planned ahead of time. Logan wanted her to be far enough away from the enemy forces to use her bow and arrow.

The horseman with Diana took off. Micheil rode directly behind him, which prevented Gwyneth from being able to hit the fool, but she would not have taken the chance anyway with Diana on the horse. Four Grant guardsmen rode alongside Micheil, killing two of Gow's men easily on the way, and the remaining six held back to fight with Logan.

Gwyneth found a spot away from the group, nocked her arrow and released. She caught one man square in the chest. A big ugly one took her arrow between the eyes, falling off his horse in a matter of seconds. Logan took on the next one, stabbing him in the leg, then catching his sword arm and pulling him off his horse. Two Grant men ran through one warrior each. Only five were left, and one took off without a backward glance, choosing to flee instead of face death.

Gwyneth shot one of the men in the belly, while Logan speared another in the side of his chest. The last two were taken down by the Grant fighters. Logan headed off after Micheil.

Gwyneth glanced at the lassies, who were still behind the huge rock in front of a copse of trees. Molly peeked out and left the cover of the rock once she saw things had quieted. Maggie followed, Sorcha happy in her arms.

Emerging from the trees at a full gallop, one of Gow's men headed straight for the girls. Gwyneth screamed, but she forced herself to steady her hands enough to nock an arrow and release it. She missed the lout. Her heart sat in her throat as she watched him reach down and pluck Sorcha out of Maggie's arms, holding her in front of him so Gwyneth couldn't fire another arrow at him.

He headed toward Gwyneth before rotating back around, Sorcha screaming in his lap. He chuckled and headed back toward the group of trees, the same direction from which he had come. Gwyneth, sick with fear over her bairn being kidnapped, set herself to fire another arrow. A fear like she had never felt before gripped her, but she pulled another arrow from her quiver and nocked it. She noticed Logan was returning from the other direction, but he was still too far away to use his sword.

The brute was still within range, thankfully, and she waited until he gave her the square of his back before she released, hitting him on the left side near his kidney. Her next arrow struck him on the other side of his back and he froze. Lifting the bairn off his lap, he held her by her arm so that she dangled off the side of the horse, her legs flailing.

Gwyneth held her breath and spurred her horse, all the while haunted by visions of the fool dropping Sorcha onto the ground before falling on top of her, crushing her. Logan charged in the same direction.

What neither of them had expected to see was a wee fairy with a mass of dark curls charge out from behind the rock like a bolt of lightning just as the warrior was about to pass her. She reached up to tug Sorcha out of his weakening grasp just before the fool fell off his horse.

Logan, who was closer, yelled, "Wife, she's fine." Sorcha's screams changed to laughter as soon as Molly righted the bairn in her arms.

With a sigh of relief, Gwyneth headed toward the girls.

"Sorry, we're so sorry." Molly's breath hitched over and over as she glanced from Logan to Gwyneth.

Logan reached down and picked up Sorcha, placing her back in her sling after he kissed her into a fit of giggles. "She's fine, wife, no wounds."

Molly stood crying between the two horses, clutching at Maggie. Gwyneth jumped off her horse and moved toward the sisters. "Well done, lassies. 'Tis naught for you to apologize. You saved our bairn, and you have our thanks."

Molly finally let go of her sister and ran into Gwyneth's arms, burying her face in her tunic.

"You ran like a deer, my sweet. We are grateful for your quick thinking." Maggie ran over and grabbed Gwyneth's leg. She kissed both of their heads and held them close. "Now I can relax. I have my three daughters back safe."

※

Micheil made death quick for the two fools who sat between his sword and his wife. As soon as he cut them down, he spurred his horse into greater speed, leaving the other two for the Grants and his brother. Why had he relented? He should never have allowed her to ride alone.

The bastard took a different route through the trees, and Micheil held out his arm to prevent the branches from taking one of his eyes out. Daylight was near gone, and he did not know the area, but he could hear the fool ahead of him. He thought Diana had her dagger in the folds of her skirt, so he wondered why she hadn't used it yet. The fool must have her completely pinned and unable to move.

"Diana, keep talking and yelling so I know where you are. I'm right behind you."

Diana's bellows echoed in the trees, and he couldn't help but smile at her gusto. His wife was one strong woman, and she wouldn't let Baron Gow's men get the best of her. He prodded his horse until they broke free of the forest, and he realized he had gained ground on his adversary. Another short distance and he would try to leap far enough to knock the lout off his horse.

Diana was a strong enough horsewoman to right the horse once he set her free. He would pummel the brute until his last breath for daring to touch his wife.

Fired with enough fury, he managed to gain even more ground. Soon he was almost riding alongside Diana and the man. A couple more feet and he would have him. As soon as he could, he leapt sideways, catching the lout with all his weight, sending them both tumbling to the ground. His fist flew into the fool's face first, followed by another uppercut to his jaw. Images of the man's hands on Diana fueled his ire even more. He grabbed his dagger and planted it in the guard's neck, only then noticing that another dagger jutted from his belly.

Well done, wife. It had not killed him, but it had slowed him enough for Micheil to catch up to him. As soon as he was able, he pulled himself off the dying man, only to feel the vibration of a herd of horses headed in their direction. His wife had slowed the horse she was riding and righted herself. Headed in his direction, she turned her head to see the massive number of warriors riding toward them.

Micheil yelled, "Diana. Come here. Do not stop for anything." His horse seemed discomfited by the approaching force, but he came to him when summoned with a whistle. Diana was riding fast toward him, close enough for him to see the panic in her face.

The Grant warrior whoop echoed across the meadow, and Micheil breathed a sigh of relief as he helped his wife down from the horse and wrapped his arms around her, burying his face in her hair. Her posture sat rigid in his arms until he said, "'Tis the Grants. Do not worry."

She melted into his arms and whispered his name. "I was so frightened. I will ride with you forever. No more strange men. Please." Her breathing still ragged from the stress of the kidnapping, she clung to him.

"You're not hurt? No wounds?" His gaze searched her face for anything, running his hands over her body to make sure there was no reason for concern.

"Aye, I am fine. Micheil." She buried her face in his chest. "No more, please. I wish to go home to my sire and my clan. No Baines, no Gow. When will it stop? And what of the weans? We have to check on them. They may need your assistance."

"Logan and Gwyneth had six guards with them. Alex will be here in a moment." He held her, not yet willing to let her go.

Alex Grant pulled away from the herd and found his way over to them. "Are there others?"

"Aye." Micheil pointed. "Send a few back to assist Logan, though I hope he is not in need of assistance by now."

Alex nodded, splitting his warriors up. "Congratulations are in order. 'Tis true? Another Ramsay has married into the Grant family?"

Without releasing her from his arms, Micheil swung her around until she faced Alex. "Aye. We married at Edinburgh Castle with the king's blessing. Did you not receive his missive?"

"Aye, we did, but Baron Gow burned his without reading it, claiming the seal was broken. As soon as he heard you were in Edinburgh, he dispatched a group of his men to bring Diana home. That done, he left for Drummond Castle, a priest by his side. He hopes to annul your marriage and claim you as wife as soon as you arrive home."

"And my sire?" Her gaze was hopeful enough to break Micheil's heart. How he wished he would have the opportunity to meet the Drummond Chieftain.

Alex shook his head. "He is still alive, cousin, but he does not speak. He is close to death, and I fear Baron Gow will encourage it if given the chance. I left Robbie and a few others as his guard in hopes we could find the two of you and return you to his side before he passes. Baron Gow will not make this easy. Though with all of us there, he will not be able to refute the missive as he attempted to do when we left."

Diana nodded and leaned into her husband. "Please take me to my father."

Micheil kissed her cheek. "Of course. We will leave as soon as we have ensured Logan and the lassies are safe. Alex, will you spare a few more men to accompany us to Drummond land? Your warriors have been indispensible. Logan and Gwyneth joined us in Edinburgh, but now he needs to get his new family home. He is traveling with many lassies, and I want to ensure they are safe."

Alex quirked a brow. "Aye, my guards go with me to Diana's sire, but I am happy to send some as protection for Logan's family. I have enough to guard both. New family?"

"He and Gwyneth adopted two lassies along with their new bairn, Sorcha."

Micheil helped his wife mount, then climbed behind her, eager to check on his brother now that Diana was safe.

"We need to see how they fare. They had to battle a few of Gow's men on their own."

CHAPTER TWENTY-ONE

They found their family settled in a clearing, cooking rabbits that Gwyneth and the guards had caught. All were safe, much to Diana's relief. The large group of guards and little lassies sat around the fire while the men cooked the meat.

Molly and Maggie both hid behind Logan as soon as they saw Laird Alexander Grant stroll into the clearing. His voice bellowed his greetings. Once both sides shared their stories, a plan was agreed upon for the morrow—one group would break off to Lothian and the Ramsay keep by midday while the rest headed to Drummond land.

Diana had not left her husband's side. She huddled next to him on a tree stump, so thankful to be with him after yet another brush with danger.

As soon as they finished eating, Alex strolled over to Gwyneth, who was holding Sorcha on her hip, and said, "May I, my lady? I miss my own wee lassie."

Molly and Maggie peeked out from behind Logan at the tall Highlander as he picked Sorcha up and settled her in his arms so she could face out and look at everyone. He sat on the ground and set her down on his lap, wrapping his plaid around her as she watched all the antics of the crowd.

Finally able to sneak away, Molly and Maggie ran off to the opposite side of the clearing and clung to each other, whispering in frantic tones. She wondered what they were about, but felt it was not her place to ask.

Some fell asleep on their plaids, but Molly and Maggie still held each other, their faces agonized. No matter what Gwyneth said to comfort them and convince them that they were not in trouble, that she was proud of them for acting so quickly to save Sorcha from the bad man who had threatened her, it did not seem to work.

Finally, Molly stood and marched off into the trees, leaving behind a sobbing Maggie. A few minutes later, Molly returned with a branch in her hand. She strode over to Logan and Gwyneth with a purposeful expression, then halted in front of Logan, her eyes cast downward.

Logan gave Gwyneth a puzzled look. The entire area quieted as their curiosity about what wee Molly had to say got to them all. The agonized look on the girl's face broke Diana's heart.

Diana reached over and squeezed Micheil's hand as they watched the wee lass.

Logan spoke first. "Molly, what is it? Why do you carry a branch?"

Molly's face, never more serious, scrunched together as her wavering chin lifted a bit. She held the branch out in front of her. "Here is the switch. I wish to take my sister's punishment now if I may."

Logan, a shocked expression on his face, uttered, "What?"

Molly stared at the ground. "I know we are to wait until morning for our beating, but I wish to have Maggie's now so she will not cry all night in waiting."

Logan turned to Gwyneth. "I know not what to say."

"Please, may we do it quickly?" Molly asked, her hand trembling as she held out the branch.

Logan took the branch from Molly and said, "Lass, I told you before, I do not beat people smaller than me, especially not lassies."

Molly glanced at him, her eyes bright with hope.

Gwyneth held her hand out to Maggie, who was now sobbing loud enough for all to hear. The wee lassie rushed over to her and allowed her to pull her close. Rubbing a gentle hand over her shoulders, Gwyneth turned to look at Molly while she consoled Maggie. "You saved wee Sorcha. Why would you think we would beat you?"

"Because I was holding Sorcha when he took her." Maggie sobbed. "I was not holding her tight enough, or he would not have been able to grab her. It is all my fault, not Molly's. But I don't like the switch." She tipped her head back and wailed. "It hurts when I get hit. I'm sorry. I did not mean to let go of her. Please don't send us back. You can hit us both."

Logan pulled Molly into a hug while Gwyneth comforted Maggie.

"Shush," Logan said. "I will not use the switch on either of you." He took the tree branch and broke it over his knee, throwing it over his shoulder. "There,'tis gone. Now cease your crying. I cannot tolerate lassies crying."

Maggie gazed up at him. "Truly? You will not hit either of us?"

"Nay, lass. Did you not hear me tell the king I would not beat you?"

Molly whispered, "But Lady Raines told my sire they would not hit us, and they used a switch on us all the time, and they made us wait until morning."

"No beatings. Ever," Gwyneth said. "Now cease crying and play with your sister. She's getting upset over there on Laird Grant's lap listening to you two cry."

They all looked at Sorcha's contorted face and broke into peals of laughter, Sorcha joining them once she sensed the change in everyone's mood.

Logan crouched down until he was level with Molly. "You had a choice. You could have stayed behind that rock and protected Maggie, your own sister, or you could have run out, putting yourself and Maggie in danger to try and save Sorcha. Which did you choose to do?"

Molly hung her head, but not before they noticed the smile on her face. "I wanted to save Sorcha from that mean man."

Reaching over, Logan smoothed her wild dark curls. "And you saved our daughter's life. I will never beat you or your sister. We don't beat our daughters, and you and Maggie are now as much our daughters as Sorcha. I promise."

Molly and Maggie grinned at each other, gave their new parents big hugs, and ran over to play with Sorcha.

When they scampered over to pick up Sorcha, Alex Grant told them, "And if anyone else tries to beat you, you let me know. I'll take care of them." Alex's expression was the most serious Diana had ever seen on him. "Do you hear me, lassies?"

The two looked at him and nodded, breaking into giggles.

Diana leaned over to her husband. "What a soft-hearted man Alex is, though you would never guess it to look at him."

"'Tis true. You should see him with his own daughter."

"I have. He is so wonderful with his bairns." She smiled.

Micheil stood and held his hand out to his wife. "Come, we have a long day ahead of us. 'Tis time to rest."

Diana followed her husband behind a tree, where he had found a soft, grassy spot for them to sleep. They arranged their furs and settled onto the ground, and he wrapped his arms around her.

"Husband, I know what you like to do, but there are too many nearby tonight." She glanced at him, an anxious set to her eyes.

"Diana, tonight I wish to just thank the Lord for our good fortune and hold you tight. May I do that?"

"'Tis naught I would rather do." She tucked her head under his chin and fell asleep in a manner of seconds.

It was just after dark when they arrived on the Drummond lands. Alex and Micheil ensured Grant warriors protected Diana on all sides. Baron Gow had proven over and over again what a stubborn old fool he was. Diana's heart pounded in her chest as they neared the portcullis. She prayed to God that her dear papa was still alive. Though she knew he wouldn't be well, she at least wanted him to meet Micheil. She wanted her sire to know she was happy and to be proud of her chosen husband. It would mean so much to her if he blessed their union.

Or was she too late?

The guards at the gate were the baron's, not her father's. This did not bode well for the status of her castle.

"Micheil, do you think he has overtaken all my father's men?"

"I hope he has ordered them at the portcullis to advise him of your arrival, and we'll see your guards elsewhere."

"Do you still possess the missive from the king? I fear I will be yanked from your arms in short order." She glanced over her shoulder at him, then at Alex Grant seated on his destrier to her left, the largest sword she had ever seen strapped within his grasp.

Micheil whispered in her ear. "Sweeting, he will need to strike me dead to tear you from my arms."

"Micheil, I love you."

"I love you, too. I will not give you up." He wrapped his hand around her to calm her trembling. Knowing Baron Gow, she was certain this would be a trial. He was not about to give up her or the Drummond land. Clearly, he was already attempting to stake his claim.

Unfamiliar stable lads rushed over to take their horses. At the last moment, her favorite stable boy ran up to her and whispered in her ear. "My lady, he lives. Do not believe him. He is not well..."

An arm reached out and yanked the lad away from her. A burly man she had never seen before cuffed him, and he ran off a distance, stopping to give her a nod. "Be off with you, you scum. Do as you are bid."

"Do not hurt him. He is my stable lad. Fergus?" She reached for him but the man stepped in the way.

"He is no longer your stable lad," the man sneered with contempt. "He will do as I direct him, or he will find himself out of a home *and* a job." He reached for Diana, but Micheil's sword stopped him.

"Do not touch her if you wish to keep your hand," Micheil said.

The man snarled and stalked off, muttering to himself as he went.

"Grant, this is not going to be easy, is it?" Micheil glanced at his friend.

"Nay," Alex said, but a smirk danced across his face. "I think we will quite enjoy ourselves. Naught would please me more than to put Baron Gow in his place. I have the king's missive giving you and Diana rights to the castle. Gow doesn't hold any rights at all. We'll see how foolish a man he is since to continue this pursuit of Diana will mean going against the king's edict. If so, we will just have to remove him in the name of King Alexander."

"But do we have enough warriors?"

"I have around fifty, and I sent for two hundred more the moment I received the king's missive. They'll get here in at most a day or two. I think we can handle Gow's paltry guard without them, but I was eager to guarantee my cousin and her husband get all that is theirs, not to mention that Gow will get his just due." Alex smiled and winked at Micheil. "Trust me, we will enjoy this one."

Diana stared at her cousin in awe as he sat on his now prancing destrier. She sensed he would not give up his horse until the last possible moment, reminding them all who was in charge.

"Remember, Gow does not treat his men well. They will be quick to run." Alex finally dismounted and patted his mount to calm him.

Diana watched as the huge Highlander took an apple from his sporran and fed it to his fine horse. "Aye, Maddie sent you your sweets. Now behave, Midnight." The horse nuzzled Alex's hand before chewing on his apple. He glanced at Diana. "Maddie spoils my horse, always promising him treats if he brings me home safely. I try to explain to her that the horse doesn't comprehend a word she says, but she does not believe me. 'Tis easier to humor her." He patted Midnight's muzzle one more time before handing him over to Fergus. "My wife thinks Midnight has magical powers."

He held his arm out for her and she grasped his elbow, holding Micheil's arm on the other side. "Shall we, cousin?"

They strode across the courtyard and up the steps to the great hall. Alex stepped inside the first, his sword drawn. As soon as ten warriors had filtered into the room, he allowed in Diana and Micheil. Then they turned to face Baron Gow, who was standing on the dais with his arms crossed, silently watching them, two guards on each side of him.

Micheil whispered, "Do you see any of your guards?"

She shook her head. "Nay. What has he done to them?"

"Unhand my betrothed, Ramsay," Gow bellowed.

Micheil and Alex moved in front of the dais, surrounding by Grant warriors. Micheil addressed him. "She is my wife, Gow. I'm sure you have received the king's missive by now declaring Diana as my wife, relieving you of your obligation."

Diana was anxious to hear if he would deny receiving the missive.

"I have received a missive with a broken seal and burned it since it was false. The Drummond is dead, and he blessed this union. No one can put our marriage asunder. The king was set to arrive for the ceremony, but we will marry first."

"Papa?" Diana's legs buckled at the words she most feared.

CHAPTER TWENTY-TWO

Micheil caught her and whispered in her ear. "Remember what the stable lad said to you. 'Tis a trick. I need you to be strong, and so does your sire." Then, loud enough for all to hear, he shouted, "You cannot marry her. Our union took place in Edinburgh Castle, presided over by the king's very own priest. We are husband and wife, and the marriage has been consummated."

The baron stared down his nose at Diana with beady eyes, fussing with his fine clothing, attempting to use his tall countenance to intimidate. "I will accept these tarnished goods in return for a fee from you for taking advantage of my betrothed. The lass was a slut, but she will soon learn to repent her ways."

Two swords were pressed to his throat moments later—Micheil's and Alex's. "You will speak of *my wife* with respect," Micheil hissed, pressing the point of his sword against the man's skin until a thin line of blood slid down his neck. The hall fell silent as Gow's men and all of Grant's men immediately unsheathed their swords, but no one moved, awaiting direction from their respective leaders.

The baron wheezed. "Remove your swords, I will control my tongue."

Alex nodded to Micheil, and they dropped their swords to their sides, the others following their lead.

Diana could not stand the suspense any longer. "Where is my sire? I cannot tolerate waiting any longer. Please. I must see him."

"I told you, he is dead. He died in his sleep last night. His last request was for you to marry me, and I would expect you to honor his dying words."

"Nay, he would not. And I do not believe you. He would wait for my return. He promised me." Tears coursed down her cheeks as she spoke, her hands wringing her skirts. "Please."

"Anyone here will tell you he is dead. Ask and you shall see. Search the entire keep. Summon the kitchen maids, the serving wenches. They will all tell you he is dead." He waved his arms, and his guards made their way to the kitchens, ushering the help out. "Ask them and find out for yourself."

Diana's gaze searched for a familiar face among the help, but she did not recognize anyone. They all nodded their heads in agreement with the baron, their eyes cast downward in fear. A door burst open, and one of her mother's maids tore across the room toward Diana.

"Seize her!" Gow shouted. His men moved, but Micheil moved faster, protecting the woman as she made her way to Diana. Alex raised his hand and pointed, sending his guards to offer further protection.

His men held each of Gow's men at swordpoint until the woman finally made it over to Diana and fell at her feet, sobbing as she crushed her skirts. "He lives yet. The guards took him to Duncan's cottage, my lady."

Suddenly, one of Gow's men swung at one of Alex's guards, and chaos erupted in the great hall. The ring of swords from scabbards ripped through the hall as the two groups finally clashed.

Diana held fast to the back of Micheil's tunic, and as soon as she saw her chance, she ran for the kitchens. Her men must have taken her sire out the tunnel used for escape from attack, the entrance hidden in the buttery. She unsheathed her dagger, prepared to fight her way to her father. Two of the baron's men reached for her, and she swung around with her dagger in hand. "Do not touch me. I go to my sire." One attempted to grab her and she stabbed his arm. Micheil rushed to protect her and struck a death blow to the other man, causing him to crumple to the ground.

"Go," Micheil said. "I will protect you. Search for your sire." He ordered two of the Grant guards to follow her while he guarded the entrance to the kitchens.

Diana whirled and grabbed her skirts, returning her dagger to her pocket while she found her way to the buttery as fast as she could. Screams rang in her ears, and she prayed for her husband and the Grants. Fear shook her like a leaf, but she had to have faith that good would prevail over evil.

Diana instructed the guards to move the chest hiding the door, and managed to tug it open on her own. She flew down the steps and through the tunnel that her father had taken her through many times to prepare her for just this circumstance. By the time she climbed the steps at the end, she threw her shoulder against the rickety old door, stumbling through the opening when it finally gave way.

Once outside, she stood panting, her hands on her hips, staring up at the sky and the beautiful stars, willing them to help her recall which way to go. The guards finally came through the door behind her, but they needn't worry. They were completely alone.

Instinct sent her east toward Duncan's cottage. A short distance later, she found it, noticing many of her guards scattered in the periphery, some sleeping on the ground, some in place checking the area. She squealed when she recognized her father's favorite guards protecting the door, tearing up the walkway to hug each of them.

"Papa?"

One guard smiled. "He lives. Go inside, my lady."

Her heart pounded in anticipation as the guard held the door for her.

Once inside, she closed the door and leaned her back against it, taking everything in before she moved. Her father was asleep in the bed, the rise of his chest barely visible. A table and four chairs sat in the corner, and two cushioned chairs sat in front of the hearth on the far wall. Robbie was busy banking the fire. He jumped up and placed his hand on his sword, only to take it away when he realized who it was.

"Diana, you're finally here. I heard some commotion and hoped it was you and Micheil, but I did not dare leave your sire's side. Laird's orders."

She ran to the bed. "Robbie, how is he?"

Robbie brought a chair over for her, then returned to the other side of the bed. "He's not gone yet. I'm sorry to tell you that I do not think he has much longer."

Diana grabbed her father's hand. "Papa, Papa. It's me. Wake up, please. I must talk to you. I have so much to tell you." She stared at him, finally realizing there was no response. His eyes were closed, his color dusky and pale. "Papa?" She could see he was still breathing, but his breaths were shallow, barely visible from the rise and fall of his chest.

Looking up at her cousin, she shook her head as her tears pricked her eyes. "How long, Robbie? How long since he has spoken?"

"A couple of days. He has barely moved, and he has not opened his eyes in my presence. But I try to keep the room warm for him. The last thing he told me was he was cold. He also gave me a message for you."

Holding her father's hand in hers, she stared at her cousin as she settled into the chair. "What was his message? That I'm a horrible daughter for not doing as he asked, that I should have married Baron Gow?"

"Nay, Alex and I told him about our trip. Alex explained about the baron's cruelty and how he allowed Micheil to take you to Edinburgh."

Diana prodded Robbie. "Go on, the message?"

"He said to tell you he was sorry for choosing the wrong man for you. Had he known about the truth about the baron, he never would have allowed you to go."

"Oh, Papa." She leaned over and kissed his brow. "I know you only wanted what was best for me."

"His goal was to stay alive until you returned. He was hoping you would find your knight." He smiled. "He told us of the stories you and your mother loved."

She leaned her cheek against her sire's. "Papa, I have. I have found my knight and I married him. Why couldn't you have waited a bit longer? He's here. Micheil Ramsay is my husband. His brother is married to Brenna Grant. He is a kind, strong, braw man, and I love him so." She lifted her head back to Robbie. "Did he say aught else? Did he speak to Baron Gow?"

Robbie nodded. "He did. He told the baron he wanted him gone. Once Alex left with his warriors, he had a large army attack your keep, so we fled here. I knew when the rest of our guards arrived, we would take the castle back. My priority was keeping your sire alive for you. I heard that since we left, the baron has tried to declare him dead, but I stay sentinel by his bedside in case he discovers this place. But you are here now. Why do I not leave you alone for a while? Duncan has moved to another cottage, so I will update him, then I will return to the keep to see if I am needed. If you need anything, just send one of the guards for me."

Robbie kissed her cheek and stepped out of the chamber.

She turned back to the bed and placed her hand on her sire's cheek. "Papa, please come back to me. Please, just for a few moments. Micheil will be here soon. He is so strong. He will protect me, just like Mama told me my knight would. Come back to me, please. I will be lost without you."

Diana climbed on top of the covers and lay down next to her father, holding his hand in hers and resting her other hand on the top of his head. "Papa, you would love Micheil so much. Please tell Mama how right she was about my knight. I fell in love with him in Edinburgh, and we married there, just as she predicted. He is everything she said he would be, except he is Scottish, not English. Our clan will love him, I know they will." Her tears continued to flow until she could barely speak.

"Papa, don't leave me yet. I am sorry I left."

She sobbed her heart out as she held her father, telling him how much she loved him, eventually tiring. It did not matter, she would sleep right here with her father. "I won't leave you again, Papa. I promise."

She could swear he squeezed her hand.

⚮

Micheil stood in front of the entrance to the kitchens, guarding his wife's search for her sire. He prayed she would find him before it was too late. The door pushed against him, and he jumped, only to see Robbie Grant come through the door.

"She's with him. I thought you could use my help. Go to her soon, follow the tunnel in the buttery and head east."

His gaze took in the chaos all around him, and he watched as Alex and Robbie Grant fought Gow's men in a fury, cutting them down with a vengeance. Chairs flew along with blood, but the Grants' energy never waned. They fought on, eventually causing some of Gow's men to run out of the hall, grasping their wounds in fear for their lives.

Micheil was only occasionally called upon to use his sword. Few dared to try to gain access to the kitchens. He had checked inside only to find a few timid servants hiding, just waiting for Diana to be reinstated. He swung his sword in front of him a couple of times, catching a Gow fighter by surprise so that a Grant aggressor could finish the job. Mostly, he just watched the Grant men in all their glory, every bit as powerful as they were reputed to be. Alex Grant fought like a man possessed. Micheil had heard about his fight at Largs against the Norse atop his mighty steed, Midnight, who had actually been clad in chainmail. The stories were clearly not exaggerated. Naught stood a chance against the mighty warrior, whose focus and strength were unparalleled.

Suddenly, two of Gow's guards leapt from beside the stairwell, Gow close behind. The two guards swung at him at the same time. He flung his dagger into the heart of one, ending his attack instantly. The other came at him while the baron stood behind him, armed with a small sword.

Micheil swung his sword in an arc, coming down hard on his opponent's, but the guard was quick and he parlayed Micheil's thrusts, forcing him toward the stairs to maintain his balance. The battle carried on for a few moments, blade striking blade, swords shrieking in ear-splitting fury as the fight continued.

"He's my best swordsman, Ramsay. You will not beat him," Gow bellowed.

Micheil ignored the distraction and continued his onslaught against his enemy. No one would get past him. He would protect Diana to his death if needed. He neared the staircase, so he stepped up two steps to give himself better leverage. Sweat dripped down his brow, threatening to blur his vision. He caught his opponent's gaze and could see he was weakening. His death blow was not far away; Micheil only had to stay strong.

Apparently, the baron sensed the weakness as well. Out of the corner of his eye, Micheil saw him raise his sword, ready to use it against him, too— two against one. Micheil brought his sword directly across his body for a full swing, hoping to take them out together. Just then, another man came near the staircase and stabbed his opponent from behind before shoving him out of the way.

At the same exact moment, Micheil's sword was at the bottom of its arc, and meeting only air, it continued on with a powerful thrust, catching the baron vigorously across his side and into his ribcage. Gow dropped his sword and stared at Micheil, his hands clutching his ribs after Micheil pulled the weapon out.

"She was supposed to be mine." He stared at Micheil in shock, then glanced at the blood dripping through his fingers, his eyes beginning to glaze over. His voice came out in a whisper. "You bastard." He crumpled, landing in a heap at the base of the stairs.

Robbie Grant stood at the bottom of the steps with a grin on his face as the rest of the great hall quieted. Still panting from exertion, Micheil swept the room with his gaze, a smile creeping across his features as he realized Gow's men were gone. The baron had been one of the last men standing, apparently.

Micheil made his way down the staircase and over the bodies, pausing to clean his blade on the clothes of the dead baron before he returned it to his scabbard. Alex stood opposite him and they made their way toward each other, finally meeting in the center of the hall and grasping each other in a hug, a celebration of the combined strength of the Grant and Ramsay clans. Robbie stood behind them, raising his sword and releasing a resounding Grant whoop for all to hear. The Grant warriors, grouped all around them, took a moment to catch their breath and congratulate each other.

Micheil grasped Alex's hand first, then Robbie's. "My thanks. I will be forever indebted to you for ridding my wife's clan of these heathens."

"Your clan now, Ramsay," Alex reminded him.

As they conversed, servants sneaked out onto the balcony, out of the kitchens, and in the front doors, expressions of hope clearly evident on their faces.

As the members of the Drummond Clan hesitantly emerged, they erupted into cheers when they realized the baron was dead. Alex held up his arms to quiet them after a few moments. He pointed to Micheil. "I introduce to you Diana of Drummond's husband, Micheil Ramsay. Honor him as you do her, and let us see if we can clean this place up and make it worthy of Diana's presence, especially during this difficult time for her."

His men and the servants joined together to remove the bodies and set the furniture back to rights. Alex said, "Go to your wife, Ramsay. You must meet her sire, if he still lives. Robbie and I will direct the clan, though they are quite happy to be free of that monster, even after only a couple of days of his tyranny, and will handle everything on their own."

Micheil nodded and headed back to the kitchens. A servant led him to the tunnel door, and he rushed through the cool air, hoping to find Diana safe and warm with her sire.

Once outside, he headed east and found many of her guards not far from the cottage. He informed them of the demise of the baron and sent a group back to help with the restoration of the keep.

The men directed him to the cottage. Making his way to the front door, he said a silent prayer that Diana's sire still lived. He stepped into the dark cottage, and as soon as his eyes adjusted to the light, he found his wife asleep on the bed next to her sire.

An old weathered hand beckoned him forward.

CHAPTER TWENTY-THREE

Micheil strode over to the figure in the bed and said, "Laird Drummond? You are awake?"

"Aye, my son. I have awaited my daughter's return, but it took some time for me to gain the strength to speak to her." He patted her hand. "Seems she is tired, so I will let her rest. I would like to speak to you first."

Micheil was dumbfounded and wanted to awaken his wife. But first he would allow her sire to speak his mind, so afraid he would reject him because of his status as a third son. "Aye?"

Keen eyes assessed him. "I see you wear some blood. Does that mean you have finally rid my keep of the baron and his men?"

Micheil nodded. "Aye, but only with the help of the Grants and their warriors. 'Tis done. Gow is dead."

He shook his head slowly. "I advised him to leave before Alex Grant returned. All of the Scots know of his prowess in battle. Nevertheless, my thanks."

Micheil peeked at his wife again, settling his hand on her hip as she slept.

"You love my lassie, do you not?"

Micheil nodded. "Aye, more than I ever thought possible."

David of Drummond looked directly at him, his eyes misting as he reached out to grasp Micheil's hand. His face was drawn and pale, but Micheil could tell he had need to share before he would let go, so he allowed him to speak without interruption.

The old chieftain spoke, "Och, it does my heart good to finally meet you. Seems a man willing to fight for her would love her, too. She's a good gel. You'll take care of her for me?"

Micheil nodded, for some reason incapable of speaking at the moment.

"Promise me to care for not just her body, but her heart as well. She is a special lass."

"I will." His voice broke. He stepped away to grab a Drummond plaid from a nearby chair and covered his wife with it before kissing her cheek.

David Drummond patted his hand and said, "Lad, 'tis a pleasure to finally meet my daughter's knight. You have my blessing." He sighed and closed his eyes, folding his hands across his chest. "I am going to rest. I do wish to summon the strength to speak to my daughter one last time."

He closed his eyes, so Micheil moved into the chair by the hearth.

It was the middle of the night when something woke her. She noticed someone had come in and covered her with a plaid. Everything came back to her slowly when she realized where she was.

"Lass, could you lean a bit away from me? I am not as strong as I used to be."

Her head popped up as her gaze flew to her father. The familiar spark in his gaze told her he was entirely himself, though he clearly had not regained much strength. "Papa? By the saints above, thank you. Papa, are you truly speaking to me?"

"Aye, lass." He sighed and took as deep of a breath as he could, squeezing her hand before he continued. "I do not have much time left, but your mother made me come back, just for you," he whispered.

She moved off the bed and into the chair next to it, pulling it as close as she could. "What do you mean? You have seen Mama?"

"Aye, she awaits me and I have missed her. Your mama is my heart and soul, and I was so happy to finally see her again. I was prepared to cross over, but she wanted me to return to you one last time. She wishes she had been here to raise you, but she is so proud of you, and pleased with the person you have become. She's proud of both of us." He smiled before continuing. "'Tis my time, daughter, and I think you know it, but I must finish my mission." He paused, gathering the strength to continue speaking.

"Papa, do not overdo it. Please listen to me. I've married my knight. His name is Micheil and I love him so. I want you to meet him, please? Give us your blessing."

"Och, lass, 'tis why I came back. Your mama wouldn't welcome me ...until I met your knight. She says he is the right one, and I have one more duty I must do."

"I'll get him. Wait." She stood up, begging him. "Promise me you will wait."

Her father raised his hand and pointed behind her. "He is already here. I met him. He is a fine man, and I welcome him as a son. He covered you with the plaid, just as I would have done if I had the strength."

Micheil stood behind her, and he grasped her hand in his. "I've been sitting in the chair next to the fire, love. I did not wish to disturb you."

Diana's face flooded with tears; how wonderful it was to finally see the two men who lived so strong in her heart meet. She grabbed her husband's hand and tugged him close to the bed. "Papa, here he is. My husband, Micheil Ramsay." She pushed Micheil ahead of her so her sire could see him. Even though they had already met, *she* had not introduced them. Micheil clearly knew her mind, for he leaned down to the gentleman and said, "I am honored to meet you, Chief Drummond, and I want you to know how much I love your daughter. I pledge to protect her with my life."

David Drummond's trembling hand came up to grab Micheil's. "Och, son, I welcome you to the Drummond clan. My wife and I are verra happy to have you here." He glanced at Diana and smiled. "My lass has been everything to me since her mama's passing. She has a good mind and will do a fine job leading the clan. Do you pledge to assist her and plan to live here with us?"

"Aye, I do. She is a strong, vibrant lass who has stolen my heart. We will live here and plan to raise our bairns here. My family is not far, and we may travel some."

"Good, good." He patted Micheil's hand. "She'll challenge you a time or too, but she has a big heart. I'm afraid..."

"Papa? What is it?"

"Och, lass, I'm weary. I'm not much longer for this world, my time is near." His breathing became irregular, and he struggled to cough.

"Papa, not yet. Please." She squeezed his hand as his eyes fluttered shut. Micheil stepped back to allow her to be closer to her father.

"Your mama and I love you, Diana....so proud of you."

"Papa, wait."

The door opened and Alex Grant strode over to the bed. He reached for the Drummond's hand and said, "Uncle, do you bless this union?"

Her sire's eyes opened, and he patted his daughter's hand. "Aye. I bless the marriage of my daughter to Micheil Ramsay. Let all know 'tis my wish." His eyes closed.

Alex set the man's hand down on the covers, kissed Diana's forehead, and left the chamber.

Diana grabbed his hand again. "Papa? Nay, please not yet?" She leaned closer, unable to hear his breathing anymore, not wanting to accept the truth.

"Papa, nay. I love you." She kissed his forehead and sobbed as her sire took his last breath.

Micheil gathered her in his arms and held her while she wept.

About an hour later, Micheil scooped his wife up in his arms and carried her out of the cottage and back to the keep, nodding to Robbie Grant when they departed.

"The baron, Micheil?"

"The baron is dead. 'Tis all you need to know. Close your eyes as we go through. The battle took place in your hall. You do not need to see this."

She buried her face in his shoulder.

"Where's your chamber, lass?" Micheil whispered, once they had traveled through the tunnel and up the stairs to the second level of the keep.

Diana pointed down the passageway, so Micheil made his way down the corridor until she stopped him and directed him to the correct chamber. He set her on the bed and returned to bolt the door.

Not quite sure what she wanted him to do, he nestled in to her side and hugged her close. "Tell me what to do for you. Anything, I'll do anything you want."

Diana sniffled and laid her head on his shoulder. "I want you."

Her crying had subsided. Micheil did not think she could possibly have another tear inside her. Her answer was unexpected, but he truly would do anything to help her through this difficult time.

"It would be my pleasure to hold you in my arms all night. You must be tired after all the trials you have endured. Close your eyes, sweeting. You have been a good daughter to your sire. 'Tis time to take your rest." He buried his face in her hair, inhaling her scent, hoping she could find some peace this night.

"Nay. I *want* you." Her hand reached up under his plaid and brushed across his thigh.

Micheil did not quite know what to say, but he did not want to misinterpret her request at such a time.

"Love me, Micheil. I need you this night. I want naught between us, no clothes, naught."

Micheil lifted his gaze and stared into the eyes of his beautiful wife. "Are you sure? I'm happy just to hold you. This has been a verra difficult day for you."

"Nay, I want to be in your arms. I want you inside me as we were meant to be, skin to skin, heart to heart. Love me the way I love you." She looked at him and brushed his long hair back from his face. "Please, Micheil. I need you. But let it be different this time. I want you to love me slowly, so we can feel the power of it. 'Tis what I need now."

Micheil kissed her lips, a sweet tender kiss meant to tell her how much she meant to him. She parted her lips and teased him with her tongue. Oh, how he had missed the taste of his love. He cupped her face and gave her a slow tangle, a delicious assault on her mouth until their need for each other mounted.

He ended the kiss and climbed out of the bed, kissing her fingertips as she reached for him.

"Nay, do not leave me, husband."

"I only seek to do as you ask. I will return once I remove these cumbersome threads from my body, then I will work on yours." He kissed the palm of her hand before he stepped away and unhooked the brooch from his blue and green plaid. Once it fell to the floor, he removed everything else. His long dark hair tumbled almost to his shoulders—it was in need of a trimming, but his wife did not seem to mind. His beard was rough and unkempt since he had not had the time to tend it. He would have to be careful to keep his roughness from chafing his wife's tender skin.

Moving back to the bed, he pulled back the furs and the covers on his side, finally reaching for his wife, who still rested atop the coverings and was watching his every move with a glint in her eye. She sat up for him, and he undid the bindings on the back of her gown, tugging the laces before freeing her of her overgown, her undergown, and finally her chemise and her stockings. She held her arms out to him, and he lifted her lithe body off the covers so he could pull them back and settle her under the protection they offered from the cool night.

"Come back to me, Micheil." She gazed at him through her long lashes and licked her lips. "Please do not make me wait any longer."

Micheil climbed in next to her and nuzzled her neck. "I have instructions for you, my lady."

She arched a quizzical brow at him and he smiled. "You have been through too much, so I ask that you rest while I spend my time getting to know your body even more than I already have."

A lazy grin crossed her features as she reached a hand up to run it through his long, thick locks. "I am all yours, Micheil Ramsay. My sire has blessed our union. I am yours forever, so you may do with me as you wish."

He removed her hand from his hair, kissed her palm, and trailed kisses up her arm, forcing a shiver from her as he reached the sensitive skin on the underside. His lips then traced a path down her ribcage and up to her breast, kissing around the outside of the full mound before reaching the center and taking her sensitive bud in his mouth. His tongue took a lazy path down the curve of one breast and back up to the peak of her other, causing his wife to moan softly, her fingers finding his hair again.

He deftly brought her other nipple to a taut peak, swirling his tongue around it before he suckled her hard and was rewarded with the passionate response he'd hoped to receive. His wife grabbed his hips, trying to force him closer, but he would not give in to her just yet. His tongue traveled down her belly and into the vee of curls at the juncture of her thighs. When he came close to her bud, he moved away, meandering down the inside of her leg to her knee.

Rolling her onto her side, he kissed the inside of each knee until she moaned. The clenching of the muscles in her legs each time he touched her with his tongue told him his ministrations were heating her passion. Rolling her onto her belly, he tasted the back of each knee before traveling up the backs of her thighs and licking a path across the soft roundness of her bottom until she squealed and squirmed, kicking her legs against the bed in torment, causing him to sit up and chuckle. Massaging her back with his hands, he brought them down over her soft mounds, caressing her with a feather light touch that caused her to buck off the bed toward him.

How he loved the way she responded to his touch. "You like, my sweet?" He grinned at her in the dark, gratified to see her react this way to him. She would be calling out his name multiple times before he was done. He had so much to teach her, but there was an abundance of time. Tonight, he would tend her every need. This night was for her.

She rolled onto her back and reached for his hand. "Micheil, you are torturing me. Please finish this, now."

"My pleasure." He went straight for her core and tongued her clit, alternating between licking the nub and plunging his tongue inside of her. When her moans reached a fevered pitch, he suckled her nub and plunged his finger inside her, forcing her to go over the edge, her muscles spasming around his finger.

As soon as Diana was able, she gave him a lazy smile and tugged him to her so she could gaze into his eyes. She reached for his hardness, and after teasing the tip of him with her tongue, said only one word, telling him exactly what she wanted.

"More."

CHAPTER TWENTY-FOUR

Diana swept her tongue down his hard length, teasing the tip until he moaned, then took him in her mouth. He felt as if he had died and gone to heaven, but he could not handle the torment any longer. "Lass, enough. I would tend to *you* tonight."

"But I want you, husband."

Micheil helped her position herself, then settled on top of her. "As you wish, my lady. Naught would give me more pleasure than to join with you this verra moment." He teased her entrance, wanting to make sure she was ready for him and not still vibrating from her first release. Her splayed legs told him everything he needed to know. He plunged inside her with one thrust, forcing himself to stop to keep from losing all control.

"Do you know what I love most about you, Diana Ramsay of Drummond?" He kissed each cheek.

She sighed. "Nay, tell me, love."

He pulled back slowly before gliding inside again, seating himself completely in her. He leaned into her ear and whispered, "Your strength and your resilience. I was so proud of how you dealt with all the trauma of the past few days." He held his weight on his elbows while he waited to move.

Teasing her again, he drew his cock out and then in again, causing her to gasp when he reached her core. "You like, my love?"

A deep lusty moan was his answer. "Aye." Her voice was barely audible above the sound of their combined panting, each of them now gasping for breath.

He continued his assault on her senses. "I love your passion."

Out again with purpose, then a deep push inside her. "The way you love with your whole heart astounds me." She moaned and grabbed him, spreading her legs wide to take him in.

After he stroked into her again this time, she whimpered, "Micheil."

One more slow retreat and fast propulsion. She had bewitched him, quite simply. He wanted no other. He would take her places she had never been before, and he would enjoy every single moment of bliss with her.

"Micheil, please. I cannot take anymore. Finish this." She contracted her muscles on him, torturing him.

Almost at the point of no return, sweat dripped from his brow as he held himself in place, buried deep inside her to the hilt, wanting to pleasure her and for them to finish together.

He reached down to massage her nub. "I love you, Diana."

And he thrust into her hard, once, twice, three times as he rubbed her. He pulsed inside her, riding her hard, hoping to push her over the edge soon because he could not hold on much longer.

She screamed his name as her release came again, her muscles contracting around him, milking him to completion at last, and he shouted her name in a fierce growl, losing everything into her as he fell into a deep oblivion.

Blissfully surrendering to pleasure, he rolled to his side and tucked her to him, and they slept well into the night.

❧

When Diana awoke at dawn, she reached for Micheil, but he wasn't there. As soon as she sat up, she smiled. A steaming hot tub sat next to the bed along with a platter of fruit and cheese set on the chest nearby. She hopped out of bed and climbed into the deliciously hot water, sighing as she settled into it.

The door opened, and her husband strolled in with her maid, Effie, right behind him.

Effie flew to her side, "Och, my lady, 'tis so good to have you back. Allow me to wash your back and your hair."

Micheil winked at her. "Your maid likes to spoil you, aye?"

"Aye." She smiled. "Effie, I have missed you so. How do you fare? And the others? My apologies for Baron Gow's intrusion these past days."

"Och, do not worry. He is gone now. 'Tis all in the past." Effie circled the tub, finding the lavender oil Diana so loved and placing a few drops in her bath. She arranged towels at her side and brought a linen square over to her.

As soon as Effie handed the square to her, Diana squawked, grabbing her hand. "Effie, what is this? Your skin is worn to the bone. What have you been doing? Stop it, whatever it is."

Effie pulled her hand back and hid it in the folds of her skirt, blushing at the chastisement from her new laird.

Micheil said, "Diana, the servants worked all night to put your great hall back to rights."

Diana scowled. "All night? Effie, you know I would not work you so."

Effie looked from husband to wife, unsure of how to answer her. She finally whispered, "There was much to do, my lady. But we are so happy to have you here. We love your new husband. We are overjoyed that a Drummond will lead again. A Drummond and her husband.

Diana gave Micheil a puzzled look.

Micheil banked the fire in the hearth. "Diana, after you left the hall in search of your sire, there was quite a battle belowstairs. The Grant warriors fought hard to rid your hall of the scum that had attempted to strong arm his way to leadership. Your clan worked feverishly throughout the night to remove the dead bodies and scrub the blood from the stone and place new rushes. But they have done a wonderful job."

Diana gave Effie an incredulous look. "What? What happened?" She turned back to her husband. "Tell me all. I am ready today to hear all that transpired."

Effie gave her a surprised look. "Why, the baron is dead, my lady. Your husband ran him through with his sword"

Diana eyes widened as she stared at Micheil. "And the Grants? They are all well?" She waited for his answer.

"There were a few injuries, but none of the Grants have died. The survivors from Gow's group have taken to the hills."

"And Alex and Robbie are still here?" she asked.

"Aye, they await you in the great hall with smiles on their faces. I do believe your cousins enjoy battling for a worthy cause, and the Drummond clan is definitely that."

She stood from the tub while Effie wrapped her in a linen towel. "Effie, please have the staff prepare for a midday feast. Whatever we have we shall share with the Grants before they leave, and we must celebrate my sire's life. Find some wine for the dais and ale for the warriors. We must celebrate, for the battle, for my sire, and for my wonderful husband." Tears slid down her cheeks as she spoke.

Micheil nodded. "Go, Effie, do as your laird has ordered, and I will help her dress. My thanks for taking such good care of your mistress and our castle."

Effie beamed and stepped out of the chamber.

Micheil helped Diana into her best gown, a dark green overgown embossed with gold thread and a yellow undergown, then helped her dry her tresses by the fire. He took a quick bath before escorting her down to their hall.

As they came around the corner, a bustle of activity took place belowstairs, but everyone stopped what they were doing when they set eyes on her. A booming cheer moved across the room as she descended the steps on her husband's arm to the delight of her servants, her guards and their wives, her steward, along with the many Grant warriors. The faces beaming up at her were full of hope, happiness, and sympathy. She strode to the dais, took her rightful place there, and held her arms up to quiet the crowd.

"My thanks for working hard, fighting hard, and for continuing to support the Drummond clan. I would like to celebrate my new husband, Micheil Ramsay, and the Grant warriors for helping us in our time of need." Whistles and shouts abounded, but she quieted the group with her next statement. "Please raise your glasses to my sire, your chieftain,

David of Drummond. He will be missed, most of all by me."

She raised her glass, and together they celebrated the new laird and the old, the past and the future.

CHAPTER TWENTY-FIVE

Two months later

Diana and Micheil rode their horses through the deep forest, listening to the crackle of the branches and the leaves on the ground as they moved, watching as the mist gathered across the ground and spun a magical weave about the horses' hooves. There were three Drummond guards in front of them and several behind them.

"Do you believe in faeries, Micheil?" Diana glanced over her shoulder at her husband. They were on their way to the Ramsay Castle, both anxious to see wee Sorcha again and to see how Molly and Maggie fared. Once Diana had settled everything with her steward, they had decided it was time for her to meet Micheil's mother and the rest of his family.

"Nay, I cannot say that I do, sweeting. You do?" He quirked a brow at her.

"Aye, sometimes. When I was a wee lass, I believed the faeries were my friends. Probably because I did not have many friends my age. I often spoke to them in the forests when I rode, and I believed that each star in the sky was a faerie waving at me." She stared at the stars just visible in the night, and the memory made her smile. "Most often after Mama passed."

"You missed your mama." He pulled his horse abreast of hers, reaching for her hand. "And I sense you are missing your sire today."

She squeezed his hand before releasing it. "Aye, I miss my da, but I am excited to meet my new family. Tell me about them again. Please?"

Micheil grinned. "With pleasure, lass. My mother is Arlene, and I have two brothers and a sister. The eldest is Quade. He has two bairns by his first wife, Torrian and Lily, and now he and Brenna have a daughter, Bethia."

"Aye, I am excited to see my cousin, Brenna, though she did travel to check on my father not too long ago. But this will be joyous, not a sad occasion. She is wonderful."

"Aye, she is, and marriage to her has been a wonder for my brother. Then there are Logan and Gwyneth, of course, but you are familiar with them. Last is my sister Avelina."

"Is Avelina the youngest?"

"Aye, and spoiled by my brothers."

She chuckled. "But not by you?"

"Aye, a wee bit, mayhap." He gave her a sheepish grin.

"How do you think Molly and Maggie have fared at your keep? Do you think they are happy? My heart ached for them. It is hard to imagine how their family could ever have turned away two such sweet lassies." She shook her head in distaste.

"My mama always wished for more granddaughters, so I am sure they have been welcomed. Molly is old enough to be a friend to Avelina, though they are at least a few summers apart. Aye, I think we will find them to be quite happy there."

"Does Avelina look like you?"

"I suppose she looks more like me than Logan or Quade do. She is tall and thin, like my mother. And Avelina will be good for Molly and Maggie. She will help fix Molly's hair, so she will feel beautiful."

"Truly? You think so?" Diana's face lit up at the thought. Molly was in the gangly stage, and her hair was a mass of dark curls, unruly but beautiful.

"Aye. Avelina was gangly like Molly until she grew into her feet."

"Och, husband, I am so excited to meet your relatives. Though I loved having my parents' attention, I have always wanted to be part of a large family."

"You will not have to wait much longer." He pointed off into the distance. "You can see the peak of the tower off to the left. Good timing since it is dusk."

"Race you." Diana spurred her horse and flew down the path toward the Ramsay castle, laughing.

As they drew close, a horn sounded, signaling that their group had come into view of the guards. Micheil took the lead, and when they were close enough, he yelled to the Ramsay guards. "Lads, open up. Tell my brother to get down here and greet his family."

They made their way through the portcullis into the inner bailey. It was a clear night, and the stars cast a magical hue on the keep. Illuminated by torches against the stone walls, the building looked beautiful to her. It was quite a bit larger than the Drummond castle, but not as large as the Grant keep.

The bailey turned into a bustling flurry of activity as Micheil dismounted and helped Diana off her horse. Their twenty warriors surrounded them, guarding their chieftain and her husband. She glanced toward the steps of the keep just in time to see the boisterous group headed their way.

She noticed Brenna right away and greeted her first. After hugging her cousin, she was introduced to Quade, Torrian, Lily, and wee Bethia, presently in Brenna's arms. Logan and Gwyneth followed with Molly and Maggie. Avelina stood in the back holding Sorcha, a shy look on her face.

Micheil tugged her forward. "And this is my wee sister, Avelina."

Avelina scowled. "Micheil, I am not so wee any longer."

Micheil kissed her brow and said, "Forgive me. You are correct. With all the new additions to the family, you are hardly wee any more, are you, lass?"

Avelina blushed and curtsied to Diana. "Pleased to make your acquaintance, my lady. Welcome to the Ramsay keep."

Avelina did indeed look like her brother, but she was not a gangly girl and longer. Sable brown curly hair, emerald eyes, and full lips all made her quite a beauty. Tall and willowy as Micheil had said, she did resemble him more than Quade or Logan. Diana crushed her in a warm embrace, careful not to squash Sorcha, who giggled at all the activity around her, her thumb popping out of her mouth.

Micheil grasped her hand and said, "Come, I'll take you to greet my mother."

They made their way across the cobblestone courtyard toward the entrance to the keep, Micheil greeting his clansmen along the way. A tall woman stood at the top of the steps, her keen gaze following Diana as she made her way up the steps.

"Lady Ramsay." Diana curtsied as Micheil grasped the woman's hand. Tall, thin, and elegant, Lady Ramsay was as regal as any queen, but the kindness in her eyes was unmistakable. Tears pressed against her eyes as she thought about having a mother figure in her life once more.

Micheil kissed his mother's cheek and said, "Mother, I'd like you to meet my wife, Diana of Drummond."

Lady Ramsay smiled and grasped her hands. "Welcome, my dear. I am so pleased you and Micheil have found each other. My family is now complete." She gave her a brisk hug and stepped back, but she grasped Diana's hand in hers. "Please, come inside. You must be weary from your travels. I'll find some refreshment for you."

Diana smiled, feeling overwhelmed but welcome. She had lost her beloved parents, but at least she had a new family to call her own. While his mother headed toward the kitchens, Micheil led her to a table near the hearth, one where they could sit across from each other, rather than sitting side by side at the dais. Diana noticed how warm and inviting the great hall was, fresh rushes on the floor, clean tables with dried flowers centered atop the table runners. The hearth was huge and blazing, the blue and green Ramsay crest proudly displayed in a tapestry above it.

In the corner sat a heap of child's playthings. Brenna set Bethia down, and she waddled over to find her doll, Lily and Maggie right behind her. The rest of the family joined them at the table. Molly took a seat next to Gwyneth and held Sorcha in her lap. Brenna and Quade sat together, Torrian on his other side, looking so much like his father.

Diana listened to all the chatter, happy to finally meet her new family. She leaned her head on her husband's shoulder and fell fast asleep.

Diana awoke the next morning alone in a strange bed. She sat up and stared at her surroundings, unable to recall anything about the night before beyond their arrival. After climbing out of bed, she pulled the fur from the window and stared out, shocked to see how high the sun was. Micheil was nowhere to be seen, and she had slept way beyond the time when the others must have broken their fast. She was standing in the middle of the chamber trying to decide what to do next when a knock sounded at the door. She opened it and peeked out.

A maid stood outside, talking with someone out in the corridor. As soon as she saw her, she said, "My lady, Lady Ramsay has sent a bath for you and some food."

Diana stood back to let the maid inside.

"Good morn to you," she said as she came into the chamber. "My name is Finella. I brought bread and cheese for you and a bit of ale." She set the platter down on the chest next to the bed. "The lads will be right along with the tub and the pails of water."

Diana said, "Have you seen my husband, Finella?"

Lady Ramsay lightly knocked before sticking her head through the doorway. "Good morn, my dear. I hope you slept well. Micheil went off hunting with Logan, Gwyneth, and Quade, hoping for a deer or a wild turkey for dinner tonight."

"Aye, 'tis acceptable since I slept half the day away." She hung her head, unable to quite believe the lateness of the hour.

Lady Ramsay moved behind her and gathered Diana's hair, running her fingers through the tendrils to straighten them. "Traveling is very tiresome, my dear. You fell asleep at the table last night. I gave Micheil a talking to about overtiring his new wife."

Diana blushed. "We hoped to arrive while the weather was still good."

"No bother. You are here and 'tis what is important. Relax in a nice bath and come downstairs afterward. Avelina is busy fixing everyone's hair while we await our next guest."

"You have more guests arriving?"

"Aye, Jennie Grant shall be here soon. She oft stays a few months with Brenna for training as a healer and because she misses her sister so."

"Wonderful. I haven't seen Jennie in a few summers. I'll hurry down." She loved her two cousins, Brenna and Jennie. The two were both such talented healers, much like their mother. When she was younger, she used to daydream about being a sister to them.

Lady Ramsay stood to the side while Finella directed the lads filling the tub. "I'll see you belowstairs. If you have need of aught, please advise Finella or me." She kissed Diana's cheek and left.

After Finella left, Diana sank into the warm water with a sigh, still in shock that she had slept so soundly she'd missed her husband's departure. It was unlike her. Once she finished washing her hair, she rushed down to the great hall and found a gaggle of lassies gathered by the hearth.

Avelina was plaiting Maggie's hair, and Lily stood to the side, inspecting Avelina's work with a serious expression on her wee face. Sitting nearby, Molly was playing a game with wee Sorcha.

Lily jumped and scampered up to her as soon as she entered the room. "Good! We need more to practice. You have such beautiful hair, my lady. May we plait your hair?"

"Lily, do not tire our guest." Lady Ramsay entered from the kitchens, carrying a platter of food for the table. "Be polite."

Lily stopped and smiled, then curtsied. "Sorry, my lady. May we plait your hair?"

Diana stared into the biggest pair of green eyes she had ever seen, a face alight with excitement at the prospect of fixing her long tresses. How could she turn down such an offer from the little lassie? "Call me, Diana, Lily. I am your aunt, and I am thrilled to have so many nieces. Aye, if you like, you may do my hair. But are you not going to do Molly's hair?"

Lily hopped a circle around Diana as they moved over to the table. "Molly doesn't want us to plait her hair. She says 'tis too messy."

Avelina glanced over at Molly as her fingers worked their magic on Maggie's tresses. "I think her hair would be beautiful tied at the back of her neck instead of plaited. I have heard of women in the court wearing their hair up like that. I think Molly would look so lovely that way, do you not agree?"

Glancing over at Molly, Diana took notice of her long, slender neck and graceful shoulders. "I think you could be correct, Avelina. Molly, why don't you let her try it?"

Molly blushed and stared at the floor. "I'm taking care of Sorcha while Mama goes out hunting."

"Well, I could help with Sorcha so you could get your hair done." Diana settled in a chair in front of Avelina, who had just finished plaiting Maggie's hair. She was glad to hear Molly refer to Gwyneth as Mama.

Molly seemed hesitant, but she finally nodded her head.

Avelina brushed Diana's out hair while Lily and Maggie chose the right ribbons for her. Lily jumped in front of her. "Diana, I have these dried flowers I can put in your hair. 'Twill look beautiful in your red tresses. May I put them in when Lina finishes?"

Lily's wee face, so full of hope and excitement, could not help but brighten Diana's morning. Micheil had told her how the wee lass had ensnared all their hearts, especially Logan's. Now she understood. "Aye, I would love to see your creation."

The lassie jumped and clapped her hands. "And will you let us do yours next, Molly? Please?"

Brenna entered the room with Bethia and set her down by the table. "Avelina, you do a beautiful job," she said with a soft smile.

"May I do yours, Brenna?"

Brenna shook her head. "Nay, I'm fine. But what about Molly?"

They all convinced Molly to allow Avelina to do her hair while Lily artfully arranged the tiny flowers in Diana's mane. Lady Ramsay and Brenna discussed the proposed menu for dinner. The corner bubbled over with feminine laughter and chatter, something Diana had not experienced in a long time. Once Lily was through fussing with Diana's hair, they played with Maggie and Sorcha, who was now sitting on Lady Ramsay's lap. All were too distracted to keep an eye on Avelina and Molly.

Mid-sentence, Lady Ramsay stopped talking, turned to Molly, and said, "My word, child."

Everyone stopped to see what had caught her attention. Avelina had turned Molly around. She had woven her wild curls into a loose bun at the base of her neck, instead of braiding it like she had done for the others, and had then woven strands into the side of her hair.

Lily smiled. "Molly, you look beautiful."

Molly's eyes widened, clearly not used to hearing such talk.

"Look, see your reflection in this platter." Lily held the platter up and Molly inspected herself. Diana was pleased to see her eyes light up with pleasure and surprise.

"Grandmama, what do you think?" Molly whispered, her gaze on her hands clasped in front of her.

"Lass, you are stunning. 'Tis a lovely look for you. Come here so I may look at it closer to see exactly what Avelina did with her weaving."

Molly could not stop smiling, which meant that no one else could either.

CHAPTER TWENTY-SIX

The door burst open and Lily swung around and shouted, "Jennie!" She tore over to the door and threw herself into Jennie's arms, her laughter bouncing off the rafters.

Jennie Grant was not quite as tall as Avelina, and her hair was straight and a shade darker. Freckles dotted the bridge of her nose, but she was clearly a little younger than Avelina. Diana greeted her cousin. "Jennie, you are so grown up. Look how tall you are, and your hair is so beautiful, straight and silky. You are almost a full grown woman." She hugged her. "Tis lovely to see you again."

The door opened again and some of the hunting group entered. Laird Alexander Grant had escorted his sister and brought his twin lads with him, Jamie and Jake. Micheil introduced Diana to the wee lads, then made his way over to her and kissed her in front of everyone. "My, you look lovely, wife. Are you rested yet?" His eyes held a teasing gleam.

"Micheil, I can't believe I slept through everything. I am so sorry." She gave him a sheepish look.

"Nay, you needed your rest." He kissed her brow and wrapped an arm around her waist.

Lady Ramsay stood, settling Sorcha on her hip and glancing at Logan. "I need to ask whether or not you were successful, Logan. Did you manage anything for dinner? 'Tis time for a family celebration this eve."

Logan wrapped his arm around his mother's shoulder and kissed Sorcha's cheek. "Aye, how does two turkeys and a pheasant sound? Gwyneth was at her best today."

She clapped her hands. "Wonderful."

Quade was the last to make his way into the room, Torrian and Growley at his side. Jamie and Jake, whom Diana guessed to be around five or six summers, ran over to Torrian, one petting the dog and the other tugging on his arms. Silence descended across the room as Logan and Gwyneth both stared speechless at their daughter.

Logan strode over in front of Molly, his hands on his hips. Her gaze cast down in embarrassment, Molly almost looked as if she were about to burst into tears. He reached down and lifted her chin. "Gywnie, what do you think?"

Tears misted in Molly's eyes as Gwyneth came over to join them. "Nay, lass," she said gently. "Do not cry. Have you not seen yourself? You are beautiful."

Logan said, "Wish your father was here to see you now."

Molly whispered, "Would you give me back?"

"Not a chance, lass. Not a chance." Logan kissed one cheek while Gwyneth kissed her other.

Molly beamed and wiped the tears from her eyes. Diana was so pleased to see how happy Molly and Maggie were in their new home. She noticed Molly was quite attached to her new grandmother.

"Not even if they begged for you to return, Molly. We need you here. You're a member of our family now. We all love you and Maggie." Quade strode over and patted her on the back. "Plus, you have to be here for the first annual Ramsay Festival."

Quade had garnered everyone's attention with that one statement. Lily, Torrian, Maggie, Molly, and Avelina all gathered in front of him, trying to contain their excitement as they waited for him to tell them more.

"For what, Da?" Torrian finally said.

Gwyneth announced, "Micheil has convinced us all to plan our first annual Ramsay Festival. Three contests—archery, an obstacle course for horseback riding, and..." She turned to her husband. "What was the other one?"

Micheil grinned and peeked at Diana. "Jousting."

She stared back at her husband, her eyes big as saucers. "Nay...." He couldn't be serious. How could he expect her to sit through the torture of waiting until he was hurt? The last jousting match had been enough for her. She never cared to see it again, especially with her husband competing. Somehow she would have to talk him out of this.

Gwyneth added, "And an obstacle course for those under twelve summers."

Quade turned to Alex, "Will you stay a sennight and join us?"

Alex glanced at his lads, their eyes wide with excitement. "Surely, we would love to stay, 'twas a bit chaotic when we left my keep. I brought Jennie to give her a rest and the lads to give Maddie some peace. When you return Jennie this time, you will all have to come along. Brenna has two new nephews."

"Already?" Brenna ran to grasp Jennie's hands in hers. "Both bore their bairns? All are well?"

Jennie nodded, her face beaming. "Aye, Caralyn and Celestina both gave birth to laddies. Robbie and

Brodie have sons born within a moon of each other. Robbie's is the biggest."

Brenna hugged Jennie. "I am so proud of you. You are a healer, just like Mama."

❧

Micheil had talked his brothers into running this festival for him. He had planned this all along, wanting to come to his land to gain assistance for this special festival. After listening to all the talk of his wife marrying a knight, he designed this to make all of her dreams finally come true. He would enter the field in his armor and defeat all the challengers to win her favor. Perhaps he wasn't an English knight, but he could prance the field as her knight and declare his love for her in front of all. Thus, Quade agreed to be in charge of the festivities to cover for Micheil's ultimate plan that was to take place at the very end of the competition. The rest had been added for fun.

Quade gathered the group in the center of the courtyard. "Are we ready?" Logan, Gwyneth, Torrian, Lily, Jennie, Avelina, Molly, Maggie, Alex, Jake, Jamie, Diana, and Micheil all stood, awaiting their assignments.

At the last minute, Father Rab came running out to join them. Gwyneth introduced her brother to Diana. Father Rab added, "I am here to help, not to be in charge."

As soon as the group quieted, he began. "Each of you will be a part of a group. Your job is to design the competition, find a location for it, then return here in a couple of hours to report your findings. Once all of the details are settled, we will allow two days for set up and practice. Any questions?"

Micheil glanced around at the others in the group, but no one spoke. He peeked at Diana again, noticing how tired she looked. She had overslept again, but they had waited for her. Now he wondered if she belonged abed. Meeting a new family had to be exhausting.

Quade started. "Gwyneth and Logan, you are in charge of archery. Torrian and I will build the obstacle course for the younger ones, and Lily, Molly, and Maggie can help us set up. Alex, Diana, and Micheil, you are in charge of the horseback obstacle course and the jousting, and the lads will help you set up the course."

"Jousting? You cannot be serious. Micheil?" Diana stared at him, obviously waiting for an explanation. "I really thought you were jesting. 'Tis way too dangerous for all of you."

Micheil said, "We'll be verra careful. 'Tis just for fun. Will only be Quade, Logan, Alex, and I along with three or four of our guards. The lads and lassies all love it. 'Tis just for show."

"You are going to put me through this again?" Diana stared at him, her eyes wide with anxiety.

Quade said, "Apparently, we missed out on something, Micheil?"

"Aye," Diana said. "You missed seeing your brother be the only one to take on an English knight, and a cheating one at that."

Quade grinned. "Och, I'm sorry we missed it. Tell us more."

Alex laughed. "'Tis some tale, in my eyes. We heard about it in Perthshire. You must tell it true to your brothers."

Micheil chuckled. "Diana, it was not that bad. I succeeded, did I not?"

"Aye, you were on the ground, bleeding all over. I thought you were dead." Diana's chest heaved as she glared at her husband.

"There's naught to worry about here, my love. No one in the family is likely to have a dagger hidden at the end of a jousting stick." Micheil was surprised at how upset Diana appeared to be.

Logan said, "Diana, we're family. We don't hurt each other."

"And your cousins are wonderful healers," Quade offered.

Micheil glowered at Quade. How in the hell was that supposed to help? "Continue, Quade. Finish the assignments. My wife and I will talk while we plan the horseback course."

Quade finished his instructions and sent everyone off to complete their assignments. When the others had left, he strode over to Diana's side. "We do not have to host a jousting contest if it will upset you." He looked from his brother to Diana.

Diana nodded. "I'll get my horse so we can locate a field for the obstacle course." She strode away from Micheil toward the stables.

"Was it that bad?" Quade asked.

"Aye, I had been hit with the dagger a few times. But they were superficial wounds. They looked worse than they were. But I did lose quite a bit of blood. Must be it upset her."

"Mayhap you should be the judge instead of a competitor."

Micheil took off to follow his wife. "Nay, she'll be fine. I'll talk to her." Besides, this would ruin all his plans. He wanted to be everything she had ever wanted.

Quade raised his eyebrows at his brother. "Tread carefully, you are newly wed."

By the time Micheil made it to the stables, Diana was through the gates on her horse. He did not understand why she was being so temperamental.

She was not usually so sensitive, so emotional about everything. Apparently, coming to his family's house had brought up some memories that were bothersome for her.

He mounted his horse and followed her through the gates, trying to catch up to her. "Diana, wait, please," he bellowed, but she continued on, barreling across the meadow as if possessed.

He was almost to the point of getting angry, when her horse stopped quickly and she froze. Finally, something must have made sense to her, and she was thinking normally again. As he came up abreast of her, a lump found its way into his throat. She had turned her horse around, and the expression on her face scared him like nothing he had ever seen before.

"Diana?" He reined in his horse. The look on her face was horrifying. "Diana, what's wrong?"

She burst into tears and said, "Micheil, help me."

CHAPTER TWENTY-SEVEN

Hellfire, he would do anything for her. He jumped off his horse and ran to her side. "What's wrong? Diana?" The expression on her face was full of fear.

"Micheil, take me home, please."

"What's wrong? Tell me why you look like that?"

"I need to see Brenna. I don't know if I should ride."

"What? You are talking in riddles, love. Tell me."

"I cannot, Micheil. 'Tis womanly issues. Just help me get back, but I must go slowly, no bouncing."

"We can do that. Do you want to ride with me? You can ride on my lap."

"Aye, but do not bounce, please."

Micheil helped her down and got her on his horse before he climbed behind her and settled her against him, at the last minute grabbing the reins of her horse to follow them. He had no idea what she was talking about, but he trusted her judgment and rode as slowly and carefully as he could. She sat sideways and leaned against him, staring into the distance as she gripped his plaid.

"Are you hurt, Diana?"

She shook her head. That was when he finally took the time to glance at his arm, at the wetness that had been there since he lifted her onto his horse. At the time, he had been too upset to notice.

Blood, not much, but there was no mistaking it. Now he understood—these were the kind of womanly issues he knew nothing about. He had to get her to Brenna quickly.

Wiping his arm on his plaid, he reached for her and tugged her in close. Logan headed toward him from the field they had been working in, concern etched on his features. Micheil maintained a slow steady pace without stopping, and Logan turned to ride next to him.

"Do you need help?"

"Aye, find Brenna and tell her I'm bringing Diana to her." Micheil turned his head to catch Logan's gaze. "Womanly issues."

Logan spurred his horse. "I'm on my way. Alex and his guards are with Gwynie and the rest of the group."

Logan must have stopped to explain to the others because he had a few who joined him as he passed each field. Quade pulled alongside him and said, "Anything I can do?"

"Just make sure your wife is ready for her. Mother also."

"I will."

Avelina and Jennie came on either side of him. "Micheil, what can we do?" Lina asked.

He shook his head, so they continued along with him. Avelina said, "In case you think of anything."

Micheil was touched with the way his family surrounded him to follow them back to the castle. Little was said, but their support meant everything.

Diana clung to him and buried her face in his chest, and he did not know what to do for her. He was totally lost, a feeling he did not like one bit.

Micheil stood outside his chamber with his brothers, waiting for Brenna to come out and tell him what was wrong with his wife. "What is taking so long?"

Quade said, "You must be patient. Brenna is verra thorough, you know that. Why don't we go downstairs and have an ale while you wait?"

"Nay, I'll stay here. I need to know what has happened to her. Why was she bleeding?"

Logan grasped his shoulder. "Womanly problems are something I know naught about, and I do not wish to know. Let Mother and Brenna take care of her. She's in good hands."

Just then, Lily and Torrian both popped up at the top of the staircase and rushed down the passageway toward them, eager for information about their new aunt. Quade shook his head and waved them away. Before Lily ran back down the stairs, she ran over and hugged Micheil. "Uncle, you know I love both of you. Lady Diana is so nice. She will get better."

Micheil picked Lily up and hugged her before setting her back down. "Thank you, sweets."

Logan put his arm around wee Lily and said, "Let's go back downstairs and see how the bairns are doing. You need to help with Bethia and Sorcha, and they will get upset if you're upset."

Lily said, "I know. I love you all." She turned and ran down the passageway to the stairs, Logan following her at a statelier pace.

Once he and his eldest brother were alone together, Micheil stared at the floor, then searched his brother's gaze. "Do you think her bleeding indicates she has lost our bairn?"

Quade whispered, "Possibly. But we don't know that yet."

Just then, the door opened, and his mother and Brenna stepped outside.

"May I see her? Is she all right?" Micheil's gut was doing somersaults. He knew his stomach would never settle until he saw his wife.

Brenna nodded. "She's resting. I gave her something to help her sleep. She cannot remember the last time she had her courses, do you?"

Micheil stared at her blankly as Quade coughed and said, "Brenna, must you?"

She glowered at her husband. "Aye, I must. I am trying to assess her condition. Do you, Micheil?"

He shook his head, not wanting to discuss the topic at all. "Nay, I don't recall."

"It is verra possible she is carrying your bairn. If so, 'tis early, so 'tis not uncommon for there to be some bleeding. I want her in bed for at least a sennight. We will take turns tending her, but I do not think she has lost the bairn yet, so she needs to make sure the babe is well set in her womb. The beginning can be a fragile time, so we must be careful.

"You may go in with her. When she awakens, I do want her to eat. 'Tis verra important that she eats enough for two, so you are to watch her for that. Has she seemed different to you at all?"

Micheil wanted to deny it, but then he thought again about her behavior these last few days. "She's been verra tired, oversleeping, but I thought it was the trip. And she has been extra sensitive." He turned to look at Quade. "The jousting, remember?"

Quade nodded. "I can attest. She was a little overbearing about it. Almost ready to cry at the mere mention of the contest."

Brenna and Lady Ramsay smiled at each other. "Congratulations, Micheil," Brenna said. "It does indeed sound as if your wife carries your bairn. We just have to make sure he or she likes their new home." She patted his arm and said, "Go sit with her. We'll send up some food and ale for you. She will sleep for a bit, so Quade can keep you company. But no weans for a while. I want it to be kept quiet for her up here."

She headed down the passageway before turning to look back at him. "Oh, and Micheil?"

"Aye?"

"No horseback riding till the bairn is born."

Micheil's eyes widened, but he nodded. "We can do that."

His mother leaned over to kiss his cheek. "Congratulations, son. She's a lovely lass and strong. I have seen it many times over the years. Some women just need to spend the first little while in bed. You will both need to be careful."

Heading toward the end of the passageway, Quade shouted, "I'll bring up some food in a wee bit. Go see to your wife."

Micheil nodded as Quade and his mother disappeared down the stairs. He stepped into the dark chamber. Brenna had left one small tallow lit. Once inside, he stared at his wife. She was sound asleep and looked so small in the bed, it broke his heart. Damn, he had pushed too hard to get to his family. She had done too much horseback riding, though neither of them had known there was a reason to refrain. Diana loved riding.

He sat in the chair, content to watch her while she slept, and folded his hands in his lap. A bairn. He was going to be a father. Was he ready for that? He thought of his two brothers and realized he would love nothing more than to see their bairn in his wife's arms. A wee laddie or a lassie, he did not care, so long as the bairn was strong. Lily and Torrian had gone through such an ordeal, he would have to pray their bairn was born robust, not weak or sickly. Thank the Lord that Brenna had saved his niece and nephew.

He prayed Brenna could save their bairn as well.

When Diana awoke, she breathed in the scent of her husband and relaxed. He smelled of pine and the outdoors, that special aroma of Micheil Ramsay she had come to love so much. He was here with her. Together, they could handle anything. She moved her head back on the pillow to see if he was asleep or not. His breathing was deep and regular, and his long dark locks were in a tangle around his head. Her ordeal must have upset him.

Brenna had told her that she was probably carrying their bairn. Her hand settled on her belly as she willed the wean to grow strong inside her, where it could be protected for many moons. Somehow, through the chaos of being newly wed and losing her father, she had not noticed it had been a while since her courses had come.

A deep rumble interrupted her thoughts. "Sweeting, how do you fare?" Micheil leaned up on his elbow to look at her, wiping the sleep from his eyes.

She smiled up at her husband, the moonlight from the slit in the window just bright enough to illuminate his dear face. "I feel fine, Micheil. Did Brenna give you the news?"

"Aye, she said we're going to have a bairn. How do you feel about that?"

"Micheil, naught would make me happier. I did not think it would happen this quickly, but I had hoped we would have several bairns some day. We need at least one laddie for the clan." She reached for his hand and intertwined their fingers.

"A lassie much like her mother would be pleasing to me." He kissed her softly. "You frightened me, wife."

She breathed in a deep sigh and rolled onto her back, staring at the ceiling as she held her husband's hand in hers. "Micheil, what if I lose the bairn?" She blinked several times in an attempt to stop the tears she felt pressing against her eyes.

"I think we must do as Brenna said. I have faith in her healing skills. She has delivered many bairns in our clan and her own. You will not have it easy because I know how you hate staying abed, but she thinks it is best that you do so for a sennight."

A tear slid down her cheek. "I know, and my horseback riding days are done for now. That does not upset me. Do you think it is my fault for racing you to the castle when we arrived?"

"Nay, what was meant to happen, will happen. If we lose this bairn, we will make another."

"Micheil?" Tears flooded down her cheeks now as she stared at the beams above.

"Sweeting, don't cry. You know how I hate to see you cry."

"What if I cannot carry a Drummond lad? What if I can only carry lassies? I want my father to see his grandson. I know he can see from heaven."

Micheil rolled back down flat on the bed and tucked his wife into his embrace, resting her head on his shoulder. "Sweeting, I will be just as happy with a lassie as I would be with a lad."

"I do not want to disappoint my sire again."

"Again? I do not think you ever disappointed your sire. Not the man I met."

"Aye, I did." She sighed before she continued. "The day I was born. He wanted a son." She swiped at the tears, likely making a mess of her face, but was unable to stop their flow. It was impossible to count how many times she had heard the story of her father's disappointment the day she was born a lass.

Micheil whispered, "The man I met adored his daughter, so much so that he admitted to spoiling you terribly. Does that sound like a sire that was disappointed?"

She giggled. "Papa did spoil me, aye. And I loved every minute of it. He was a wonderful sire."

"Then fear not. He will be proud of you no matter what. Now cease your tears. I am trying to imagine how you'll look with a swollen belly, ripe with child."

"Micheil. I do love you so." She kissed him and rested her head back on his shoulder, falling asleep in a matter of moments.

Micheil stared at his wife, who lay fast asleep in his arms. He had planned everything so carefully, but he hadn't planned on this. How could he have guessed she was carrying their bairn? He had hoped to joust in the tourney, then present himself to her as the knight of her dreams.

He remembered how excited she had been in Edinburgh at the thought of seeing the English knights joust in the tournament. Diana had loved sitting in the stands, and according to Aunt Elspeth, her cheeks had flushed a pleased pink when the knight presented himself for her token. It had been such a wonderful day for her—except for one thing. The knight had been unmasked as the odious Randall Baines.

Now Micheil wanted to be her knight. His wife had loved her mother's tales of chivalry, so it didn't seem right that the only tournament she'd seen in person had starred a cheating knight. He wanted to fulfill her dreams, and doing so at their festival seemed a perfect plan. But could she handle watching him joust in her state? The last thing he wished to do was cause her undue worry, so he'd tried to explain how careful he would be, but her fear seemed very real. Was he making a mistake?

CHAPTER TWENTY-EIGHT

Diana sent Micheil out to take part in the planning for the festival. Father Rab had been by to pray with her and had agreed to assist in the contest planning in her place. Logan was going to do double duty and help Micheil out with the horseback obstacle course since Gwyneth had the archery field under control. The first practice was set for the next morning.

Lady Ramsay had just left with her finished meal platter when a quiet knock sounded at her door.

"Come in." Diana had no idea who it could be. She had seen most everyone this morning, though not many of the bairns.

Torrian stuck his head through the cracked door. "May I come in, Lady Diana?"

"Of course, Torrian." She waved him inside and over to the chair next to the bed. "I would love to talk to my only nephew."

Torrian was at an awkward stage—still young, yet trying to act like an adult. His shoulders were broadening, and his voice crackled when he talked. She could tell his voice would deepen a couple of octaves over the next few moons.

He sat in the chair and asked, "Is there aught I can get for you?"

"Nay, your grandmama just left, so I have everything I need. 'Tis thoughtful of you to come check on me."

"We just finished our meeting about the festival, and I wanted to give you an update. We have all decided to postpone for a sennight so that you will be well enough to come and watch. Alex agreed to stay with the lads until after the festival. Actually, I was hoping you would consider being one of the judges in the obstacle course for the young ones?"

"If Brenna says it is all right, I would love to judge. Tell me what you have arranged for them in the course." Diana thought it was a wonderful idea and could not wait to see the lads and lassies compete, though she tried her best not to think about her husband jousting. "Will those older take part in the other competitions?"

"Molly wishes to stay in the younger competition. Jennie and I will try the horseback obstacle course, and Avelina will join us for the archery contest."

"So is Gwyneth training everyone in archery?"

"Aye, practice starts tomorrow. Mama and Papa will walk the young ones through the obstacle course while the rest of us practice the other two courses. Do not worry about the horseback obstacle course or the jousting, Alex and Micheil have it under control."

"Torrian, I must confess, a short while ago naught would have excited me more than a jousting competition, but now naught frightens me more." She studied her fingers as she realized how much she had changed in such a short time. She had been delighted to attend in Edinburgh.

"You worry about Micheil? You should not, he has always been our strongest. Papa and Logan are better with the bow, but Micheil is the best at jousting."

"I will try to trust in my husband's skills. Tell me about the obstacles for the lassies, though I expect Alex's lads will join in."

"Actually, Papa has opened it up to any of his guards' families."

"Oooh, this is exciting, do you not agree?"

He nodded and grinned. "So far, we have a log set up over a wee stream, then two barrels they must crawl through, then a long field they must run across, then we plan to set a tent really low that they must crawl underneath without knocking it over. The last thing they must do is throw hazelnuts toward a target. At first, we were going to do rocks, but Papa said Jamie and Jake can be a wee bit wild. He didn't want any rock throwing with all the bairns around. What do you think?"

"Torrian, that sounds wonderful. I agree with your da that the nuts would be safer than the rocks. Either way, the wee ones will have great fun."

Torrian stared at his hands for a moment and scowled. Then he raised his gaze to hers. "Would you mind if I asked you a couple of questions? They are a bit unusual."

"Sure, 'tis what an aunt should do. I would like to help you if I can."

He thought for a moment, then said, "My apologies for losing your sire, but I would like to ask you something. Are you concerned about being the laird now that your sire has passed?"

Diana smiled at her nephew, trying so hard to grow up, yet still so young at heart. "Torrian, I am petrified most days that I will make a mistake. I am verra thankful to have Micheil by my side for guidance." She glanced up at the beams overhead.

"Before my sire passed, I thought I would never be able to act in his stead. It frightened me to think of my decisions affecting so many. Is that how you are feeling?"

He nodded. "Aye. Papa has asked me to follow him everywhere now to learn from him, and I do not know how he does it all. Some days, I think I could never do it. He must live forever because I will not be able to handle the pressure."

"Come sit on the bed next to me." She patted the covers, and he sat down with a sheepish expression on his face. "One thing you must remember is that your sire rarely ever acts on his own."

He gave her a puzzled look. "Aye, he does all the time. He decides punishment for anyone who commits a crime against the clan, he decides how to spend our coin and what crops to grow. 'Tis his decision for everything."

"Mayhap you are correct, but I'm sure he discusses many of these things with others."

"Who? I do not see him discuss aught with others."

"Does your father not have a steward? I know I would be lost without my steward."

"Aye, he handles most of the coin and the crops, but not without my sire's instructions."

"True, but I would presume they discuss many things, maybe when you are not in the chamber."

He thought about this before nodding slowly. "Mayhap you are correct."

"And your grandmama? I am sure she is a wealth of information. She has been here for many years, and she stood at the side of the previous laird for a long time, aye?"

"'Tis true." His hand came up to rub his chin, though no whiskers were there for him to stroke yet.

"And what about Brenna?"

"Och, he talks to her all the time."

"Aye, because she was verra close to another laird."

"Hmm, my thanks, Diana. You have given me much to consider. I will pay better attention to Papa when he is about."

"You have to remember that your clan is made of many people, and you must all work together for it to succeed."

"I am so afraid I will not be strong enough..."

"Why would you say that, Torrian?"

"You did not know me before, but I had a sickness that kept me abed for a long time. I try so verra hard to eat and build muscles like my da and my uncles. I want to be a strong warrior like the Ramsay guards and the Grant warriors, but naught seems to help."

"You are not full grown yet, Torrian. I think you have quite a bit more growing to do. Do not worry about that yet. When lads grow, their muscles grow with them."

"Truly? Do you believe it?"

"Aye, I do. But keep learning as much as you can from your da. You will not regret it. You will be a fine laird someday. I know it."

He quirked his brow. "How can you tell?"

"Because you care, lad, and 'tis the most important thing of all."

Two days later, Jennie and Avelina were on the training field, learning archery from Gwyneth. Jennie glanced at Avelina, surprised to see how intent she was on her task. Torrian had been there for a while, but he'd left with his da.

Jennie nocked and released another arrow, missing the target by a long shot. "Why do I even bother? I don't need to know how to shoot, do I?"

"It cannot hurt you to know how to protect yourself," Gwyneth retorted. "It is something you have to practice. Lina has been coming out here for some time, haven't you, lass?"

Avelina sighed. "Aye, for six or seven moons. I started early last spring, and I can still barely hit the target. My arms are too weak."

Jennie laughed as she released another wild arrow, way off target. "At least you come close to your target, Lina. I am terrible at this. I concede to you and Torrian."

"Nay, do not quit. I want you trying with me."

Gwyneth shot two more arrows before she put her things away. "Lassies, I have to go feed Sorcha, so I will leave you to practice. Do you have any other questions?"

"Nay," Jennie sighed. "I will keep trying."

"Alex is in the next field, so if you need anything, holler. He's close enough to hear you, and there are a few guards still in the area. I'll pass by him and advise him you are still out here."

"Thanks, Gwyneth, for your patience," Jennie said, a defeated expression on her face.

"You're welcome. Now make me proud, lasses. Aim and release!" She gave them each a pat on the back and left.

Jennie dropped her bow. "I've had enough. I cannot do this. I'm ready to quit right now. How about you, Lina?"

"Nay, I have a few more left. Come, do not make me practice alone. You have three arrows in your quiver. Shoot them. It can only help to practice." She pulled her bow back and released another arrow, hitting the outside area of the target.

"Nice shot! I could not do even that." Jennie watched in amazement as Avelina hit the target twice more. "All right. You've inspired me." She nocked her arrow, pulled it backed, and aimed carefully before releasing it, Lina watching her with an encouraging smile.

At the last second, her arm twitched and the arrow flew way off course into the woods. Jennie started laughing and Avelina grinned, but as soon as the arrow landed, a yelp came out from the copse of trees the arrow had disappeared into. Immediately after the yelp, a deep bellow rang out. "Who shot me? Hellfire, who is it? Come out and face me like a man!"

CHAPTER TWENTY-NINE

Jennie stared at Avelina wide-eyed. Without hesitation, her healer instincts took over and she ran into the trees to find her victim.

Avelina followed, yelling at her all the way. "Jennie, be careful. You have no idea who that is. He could be dangerous!"

As soon as she made it past the line of trees, she saw five men and five horses. Four of the men stood gathered around the fifth, a dark-haired lad who was prostrate on the ground. His friend reached down to assist him.

"Help me up," he groaned. "I'll find out who did this, and I'll fix the rotten bastard. Since when do you fire wild into the trees with naught around to shoot at?" He stood up and limped around in a circle.

Jennie ran into the middle of the circle of men. "Are you all right? My apologies. My arm jerked and my arrow flew wild. I did not intend to hurt anyone." She came up behind the man she had shot, stopping abruptly as soon as she saw her arrow, right in the middle of the right side of his arse. "Oh!"

He whirled around, his long dark locks tossing high into the air, and her gaze met the deepest blue eyes she had ever seen. They were filled with fury.

"Seems you are correct, lass. You hit me in the arse. What in hellfire are you doing?" The more he spoke, the louder his voice became, and his arms

flew up at his sides, swinging in the air close enough
to hit her. "You belong in the courtyard, indoors
tending the bairns, or in the kitchens, not out here
shooting good lads for naught. Foolish wench!"

Avelina charged in behind Jennie, but came to an
abrupt halt just outside the circle.

Jennie said calmly, "I'm a healer, not a wench.
Mayhap I can be of assistance." He stood a good
head taller than her, but she refused to cower before
his ire, instead choosing to wait until reason
returned to his head.

"You wish to assist me?" He glowered at her,
bringing his face down toward hers. "I think you
have *assisted* me enough."

Heat shot from his body to hers, traveling through
her face and down to her core. Who was this lad? He
made her feel strange things, and she did not like it.
His gaze left hers for a moment, running down her
body and back up again. His expression changed to
one of admiration, but she had no idea why. Her
brother allowed her little contact with lads, and she
had never seen a reaction like he had.

"I say let her assist you," one of his friends said
with a shrug. "She should pull it out, not me. Better
than you pulling it out."

Another lad chuckled. "Aye, let the lass pull it out
and we'll watch."

A third whistled as he stared over Jennie's
shoulder at Avelina. "Please, Cameron. Let her
assist you, and I'll let the beauty behind her assist
me. I think I have an arrow in my arse, too. Come,
lass, check it out for me."

The others chuckled and stepped back, pushing
Avelina up next to Jennie.

"So you want that one, Drew, and I'll take this
one? Is that the plan?" the man referred to as

Cameron asked, his eyes never leaving hers. He took a step closer.

Jennie could breathe in his scent—he smelled like horse, leather, and something else, something that made her move in closer to place the other pleasant aroma.

"See something you like, lass?" He quirked a brow at her and grinned.

Jennie was not amused, not even when his breath hit her with the fragrance of mint leaves. Aye, he was pleasant looking, but there was something about him she did not like. "Do you wish my assistance with your wound or not? Otherwise, we will take our leave." Rather than backing away from him, she stood tall, daring him to insult her again.

Lina whispered behind her, "Jennie..."

"Do not be afraid of them. I am not." Her gaze hardened.

The other four circled Cameron and the two women, whistling and hollering, attempting to instigate something.

From outside the copse of trees, Alex bellowed, "Jennie!"

The five lads turned around in time to see Alex Grant approaching at full stride on Midnight, his destrier. Three of them hopped onto their horses and took off, but Cameron reached for the arrow in his arse and yanked it out.

"This isn't finished. I will find you someday. You owe me." Cameron tossed the arrow at her before jumping onto his horse, Drew mounting his steed at the same time.

Drew stared at Avelina and said, "I'll find you again, too, lass, but not for the same reasons." He winked and turned his horse just as Alex broke through the trees, cutting him off.

"Touch either lass and you can count yourself a dead man." He pulled out his sword and rode hard toward Cameron, his sword point aimed straight for his heart.

Jennie screamed. "Alex, nay! 'Twas my fault. I shot the lad."

Alex stared at him. "'Struth, lad? You are injured?"

Cameron returned Alex's glare before he answered, seemingly unconcerned about the sword poised to kill him. "Naught that I cannot handle. Hold your sword. I want naught to do with her."

"Let it be known that you have just met Alexander Grant's sister, and if anyone dares to touch her, I'll cut his heart out myself. And that goes for her friend, too. Understood?"

Cameron raked his gaze over Jennie again. "Understood."

Alex lowered his sword to allow the two to follow their companions.

As soon as they were gone, Jennie turned to her brother. "Alex, why can you not let me handle myself? You cannot do everything for me." Jennie's frustration with her brother grew each year, but he did not seem to care. She loved him dearly because he had been like a father figure to her, but he had to stop smothering her so.

"Lass, you and Lina were surrounded by five lads. They had different things in mind than you did."

"How would I know? You must stop protecting me so. I will marry someday whether you wish it or not."

"'Tis where you're wrong, lass. You will not marry without my approval."

Fury blazed in her eyes. "Then I have no hope, do I?"

The day of the Ramsay Festival had finally arrived. The sun shone bright on the late autumn day, making it warm enough to be outside. Diana was excited to finally be allowed out of the castle, but yet she had no wish to watch her husband joust. The day before she had walked inside the keep to see if she was better, and there were no problems. Brenna was confident she could walk out to the fields as a judge.

Micheil strolled alongside her, carrying a fur and an extra plaid to keep her warm. Torrian and Logan had already taken a cartload of stools and benches to the field for the ladies to sit on. Even Micheil's mother had promised she would come out to watch.

Quade had made sure everyone in the clan understood they were to come to the festival rather than working. They had planned a large feast for everyone in the courtyard after the event.

The first competition was for those under ten. Micheil and Diana were to be judges, and Quade and Torrian had everything arranged. There were ten entrants of various ages, including Alex's twins, Jake and Jamie, Lily, Maggie, Molly, and five other members of the clan. Ten separate lanes had been set up to accommodate all of them. The course was mostly as Torrian had described to her, and Micheil and Diana assigned two guards as backup judges to assist them at the end in case all ten competitors ended up throwing their hazelnuts at the same time.

The ten lined up as their parents screamed their encouragement. At the last minute, Alex held his hand up to Micheil.

"What is it, Grant?"

"Just need to make this a bit easier on everyone." The youngest competitors were his two boys, and they stood at the end of the line, shoving at each other in the hopes of getting a head start over the other. "Lads!" A loud bellow stopped all the chatter, including the twins' squirming.

He marched down the line, picked up dark-haired Jamie without uttering a word and carried him under his arm down to the opposite end of the lanes, moving all the contestants down one to make room for him. Once he had settled Jamie in a different lane, he turned to the event coordinator, Quade, and nodded. "Mayhap they will not kill each other with eight others between them. They are a wee bit competitive." He made his way off the field to the good-natured guffaws of the spectators.

"One, two, three, go!" Ten pairs of legs flew across the logs, and a couple of entrants fell right away. Micheil followed the course with them as judge, but Diana remained seated at the side with her family. Hoots and hollers followed their trail through the obstacle course. By the time they reached the tent, Jamie and Jake and another boy were way ahead of the rest. Molly was ahead of Maggie, and Lily spent too much time giggling to progress very far or fast.

The three lads hit the beginning of the long field where the race would take place ahead of the rest, but Molly was gaining on them. Logan shouted, "Come on, Molly. Show the lads who's the best." He wrapped his arm around Gwyneth, who was holding Sorcha on her hip, biting her fingernails as she watched her eldest daughter compete.

Molly was three strides behind the lads, but as soon as she hit the field, the spectators all took their eyes off the leaders to watch her race.

"Logan, she runs like the most beautiful deer I have ever seen," Gwyneth said.

Diana was in awe. "Gwyneth, I have never seen anyone so graceful. What a lovely sight." She couldn't help but pull for a lass sent out by her own sire.

And indeed, Molly sailed across the field with elegance and strength that gave her speed way beyond the others, her long strides powering her to the end way ahead of the boys. She picked up a hazelnut and flung it, missing the target by a long shot.

Logan shouted, "Come on, Molly!" He glanced at Gwyneth. "Wife, could you not have taught the lass how to hit the broad side of a stable?"

She had thrown three nuts and missed each one by the time the lads caught up with her. She had one left and flung it as hard as she could, finally hitting the very edge of the target. Micheil declared Molly the winner, while Jake came in second and Jamie won third place.

Logan ran over and tossed her into the air after they announced the winner and pinned a ribbon on her.

Molly could not stop smiling.

Diana couldn't help but notice how Molly had changed in the short time she had spent with the Logan and Gwyneth. Her eyes shone bright as she hugged her parents and listened to all the congratulations from the others. She now walked with her shoulders back instead of constantly hunched over and staring at the ground.

Which brought another thought to the forefront of Diana's mind. Had she changed as much as Molly? Two moons ago, she had nearly swooned at the suggestion of a tournament and men jousting, clamoring to get there ahead of others. Now she wished to avoid it completely. After all the trials of

Edinburgh and Falkirk, then losing her father, gaining a wonderful husband, and becoming chieftain of her clan, suddenly she viewed everything differently. Aye, she had grown and matured as much as the wee lass in front of her, she just hadn't realized it. How could she have missed it?

The next competition was the obstacle course on horseback. Diana cheered from the side, not minding that she couldn't participate. Eight different contestants had entered, but none could outdo Alex Grant atop Midnight.

Jake and Jamie sat on either side of Diana, in awe of their sire, and they jumped up and down in the air when he was announced as the winner.

The third contest was archery. They moved to a different field to observe this competition. There were two contests, one for adults, and one for lads and lassies. Gwyneth won the adult contest, with Logan coming in second and Quade third. Avelina won the contest for the young ones, with Torrian coming in second and another lad third.

Jennie refused to shoot.

The very last contest, much to Diana's chagrin, was the jousting competition. She had attempted to talk Micheil out of participating, but he had convinced her it was just in good fun. Diana's hands started sweating as soon as she saw all the competitors gathered on the field. With twenty entrants, it was the most popular contest. Micheil would have to joust nineteen other contestants if he was to win. She had agreed to say naught, but now the growing tension in her body made her verra uncomfortable. How would she get through this? The same memory played over and over in her mind, that instant in Edinburgh when Micheil had tumbled from his horse and fell bleeding to the ground.

All of a sudden, she changed her mind. She just could not do it, she could not watch her husband in any type of jousting contest. Her hand moved to her belly, calming the butterflies and attempting to relax her churning gut. What would she do if something happened to him? She rubbed her belly, wondering if she was indeed carrying their son or daughter. The more she thought about it, the more desperate she became. It had to stop.

Micheil came flying across the field with his lance in his hand, headed straight for Diana.

"Nay," Diana wailed, forcing everyone to turn their gaze to her.

Micheil stopped in front of her and bowed his head, positioning his lance for her favor in the same fashion as that odious knight had done in Edinburgh. "My lady."

"Micheil, nay, please." Tears misted in her eyes, but he did not falter. "Please do not do this, I am desperate." How could she get him to stop this foolishness?

"Desperate? You are always desperate, Diana."

She scowled at him, raising her voice with indignation. "I am *not*."

"Aye, you are." He still held his lance out, awaiting her favor.

She crossed her arms and flounced away from him, settling down on her bench.

"Were you not desperate when we left the Gow keep in the middle of the night through the kitchens wearing lad's clothing?"

Thankfully, the entire field couldn't hear what he said to her, but those around her could. She ignored him and stared off into the distance.

"Were you not desperate when we traveled from Falkirk to Edinburgh in the dark of night, just the two of us?"

She turned back to huff at him. "We were not alone. Alex's men surrounded us."

"I'll give you that one. Were you not desperate the night you dragged me to the courtyard at the royal castle searching for any English knight who would take you as his wife?"

She turned her back to him again.

"And were you not desperate, my beautiful Highlander, when you stayed up all night to sew a used gown so it could fit you? And from what I now know about you and your gowns, that was true desperation." He rolled his eyes.

"Enough. I have been desperate before, but I beg you now. Please, Micheil. Do not do this." She tried to remain strong, to stop the flow of tears again, but to no avail.

"Diana, I will be fine. This is all in fun, for show. 'Tis not a competition. You must learn to trust me."

Lily ran over and said, "Here, Uncle Micheil, I'll give you my favor."

She tied her ribbon on his lance and Micheil said, "My thanks, my lady." Lily giggled as she skipped back to her spot.

His mother stood and said, "I must give my son my favor, for safe travel."

Micheil bowed to his mother. Diana could feel him staring at her from the corner of his eye, but she was not willing to budge.

Avelina leaned over. "I must give my brother a token." She tied a hair ribbon on his lance with the other favors.

Micheil held up his lance for all to see, then circled the perimeter of the field, showing off his lance while all the lassies applauded him. Before he passed her again, he brought his horse over and lowered his lance to her.

Diana wanted to throw something at him, but she finally conceded and yanked a ribbon from her hair to tie on the blunt end of his lance. "Micheil, I will never forgive you for this."

As soon as she took her hand away, he raised his lance in celebration while the crowd roared. Then he did the oddest thing. She had expected him to ride across the field again in triumph. Instead, he dismounted and knelt before her, placing his lance on the ground in front of her. "I'll not joust. For you, my love."

He strode over to the bench and wrapped his arms around her. "I wanted to be your knight," he whispered in her ear. "I set this whole festival up for you. I wanted to give you the knight of your dreams."

Tears pooled in her eyes. "Micheil, you are my knight. I do love you so."

He settled her on his lap and said, "I love you, too. No more desperation. I want my bride happy."

EPILOGUE

Several months later

"I'm desperate! Please, Micheil." Diana's shout shook the rafters of the Drummond keep. "Get out. Look what you've done to me. I never want to see you again. Get out, get out. I hate you!"

Micheil closed the chamber door behind him, his face ashen. He heard a clunk against the door, which he judged to be another shoe flung across the room. He stood there confused, unsure of his next steps.

Logan chuckled and clapped a hand on his brother's shoulder. "I told you to stay out. Women giving birth are not the same. They're overtaken by wee gremlins, I swear it."

"But I did not wish to be there, *she* wanted it. She asked me to stay because Alex Grant always assists his wife. Now she's changed her mind." Totally perplexed, he did not know what to make of the situation. "Thank goodness you all came. I could not have handled this alone."

"Pregnant women have that prerogative, especially if they're in the middle of delivering the bairn. 'Tis a difficult job. Stop and think about what they go through. I never did appreciate it until I saw my Gwynie struggle with it, and she's tougher than most." Logan ushered him through the passageway and down the stairs to join the rest of the family in the great hall, patiently awaiting the arrival of the two's first bairn.

Micheil glanced at Quade, "Were you at Brenna's side when she had your bairn?"

"Hell, nay. 'Tis no place for me. Perish the thought. Never stepped into the chamber." His eyes widened. "And I won't be the next time either."

"Brenna's carrying again?" Micheil asked. "Why didn't you tell me?"

Quade answered, "Aye, 'tis still early. You have enough on your mind."

Logan found a goblet and filled it with ale. "Actually, Diana seems to be faring well. Gwynie told me she was going to cut my bollocks off." He guffawed as he looked at his wife. She was seated in the chair by the hearth, feeding their new son, Gavin. "Once she holds the bairn in her arms, she'll forget everything she just said. 'Tis a verra painful process. Tell him, Gwynie."

"Aye, 'tis true, Micheil. It hurts so much, it makes you daft. She didn't mean it, and she won't be angry with you once she delivers the babe. She'll be her old self in a week or two."

Micheil sat and wrung his hands. "I hope so." He downed his first ale in two swallows, all the time glancing over his shoulder to check on the balcony above stairs. He did not like this one bit. Diana was completely daft with pain. What was he to do? Was it possible she would be like this forever? How could he care for the bairn if she stayed that way?

After finding himself unable to sit in one spot, he strode over to the door and swung it open, only to be pelted with sheeting rain outside.

"Close the door, Micheil. It's storming out and I have a bairn in here," Logan yelled.

He closed the door and leaned against it, his gaze searching the Drummond Great Hall. Every pair of eyes watched him, every Drummond servant, each member of the Ramsay family, even Diana's steward.

Lily ran over and tugged on his hand. "Come, you may play a game with Molly and Maggie and me. We'll dress you up."

And he did not care one bit.

⟨∞⟩

The storm continued outside, blustery winds along with thunder and lightning that lit up the gloomy midday sky. Diana screamed as she gave the last push to finally end her labor. A sigh escaped her as the bairn slid out of her body and into Brenna's capable hands. Lady Ramsay sat in the chair next to her mopping her brow, soothing her in any way she could.

"What is it? Is it hearty? Is it sickly?" Diana stared at the reddish purple bundle in Brenna's hands.

Brenna fussed with the bairn's face, cleaning it with a damp cloth, Diana's maid and Avelina peered over her shoulder in anticipation. The bairn let out a loud yelp, followed by a long guttural cry. "It's a laddie. Congratulations, Diana. You and Micheil have a strong son."

Diana sat up as tears sluiced down her face. "We do? A laddie? Och, where's Micheil? I want him to see him. May I hold him?"

Brenna cleaned him up a bit before she set the lad on her belly, his cord still attached. She reached for her clamp, then said, "Avelina, why don't you get Micheil for us? Don't tell him that it's a laddie until he comes inside. We'll tell him. Diana, as soon as your maid and I clean him up a bit more and I cut his life cord, you may hold him. But you need to stay just as you are now, there's more to do."

Diana stared down at her son as Brenna cut the cord, then cleaned him and swaddled him up tight in a plaid. She held out her arms, and Brenna placed the babe in the curve of her arms while he still bellowed his dissatisfaction with his new status in life.

The door flew open and Micheil appeared. "Diana, are you all right?"

"Micheil, come see our son."

"A lad? 'Tis a lad?" He rushed to her side and stared at the bundle in her arms. His mother got up from her spot, kissed his cheek and stepped outside. Kissing his wife, he settled on a stool next to her and stared at the bairn enfolded close to her heart.

"Micheil, look how beautiful he is. Do you not think so?"

He nodded, a look of sheer wonder and awe in his gaze. "Aye, he is." The lad's wee fist popped out of the plaid, and he reached for his sire, his fingers outstretched. Micheil put his finger against the palm of his hand, and he grasped on tight.

He continued to wail, so Brenna said, "Why don't you put him to your breast, Diana? 'Twill calm him."

Diana stared at Brenna. She had no idea how to go about it. Aye, she had seen it happen many times, but how did one manage such a thing?

Brenna set her tools down and said, "Here. I'll assist you." She helped Diana adjust her gown to free up her breast, then brought the laddie close to her nipple, teasing it against his cheek.

Diana looked on in wonder as he opened his mouth, searching for her, and with just a wiggle of repositioning from Brenna, latched onto her nipple and suckled. She peered up at her husband as their son quieted, his hand still grasping his father's finger.

Neither spoke as they watched the new joy in their life discover his mama and papa. A few moments later, Brenna sent Avelina and the maid out of the room.

Micheil kissed Diana's brow. "I love you."

Diana clutched his hand. "I'm so sorry I yelled at you. You know I love you so." Tears slid down her cheeks. No matter how she tried to stop them, she could not.

"Have you thought of a name yet?" Brenna asked.

Mother and father both shook their heads before staring at each other.

"Micheil, I know what I wish to name him."

A light flashed through his eyes, and he nodded. "David," he said. "David after your father."

Diana sobbed, "'Tis exactly what I wanted. David Micheil Ramsay Drummond."

Micheil smiled and kissed her wet cheek before leaning in to kiss his son's head. "David Micheil it is."

She whispered, her gaze hopeful, "Do you think he knows? Do you think Da can see his grandson?"

"Aye, I think both your mama and papa are looking down on us right now, mayhap with my sire. And I am verra sure of something else."

"What?"

"There is naught you could do to make them more proud than they are at this moment."

Diana buried her face in her husband's shoulder and sobbed as she held wee David at her breast, but then she straightened to stare, her finger pointing out the window. Brenna walked over and pulled the fur back, standing to the side with a smile on her face.

The sun shone bright, illuminating the most beautiful rainbow they had ever seen.

THE END

Dear Reader,

Thank you so much for reading MY DESPERATE HIGHLANDER. I hope you enjoyed Micheil and Diana's story. I haven't decided yet which story will be next. I thought Jennie's, but now I think it may be Avelina's. There are a couple of lads who made promises to the two lassies. Which one will act on their promise first? Hmmm...

As always, let me know what you think! It's usually the readers who help me determine what I'm writing next.

Here's how you can reach me or let me know what you think:

1. **Write a review:** Please consider leaving a review. They can really help an author, particularly one who is self-published as I am. I don't have a marketing department or an advertising team backing me. These reviews are also helpful for other readers.

2. **Send me an email at keiramontclair@gmail.com.** I promise to respond!

3. **Go to my Facebook page and 'like' me:** You will get updates on any new novels, book signings, and giveaways. Here is the link: **https://www.facebook.com/KeiraMontclair**

4. **Visit my website: www.keiramontclair.com:** Another way to contact me is through my website. Don't forget to sign up for my **newsletter** while you're there.

5. **Stop by my Pinterest page: http://www.pinterest.com/KeiraMontclair/** You'll see how I envision Micheil and Diana, along with the additions to Logan and Gwyneth's family— Sorcha (the cutest EVER), Molly (with her dark curls), and Maggie.

The next Clan Grant series novel will be a surprise to both of us! You can also expect Jake's story from Summerhill sometime soon.

Keep reading!
Keira Montclair

ABOUT THE AUTHOR

Keira Montclair is the pen name of an author who lives in Florida with her husband. She loves to write fast-paced emotional romance, especially with children as secondary characters in her stories. In her spare time, she is a voracious reader and loves to take ballet classes. She has worked as a registered nurse in pediatrics and recovery room nursing. Teaching is another of her loves, as she has taught high school Mathematics, Medical Assisting, and Practical Nursing.

Her Highlander Clan Grant Series is a reader favorite and she has many other stories planned. Her contemporary series, The Summerhill Series, is set in the Finger Lakes of western New York and centers around the descendants of her historical series. She loves to hear from readers. If you send her an email through her website, **www.keiramontclair.com**, she promises to respond.

Printed in Great Britain
by Amazon